William Sumner Dodge

A Waif of the War

The history of the Seventy-fifth Illinois infantry, embracing the entire campaigns of

the Army of the Cumberland

William Sumner Dodge

A Waif of the War
The history of the Seventy-fifth Illinois infantry, embracing the entire campaigns of the Army of the Cumberland

ISBN/EAN: 9783337423285

Printed in Europe, USA, Canada, Australia, Japan

Cover: Foto ©Andreas Hilbeck / pixelio.de

More available books at **www.hansebooks.com**

A WAIF

OF

THE WAR;

OR, THE

History of the Seventy-Fifth Illinois Infantry,

EMBRACING

THE ENTIRE CAMPAIGNS

OF THE

ARMY OF THE CUMBERLAND.

BY

WM. SUMNER DODGE,

AUTHOR OF "CHRONICLES OF THE ARMY OF THE CUMBERLAND; OR, HISTORY OF THE OLD SECOND DIVISION."

———

Here the free spirit of mankind, at length
Throws its last fetters off; and who shall place
A limit to the giant's unchained strength,
Or curb his swiftness in the forward race?
BRYANT: *The Ages.*

From a conservative and progressive republic—The only one durable, the only one possible—May the unseen hand cause to bloom forth what is germinant in this kind of institution —The morality of the people and the reign of God.—LAMARTINE: *History of the French Revolution.*

———

CHICAGO:
CHURCH AND GOODMAN, PUBLISHERS,
51 LA SALLE STREET,

1866.

PREFACE.

By request of the officers and soldiers of the SEVENTY-FIFTH REGIMENT ILLINOIS VOLUNTEERS, who, upon the expiration of their term of service, partially raised the amount necessary to write out its history, I undertake the task. How well it is accomplished, remains with them to say. Illinois has sustained a proud record in the late war for the Union; and among the hundreds of regiments she has sent into the field, none have reflected greater credit upon her name than this. I have aimed to recount its marches and battles in such a manner as to do the command justice; and while doing this, have presented the outlines of campaigns, and the actions of the corps, division and brigade under which it acted a subordinate part. I have also given a sketch of other commands when acting in unison with it. To do this clearly has involved the labor of collating and examining a large mass of documents, apart from those necessary to strict regimental details. Three years of service in another division of the same army gives me, perhaps, some claim to an understanding of army operations, and also frees me from that bias which might attach to a writer who himself belonged to the regiment.

It is but justice to the brave men who have served so faithfully through our country's peril, that their services be recorded. For myself, I will state that, appreciating the desire of the members of the SEVENTY-FIFTH for such a memorial, I have, without compensation, given my time in its preparation. If it meets the approval of those interested, I have my reward. It has not been my intention to over-praise any, or to disparage any. In this matter, the official record has been my guide. Circumstances beyond my control have delayed its publication for months longer than I anticipated. Those reasons I need not explain here. The command had the good fortune to serve until the end of the war. Entering the service when the black clouds of despondency had settled over the land, it withdrew only when the sunlight of Peace illumined a clear sky, from zenith to horizon. Liberty has been won. Republican institutions now stand vindicated before the world. If, now, the brave men who have fought the battles of the Republic, will stand forth in the dignity of true manhood, and by the exercise of a just conservatism in their political ideas, abjuring all sectional parties and isms, *continue to maintain what has been gained,* sealed as it is by the blood of our martyred President, Abraham Lincoln, and *fulfil the hopes of the Fathers*—the labor of his life—then will the unity of the nation be established on a basis that cannot crumble, and the world forever feel its power for good.

WM. SUMNER DODGE.

WASHINGTON, D. C., Sept. 15, 1866.

CONTENTS.

vi.

CHAPTER VII.

CHAPTER VIII.

CHAPTER IX.

CHAPTER X.

CHAPTER XI.

CHAPTER XII.

CHAPTER XIII.

CHAPTER XIV.

CHAPTER XV.

·CHAPTER I.

THE rebellion, which our people were confident of
crushing in three short months, with a force of
seventy-five thousand men, had continued through
an entire year, rousing the nation to a realization
of the fact that a bitter fratricidal strife was upon
us; a war of sections, which augured much blood-
shed, great expenditure of treasure, ruined homes,
devastated fields, broken and sorrowing hearts.
Already three hundred thousand additional troops
were in the field; but, seemingly, the larger our
army, the more complex our difficulties—yet farther
off the termination of the dreadful struggle.

True, in the West there had been sanguinary battles, resulting in rebel defeats, and consequent re-
treats, entailing upon us the necessity of defending
longer exterior lines of operation, and more extended
highways of communication. The battles of Mill

2

Springs and Belmont had been fought, the storming of Fort Donelson effected, and, as a logical sequence, the evacuation of Columbus, Bowling Green, and Nashville by the rebel forces. Then came the terrible ordeal of Shiloh, where the united armies of Grant and Buell routed the Beauregardian hosts of the Confederacy, and drove them pell-mell within their fortifications at Corinth. Other brilliant successes on the Mississippi, and beyond it, also added *eclat* to our victorious western banners. The surrender of Island No. 10, and the blood-bought field of Pea Ridge, for a moment inspired faith in our speedy triumph. And the dashing operations of Mitchell's command in Alabama greatly strengthened that faith.

But now there was a lull in the conquering breeze. Defiantly sat the combined rebel armies of the South-West in the intrenchments at Corinth, awaiting the attack of the concentrated Union forces under Grant, Buell, and Pope. Here resulted a long and weary siege, ending in the escape of the entire rebel army, outwitting all the deep-laid plans of the military chieftain, Halleck.

But the war which, until the siege of Corinth, had been such a success in the West, had been almost one constant reverse in the East. Like the Spanish campaigns against the Moors and Turks, the Crucifix triumphed here, the Crescent there. From Bull Run to Yorktown, thence through the memorable Chick-ahominy campaign, resulting in the indomitable but ill-starred battles of Mechanicsville, Gaines' Hill, Savage Station, and Malvern Hill, up to the very gateways of Richmond, within grasp of the coveted prize, the Union cause oscillated, until every gleam of hope was dispelled; when at last the sad intelli- gence was published that the Army of the Potomac rested at Harrison's Landing — thousands of patriot men in their graves, and nothing accomplished.

Our navy, weak in numbers, but gallant in heart and purpose, invested the coast, each harbor and inlet, aiding so far as possible in preventing rebel communication with Europe, cutting off the enemy's supplies, and placing him strictly within the pale of insurrection, or rebellion. Besides this onerous duty, it maintained its olden reputation for achievement in the capture of Newbern, St. Augustine, and New Orleans.

Such was the status of military affairs. The politics of the country, which then in fact controlled the army, its movements and policy, were in a far more lamentable condition. Slavery, the cause of the rebellion, and therefore the root of discord which should have been exterminated, or rather to destroy which should have been the policy of the Govern- ment, was, strangely enough, cared for as tenderly as a child. A foreigner, not familiar with the his- tory of the conspiracy, its causes, and the ambitious motives of its leaders, would have supposed that we regarded Slavery as a tower of strength in our cause — that upon its protection depended the salvation

of the Union.   Campaigns were conducted, marches
made, the armies sustained in such manner as least
to tax the energies and resources of the South.

Our army fought for the maintenance of the Union:
the rebel army for its disintegration, and the perpe-
tuity of Slavery.   The deadly conflict was waged by
us against the latter idea, yet outside of the battle-
field no steps could be taken to thwart the foul purpose.   Rebel property was protected by Federal
bayonets.   Their homes, their fields of corn and
grain, and the slaves who sustained the damnable
cause, were each and all secured to the rebel masters.
When it was deemed necessary by military commanders
to use or appropriate any species of property belong-
ing to the enemy, this could only be done with immediate and full compensation.   And the negro, the
innocent cause of all, he who never yet through all
the war betrayed our side, and who from his position
was ever able to give valuable information relating
to rebel movements, was denied admission within
our lines, and if by chance he came into our camps,
Union soldiers were employed to force him to return to his so-called master.   So despised was the
negro, and so fearful were the politicians and military
of giving offence to their " Southern brethren !"

War is a calamity to any nation involved in its
bloody meshes.   But when it is forced upon a peaceful people, all its terrible enginery should be used to
crush the aggressor into the earth.   Every means
allowed by the law of nations should be employed to

make the conflict speedy and decisive. With us was presented the anomaly of fighting to destroy a heresy, yet protecting it behind the very shields we in vain sought to shatter. War thus waged was inhuman. It awarded a premium to butchery, without hope of good results. It was like the cannibals of the South Sea Islands, who, binding their victims, cover them with wounds, yet are careful not to pierce a vital part, lest the sufferings of the tortured cease. God had no attributes that would side with us in such a warfare.

But He had not deserted us. He suffered our people to flounder on in this sea of trouble, until calm reason should teach them by stern experience what party prejudices and passion had failed to do, *that emancipation of the negro and the fulfillment of the promises of the Declaration of Independence were the conditions of our national safety.*

Thus formidable was the power of Slavery. From the first cannon-shot which announced the fray, until July in 1862, it controlled not only its own usurped domains, but the political power of the Free States, so that no arm was yet sufficiently nerved to attack the giant criminal. Then the people, realizing that Divine favor could never be bestowed on injustice, marshalled their forces to storm the citadel. Our martyred President, who ever leaned upon the popular heart, and directed his policy in accordance with its pulsations, finally, thinking the hour had come, grasped the thunderbolt under which the iniquity should stagger to its fall. Nearly contemporary with this glorious event came the demand for more troops, to carry on war *in earnest*, and under this call of July 6, 1862, came that generous .outpouring of brave and loyal hearts, adding new strength to the armies already in the field, and constituting with them that grander force which in the future would astonish the world by its magnificent triumphs.

CHAPTER II.

Immediately upon the call of the President, July 6, 1862, for three hundred thousand volunteers, and before it was yet definitely known what would be the quota for Illinois, Governor Richard Yates, than whom no better ever served a State, full of patriotic ardor and lofty devotion to the cause, issued a stirring proclamation to the citizens of Illinois. It was the bugle-blast calling to battle — the key-note to a grand success.

In a few days after the call was made, it was announced that the Illinois quota would be 52,296 men. The Secretary of War had previously called for nine regiments as a part of this quota, and nine camps of rendezvous were at once established for the troops. Among them was one at Dixon, the county seat of Lee. This was the camp of instruction for the SEVENTY-FIFTH ILLINOIS, and was entitled Camp Dement, in honor of a highly esteemed citizen of that town, who had formerly held various offices of public trust — Colonel John Dement.

On the 15th of August, 1862, Captain Wm. M. Kilgore, who had on the previous 17th of July been commissioned by the Adjutant-General to raise a company for the service, received the following :

" *General Order No. 82.*

" GEN. HEAD QUARTERS STATE OF ILLINOIS,
" ADJ'T GEN'L'S OFFICE, SPRINGFIELD,
" August 15th, 1862.

" Captain Wm. M. Kilgore, of Whiteside county, will assume temporary command of volunteers at camp at Dixon until further orders, and make daily reports to this Department.

" By order of His Excellency, Richard Yates, Governor.

" ALLEN C. FULLER, *Adj't General.*"

In obedience to this order, Captain Kilgore took charge of " Camp Dement," and the new levies for that Congressional district were rapidly concentrated here for organization and drill.

The several companies which composed the Seventy-fifth were speedily organized, to wit :

COMPANY A was enlisted at Dixon by James A. Watson, Ezekiel Giles, William Parker, and George Putnam. The men were principally from Dixon, Palmyra and Nelson. It elected its company officers, and was sworn into the State service August 11th, and rendezvoused at Camp Dement on the 13th.

COMPANY B was recruited at Lyndon, Whiteside county, by John Whallen, James Blean, and others. Its members were principally from Lyndon, Fenton, Garden Plains, Newton, Round Grove, and Prophetstown. It was organized and company officers elected on the 12th of August, and on the 15th proceeded to Dixon.

COMPANY C was raised at Morrison, Whiteside county, chiefly by the energy of John E. Bennett, assisted by Ernest Altman and George R. Shaw. Its members were from Morrison, Prophetstown, Round Grove, Newton, Clyde, and Portland. This company was recruited in five days, commencing August 4th, and being organized by the election of officers on the 9th. It left for Dixon the 14th of August.

COMPANY D was recruited under the auspices of the Chicago Board of Trade, by Capt. A. McMoore, in the vicinity of Sterling, Colomo, Genesee, Hume, Hannahman, Hopkins, Montmorency, Portland, and Prophetstown — all of Whiteside county. This company first rendezvoused at Sterling. On the 11th of August it elected its officers, and that night proceeded to Chicago. But owing to misrepresentation or misunderstanding on the part of the Board of Trade, it returned to Sterling, and on the 15th joined the company organizations at Dixon.

COMPANY E was raised almost wholly from the towns of Lee Center and Sublette, in the county of Lee. Its organization was more the result of an outburst of patriotic ardor on the part of the loyal people, who were determined to see our cause succeed, than that of individual effort. Yet to Wm. S. Frost, F. H. Eels, and J. H. Blodgett, the officers elected, · is the company indebted for speedy preparation for the field. It rendezvoused at Dixon about the middle of August.

COMPANY F was recruited in the vicinity of Amboy, county of Lee, by Addison S. Vorrey and James Tourtillott. It rendezvoused in Amboy during its enlistment, and when ready was sworn into the State service by Samuel Brown, Esq., on the 21st of August, and on the 27th joined the volunteers at Dixon.

COMPANY G was organized at Franklin Grove, Lee county. Its members were from that vicinity and adjoining towns. Those who contributed particularly to its success were Joseph Williams, Robert L. Irwin, and James Taylor, of Lafayette. The latter, by his influence alone, raised thirty men for this company. Twenty-seven of the members were married men. Upon its organization it reported at Dixon.

COMPANY H was recruited in Sterling, Como, Genesee Grove, and Jordan, through the efforts of John G. Price, Joseph W. R. Stambaugh, and others. It remained for a short time in Sterling, but upon the election of its officers it moved to the encampment at Dixon.

COMPANY I was enlisted in Whiteside county, principally in the townships of Sterling, Erie, Fulton, and Ustick. The election of officers took place at

Wallace Hall in Sterling, on the evening of August 14th, and was made an occasion of much festivity and good feeling. After the meeting was over, the "boys" amused themselves by hauling an old "Mc-Cormick." through the streets, one of their number going through the motions of "raking off." This gave them the name of the "Reaper Company." It rendezvoused at Dixon, August 18th, and awaited further orders.

COMPANY K was organized at Wyoming, Lee county, and was enlisted by Dr. George Ryon, James Thompson, B. G. Barrett, and I. L. Hunt, in Pawpaw, Willow Creek, Wyoming, and Viola. On the 25th of August it proceeded to Dixon.

Such is a brief history of the organization of the companies which were soon to constitute the SEV-ENTY-FIFTH ILLINOIS INFANTRY. They were composed almost entirely of farmers and farmers' sons, and young men in the country towns of the 22d judicial circuit. They were emphatically citizens, but very few of whom, either as officers or men, had seen actual service in war. Now they were entered on a field of duty unknown and untried, full of fatigue, hardship, suffering, and danger. They were *men*, who, now the Republic was in imminent peril, re-solved to throw themselves into the deadly breach, that it might be saved. Forgetful of self, and rising above the sordid views of gain, they abandoned the quiet of their homes, society and its fascinations, the world at large and its constant whirl of excitement, and as soldiers were now to "gird on their armor," march forth to battle, and, breasting the leaden and iron hail of the enemy, stand the avowed champions of the national honor and safety.

On the 2d day of September, the regimental companies, having lotteried each for its *letter* designation, and also elected its field officers — Dr. Geo. Ryon, of Co. K, as Colonel; John E. Bennett, of Company C, as Lieutenant-Colonel; and Wm. M. Kilgore, of Company I, as Major — they were mustered into the serice of the United States, under orders of Governor Yates, "for three years or during the war," by Capt. T. O. Barri, of the Eleventh U. S. Infantry.

"Camp Dement" now became a grand school of instruction. Several other companies, the nuclus of other regiments, were here, and officers and men must, so far as possible, be thoroughly informed of the duties pertaining to the camp, the garrison; the march, and the field. Tactics, embracing the school of the soldier, the company, skirmish drill, and the school of the battalion, were carefully and constantly taught, and theory joined to practice. Major Kilgore and Captain Hale having seen some service, one in the 13th, and the other in the 11th Illinois, aided much in a quick understanding of those movements.

Here for nearly a month, the regiment was busied in learning to be soldiers. Schooling in positions, facings, the principles of the step, the manual of arms, loading, firing, bayonet exercise, kneeling, alignment, marching, and wheeling, was the order of the day.

The camp was thronged with visitors and friends of the soldiers, and much amusement was afforded them. But this was mere play at soldiering. It was not to last long. The Government had not called them into being as blue-dressed toys to tickle a war-like nation's pride; but for stern work, such only as heroes are fit for and die in the doing.

The country was full of dangers. Everywhere, north, south, east and west, the demons of destruction raised their hydra heads, and howled madness and wrath. Here it was open, declared foes; there it was a concealed enemy, the more dangerous because secret. But the safety of the Republic rested with its citizens, its founders and supporters. If so inclined, they could maintain it against every shock. Would they do it? History nowhere testifies to such an out-pouring of patriotism, such shedding of blood, such sufferings, and finally such triumphs. But there were dark days still in store for us; days such as, while their events are recorded in the great scroll of time, should sadden many a household hearth. And the SEVENTY-FIFTH, unable to read the dark horoscope of the immediate future, drifted rapidly into its vortex of "fire and blood."

Orders came for a movement immediately to the seat of war. And so, on the 27th of September, many a last farewell was spoken, many a lip was for the last time pressed, and many a heart mutely told what the tongue, dumb with anguish, could not utter.

But they were going forth to battle for God, Country, and Right, and they felt that they were in His good keeping; and if they were numbered with the slain, it was to serve his own wise purpose. Hence they hesitated not at duty.

CHAPTER III.

UPON the arrival of the Army of the Ohio at Louisville, Ky., whence it had retreated to save that city
from the rebel army under General Bragg, it was
thoroughly reorganized, and the new levies were dis-
tributed in the different divisions and brigades of
the old army. It was organized into three army
corps, the First commanded by Major-General A.
McD. McCook; the Second by Major-General T. L.
Crittenden; and the Third by Major-General C. C.
Gilbert. The army consisted of eleven divisions,
formed of brigades numbering from One to Thirty-
seven. The SEVENTY-FIFTH Illinois arrived at Jeffersonville, Indiana, on the 29th of September, via
Chicago and Indianapolis. Thousands of others of
the new troops were all along the Indiana shore,
rallied there to repel the threatened capture of Louisville. A gigantic task was now before the commanding General — that of supply. These great armies
of men, old and new, must be fed and clothed, and

to a great extent newly equipped. This and the
reorganization accomplished, the campaign could be
commenced with reasonable hope of success.

The SEVENTY-FIFTH was assigned to the Thirtieth
Brigade, Ninth Division, and Third Army Corps.
General Crittenden's Corps constituted the right
wing, General McCook's the left, and General Gilbert's the center. Such was the new organization of
the "Army of the Ohio."

By the 30th of September the army was consolidated, equipped, and ready for the advance. Bragg's
forces were still at Bardstown, Kentucky, and on
the 1st of October the army moved out the Bardstown, Frankfort and Lebanon pikes, with the intention of attacking them. But now, Bragg had moved
his command from Bardstown to Perryville, and the
concurrent testimony of citizens and prisoners proved
that it was his intention to move still further southward, and not to offer the "wager of battle." But,
finally, learning that the advance of Buell's columns
was moving rapidly upon the rear of his own column,
he resolved to mass his force'sand crush one or more of
them, and thus, if necessity compelled, or opportunity offered, destroy our army by detail. Bragg,
therefore, skillfully amused our generals by means
of small parties of cavalry, skirmishing at Floyd's
Fork, Claysville, Mount Washington, Bardstown,
Springfield, and Texas; inducing them to believe
they were closely upon his heels, while in reality he
was most judiciously posting his army to entrap us.

He had planted his batteries upon a range of low, wooded hills in front of Perryville, overlooking and completely commanding a large space of open ground lying immediately at the foot of the ridge. His infantry were massed around and behind his artillery, and his cavalry were prepared to charge down the slope of the hills, and sweep everything from the comparatively level ground below. Such was the position selected by the rebel general. His forces were under the immediate command of the Rev. and General Leonidas Polk. His division commanders were Hardee (who had two divisions), Cheatham, Buckner, and Anderson.

On the 7th October, the two armies well confronted each other. Skirmishing with infantry, and artillery duels were of frequent occurrence. Our own lines were gradually established, and preparations made for battle. Major-General McCook, with his two divisions, Rousseau's and Jackson's, occupied splendid ground, selected by Rousseau — ground which the sequel proved was admirably held, although with the most terrific fighting. Gilbert's Corps came in on the Springfield turnpike, and when within five miles of Perryville, the enemy appeared in force, the Ninth Division, General R. B. Mitchell's, was drawn up in line of battle across the road. No engagement, save light skirmishing, ensued, and soon after the Eleventh Division, General Phil. Sheridan, was passed to the front, and established on some heights to the right of the road near Doctor's Creek.

3

General Crittenden's corps was moving up the Lebanon pike, but was not within supporting distance. The order of battle thus established was: Rousseau's division on the extreme left, with Jackson's division somewhat to the rear; joining this on the right and in prolongation of the line, was Sheridan's division, with Mitchell's in reserve. The cavalry, under General Gay, was deployed on the flanks.

The night was a beautiful moon-light. Softly Luna shone on hill and valley, on forest and field — tinting with mellow hues the foliage of the trees. The scene was grandly solemn — solemn, because while Nature herself was so peaceful, man, enraged against his brother, was marshaled in warlike array, eager to inflict death, destruction, and woe. All through the night shot and shell went whizzing over head, crashing through the trees; constant monitors. that the enemy was present, and heralds of a bloody to-morrow.

It was hardly day-break on the 8th, for the beautiful moonlight still slumbered upon the hills, when the rebels appeared on the front and flanks of the Thirty-sixth Brigade, Colonel Daniel McCook's, and planting a battery, poured forth a shower of shrapnel, which went crashing through its lines; but although new troops, they never flinched from duty. A few well-directed shots from Barnett's artillery silenced the rebel guns. But the foe was determined, and thrice rallied round the guns and opened fire; each time to be repulsed by the deadly Parrotts, and finally to retire altogether. Thus McCook held in undisputed possession the contested ground. General Gay then threw forward a portion of his cavalry, the Second Michigan, in pursuit of the retiring rebels, one battalion dismounted, two mounted, and soon encountered resistance. The dismounted force, aided by the Fifty-second Ohio, entered into the work with energy, and drove them from the woods; but they soon met reinforcements, rallied, and in turn forced our men to retire, obstinately contesting each inch of ground.

In a few moments it seemed as if the battle had commenced. On came the rebels, pouring volley after volley into the ranks of our cavalry and advanced infantry — pushing them back to their original position. This gave the enemy courage; and with that whoop or yell so peculiar to them, they prepared to attack our main line of battle. The situation was critical indeed. Should they break the line of the Thirty-sixth Brigade, they would hold the center of our intended line of battle, and disaster must ensue. Fortunately, Mitchell's division had moved up, and was already establishing a prolongation of this line of battle, and covering securely the entire right of the hill. So far safe; but more fortunate still, the Second Missouri Infantry, of Pea Ridge fame, came gallantly to the aid of the imperiled line, and then the Michigan heroes advanced anew, the Second Missouri moving close after in line of battle, supported by the Fifteenth Missouri. Again the battle raged fiercely. A perfect hailstorm of bullets greeted them; shot and shell tore among them fearfully; and many a brave heart departed to another world. In vain this murderous fire, in vain the sleet of leaden hail. Undaunted they pushed on, the "Stars and Stripes" gloriously aloft, and soon the dismayed and conquered rebels fled from the field. Pursuit was made for more than a mile; and Hotchkiss' Minnesota battery aided much by an effective fire upon the enemy's flank.

Thus ended the initiatory engagement on this fatal day. It was ten o'clock in the morning. Our loss had been considerable; the enemy's equaled at least our own, for both had fought with tenacious purpose; but we were masters of the ground. This attack of Bragg confirmed our generals in the opinion that here we were to be met and driven back, if possible. Thus it was deemed the height of imprudence to invite attack by any offensive demonstration on our part, until our own army was all in order of battle, or at least within close support.

It is evident, however, the rebel generals chafed with madness and impatience. Their well conceived plan of drawing our advance troops into a trap had failed, owing to the judicious cautiousness of their movement as they neared Perryville. Again, the longer they delayed the battle, the more doubtful was their success, as they justly reasoned it were better to fight two or three divisions than six. Hence the order of Bragg, to "assail at once, and vigorously."

About noon, or perhaps somewhat later, everything being quiet, as all indications were that the enemy had for a time retired, General Rousseau concluded to resume his march to Chaplin Creek, anticipating by a little a verbal order of General Buell given to General McCook, to move to this point, as his men were suffering most intensely from thirst.

While General Gay was skirmishing with the enemy, he had requested support from Rousseau for his artillery, and the General had sent him the Forty-second Indiana, and Loomis with two of his long-range Parrott guns. These had remained in the position occupied during the engagement; and now, as the head of Rousseau's column was within a hundred yards of Loomis's guns, it was reported to him that the enemy was reappearing in the woods beyond. He halted the column, rode forward personally to satisfy himself of the fact, and in a few moments more the rebels could be seen plainly. The discharge of shell from three masked batteries proved unmistakably that they were in force, determined on *action*.

Rousseau ordered Loomis to reply instantly, and to hasten forward the remainder of his guns. Simonson's Fifth Indiana Battery was ordered up, and the contest opened in thunder tones. He then directed Colonel Lytle to form his brigade on the right in a strong position, and immediately learning from Captain Wickliffe, of the Second Kentucky Cavalry, that a great force of cavalry, infantry and artillery

was moving down directly on the front of Colonel
Harris's brigade, he galloped over to him and assisted
in forming his brigade in two lines of battle, on the
left of Colonel Lytle. Here the gallant Starkweather
announced by a messenger his arrival on the field
still further to the left. Rousseau's heart was gladdened, for these men were veterans, tried and true.
The Twenty-Eighth Brigade had been accidentally
cut off in the morning by a movement of General
Jackson's division at Maxville ; but Starkweather,
true to the instincts of a soldier, hearing firing in the
front, had abandoned the road, moved around Jackson's column, and halted where Rousseau found him,
and, as Rousseau says, in his official report, " on the
very spot where he was most needed." At this moment a large body of rebel cavalry was seen moving
down the road a full mile in front of Starkweather's
line, which, admirably shelled by Stone's First Kentucky Battery, was dispersed in great disorder. The
First Kentucky and Bush's Fourth Indiana artillery
were then placed on a high ridge on the extreme left
of the battle line, extending diagonally to the front.
These batteries were supported by the First Wisconsin, while the Seventy-ninth Pennsylvania, in line on
another ridge running at right angles to the one on
which the batteries were planted, delivered a splendid
cross-fire upon any troops attempting to charge them;
and this proved to be the key of the position during
all that bloody ordeal soon to follow.

    These positions were all taken in great haste, but

without the least confusion. Rousseau now returned to Harris's brigade, and found the Thirty-third Ohio already engaged, being ordered further forward by General McCook, closely supported by the Second Ohio. Rousseau then led forward in person the Twenty-fourth Illinois, which was rapidly deployed into line, and went galloping into action on the left of the Thirty-third Ohio. Harris's entire brigade now received a fearful shock in battle. Cheatham's whole division bore down upon it, three to one, and the cannonade and musketry fire was terrible. Mars, the great god of war, now held full sway. He was carrying out on the grandest scale a tragedy more direful than ever was presented on the foot-boards, to never so excited an auditorium. Tragedy had stepped into full life; all that devoted band were actors. The brightness of day had changed into the gloom of night. The demon of Death hurtled through the sulphureous canopy his ministers of steel and flame, and laid hundreds of brave men low. But right gallantly this noble brigade held the enemy at bay, hurling back each assault with desperate energy; and among those noble soldiers none displayed more valor than the new regiment, the Ninety-fourth Ohio, Colonel Frizell, which, acting in unison with the Thirty-eighth Indiana, did service worthy the eternal gratitude of the country. The men not only emptied their own cartridge boxes, but those of the dead and wounded around them.

At this juncture, General Jackson's division, com-

posed entirely of new troops, and hence lacking that
confidence which association with veteran regiments.
would naturally give them, having been terribly
pressed by another overwhelming force of the enemy
—Hardee's division—their gallant Generals Jackson
and Terrell being killed, and the chivalrous Webster
mortally wounded, yielded the field in great confusion, hundreds of their men falling meantime, under
a most merciless fire of musketry, sacrificing the
magnificent battery of Parsons, and breaking the
line of battle. At first they fought with commendable courage, and again and again checked the rebel
tides as they rolled frantically against their lines. But
the troops opposed to them were the veterans who had
taken part in the battles of Belmont, Fort Donelson,
and Shiloh, and their resolution and skill had not in
the least abated. And it is not singular that they
were forced to yield the contest. However lamentable the fact that they did succumb, impartial history
must do them justice, and state that they did all that
undisciplined men could do, regiment vieing with
regiment, and man with man, to see who should
longest withstand the fierce assaults — retreating,
rallying, reforming, again supporting the batteries
of Harris, Stone, and Parsons, together vomiting
forth a perfect lava of bullets, grape and canister,
into the very bosoms of the advancing host, literally
strewing the ground with the bodies of dead and
mangled victims.   .

Jackson's division routed, and, flushed with the deli-

rium of victory, the rebels now, under the lead of
Bragg and the infamous Buckner, were encouraged to
re-attack Rousseau's Spartan band. And here occurred
one of the bloodiest passages at arms recorded in the
annals of time. The attack was made on the devoted
brigade of the gifted Lytle. As the column appeared
from behind a belt of timber which had sheltered it
in its formation, it presented a most beautiful pag-
eant. Long lines of burnished bayonets gleamed
brightly in the already setting sun. The regimental
flags, with their fields of blue and single stars, waved
proudly in the air. Their leaders and their staffs
were splendidly mounted on spirited white horses,
and all seemed impatient for the fray. It was one
of those sublime spectacles—a picture of the "pride,
pomp, and circumstance of glorious war"—where,
too often, horror, woe, and death finally wraps the
scene in the gloom of tragedy.

Arriving within artillery range, the enemy planted
two batteries and opened a galling fire upon the
Third Ohio and Forty-second Indiana. Their infantry advanced steadily under cover of this fire, and
when within close musket range, poured a most terrific fire into these two regiments. They stood like
a rock washed by an ocean tempest; yes, stood,
although nearly one-half of their number strewed
the ground. But an accident compelled them to
that which the enemy could not. A large barn filled
with hay, near which the right of the Third Ohio
rested, took fire, and in a moment the whole was in

a blaze. The heat was unendurable, yet the heroes
stood their ground until their faces were blistered;
at last they retired to the foot of the hill, and in
doing this got into disorder. The Fifteenth Kentucky,
Colonel Curran Pope, rushed up the eminence, to
supply its place. Immediately it was greeted with
every deadly missile of war, and its ranks were decimated ere it had been there a single minute,—Lieutenant-Colonel Jouett and Major Campbell were killed,
and Colonel Pope wounded. It retired, but rallied
at the foot of the hill. The forced retreat of these
regiments uncovered the right wing of the Tenth
Ohio, and a brigade of rebels approached it under
cover of the crest where the other regiments had
been, and unawares struck that command in flank
and rear, almost annihilating it ere it could change
front and repel the attack from so unexpected a
quarter. Lytle had expected the enemy in his front,
and his men were lying down behind the crest of the
hill, and he intended to have the Tenth charge him
with the bayonet, as he came over the ridge. Oh!
it was heart-rending to see that noble regiment thus
compromised, yea, sacrificed; but it was alone, cut
off from support, and Rousseau's eagle eye was elsewhere engaged, cheering the men on the left, who were
beating back most murderous assaults. The heroes
of Carnifex soon received a withering volley from
the cat-like foe, and leaping to their feet, unable to
form line, deliberately *walked* away. Here fell, and
it was thought, mortally wounded, the noble Lytle,

the Chevalier Bayard of Ohio. One of his sergeants lifted him in his arms, and strove to bear him off the field. "*You* may do some good yet," said he; "I can do no more; let me die here." He was left there, and was captured by the enemy; but he did not die. God reserved him to fall finally in such another forlorn hope at Chickamauga. Hearing of this terrible mishap, and with his great heart bleeding at the sacrifice, Rousseau, our American Murat, galloped over to the right to cheer it by his presence, and assure them that, though left alone, they were not forgotten, but that stern necessity had compelled it. He found Harris's brigade re-formed, and though few in numbers, determined to perform their duty. While here he saw another heavy force of the enemy bearing directly down on the Fifteenth Kentucky. On approaching, this regiment rose, cheered, and again hastened to the crest of the hill, where it was ordered by Rousseau to lie down. He then ordered Loomis to open fire, which he did with terrible effect; but the rebel line moved straight on, its broken ranks closing up with alacrity, although riddled by a cross fire from the Seventeenth brigade.

Rousseau's heart sank within him. His division had been incessantly engaged for more than three hours, losing terribly; and now, tired out and with almost exhausted cartridge-boxes, it must stand another trial against greatly superior, and from appearance, fresh numbers. Could he not have help? Is there no one to come to the rescue? Gilbert is fight-

ing, but are his forces all engaged? McCook had
sent repeatedly for reinforcements, but none came.
Was his corps to be sacrificed, and an entire army
within a few miles, idly lying on its arms? Thus it
seemed. But no! Fortune smiles on the heroes!
Help is at hand. A courier announces that a brigade
from Mitchell's division awaits orders for action.
Rousseau hails the news with gladness, withdraws
Harris's worn-out men, and the fresh brigade, Colonel
Gooding's, forms its line of battle and shows what it
can do. Into the contest it hastened like

> "Many a stout corps that went
> Full ranked from camp and tent,
> And brought back a brigade;
> Like many a brave regiment
> That mustered only a squad."

This brigade was formed in line of battle as
follows: The Twenty-second Indiana on the right,
the Fifty-ninth Illinois on the right, and the SEVEN-
TY-FIFTH ILLINOIS in the center, with Pinney's Fifth
Wisconsin Battery on an eminence in the rear, bor-
dered with woods.

Instantly the battle raged anew; nor was it confined to this brigade; it extended along the entire
line. But nowhere did it rage fiercer than here.
The roar of the cannon and musketry was deafening;
the earth trembled under their shock. For two
hours a lurid sheet of fire blazed between the opposing lines, hurling destruction into each other's ranks.

Fiercer and wilder grew the contest, and almost hand to hand they fought at least three times their own number, often charging upon them with such impetuosity that they retired weakened by the deadly fire. At one time the Twenty-second Indiana charged on the enemy with fixed bayonets, completely routing them from their position on the right of the brigade, but at the same time a reserve force attacked them on the left, in which the Fifty-ninth and Seventy-fifth were engaged, and with great desperation. Soon the Twenty-second Indiana lent its aid—and then fell the gallant Lieutenant-Colonel Keith, of that Regiment, and Major Kilgore, of the Seventy-fifth Illinois. The former was killed, the latter most dangerously wounded. The tenacity with which the SEVENTY-FIFTH ILLINOIS maintained the conflict in the centre is worthy of all praise. Colonel Ryon, who had been arrested for neglect in not having the Regiment supplied with ammunition (unjustly though it was), entered the ranks, and fought side by side with his brave men. After the conflict had ended, so gallant was his conduct, his sword was restored to him, and a court martial convened to try him for "criminal negligence in not supplying his regiment with ammunition," honorably acquitted him, and he was restored to his command.

The loss of the regiment was fearful, and by it the hearts of hundreds of households were wrung with anguish. Among the many, *many* fallen, were Lieutenants Franklin H. Eels, and James Blean, killed;

Major W. M. Kilgore ; Captains John Whallon, Wm. S. Frost, and D. M. Roberts ; Lieutenants Edward H. Barber, Wm. H. Thompson, Robert L. Irwin, and James H. Blodgett, wounded. Kilgore, Roberts and Irwin were supposed to be mortally hurt, but after long suffering, they recovered and returned to duty. The conduct of the fated Blean was most noble, although rash. When wounded, he refused to be carried off the field, saying, " I'll take care of myself. Fight on; give the rebels the best you have." While lying on the ground, just in rear of the line of battle, whence he had crawled, he was again wounded, and died the next day. At times it seemed impossible to keep the men in line, so anxious were they to win a reputation for good fighting ; and, doubtless, this ambition was stimulated by the sad misfortune which occurred to General Jackson's division of new troops. They would advance beyond the line, in some instances several rods, and there remain, sharpshooting, until ordered back. Among those whose names are remembered, are Earnest Wernick, Daniel Burns, and Wm. Armstrong, of Company F. Corporal D. B. Walker, color guard, lost here his right arm. Another instance occurred worthy of mention. Corporal James L. Bracken had been detailed in charge of the guard for the regimental baggage train, some five miles in rear of the battle-ground. Hearing the cannonade and musketry, he was convinced a fight was raging, and desired to participate in it. Asking the consent of the Quartermaster, Lieut. J.

E. Remington, he was refused. Said Bracken, "You had better let me go : I must go. · I shall desert my post." Finally he consented, when Bracken double-quicked it, with his gun, for five miles, on that hot, dusty day, and reached the regiment just as it was moving into line of battle in aid of Rousseau. It is needless to add, that then, as many times since, he distinguished himself for bravery and soldierly bearing.

Lieutenant-Colonel Bennett, commanding the regiment, behaved with great gallantry, winning mention in the reports of superior officers. His horse was shot from under him, but he himself remained unhurt. The other officers did their duty faithfully, and well, so far as I know, displaying true mettle. And too much praise cannot be given the men, for their behavior in this, their first rencontre with the foe. Some captured rebels, speaking of this brigade, said, "We should have routed you, if it had not been for those regulars. They fought like devils." Forty-three were left dead on the field, and nine mortally wounded, besides one hundred and fifty more who received hospital treatment, many of whom were discharged as unfit for further service. Twelve were also taken prisoners. The brigade commander, Colonel Gooding, being taken prisoner in the heat of the action, Lieutenant-Colonel Bennett, being senior officer in the brigade, reformed it, in its second line of battle, and led it off the field. Night came on, and the battle ended. Now the horrors of the carnage began to be realized. All through the night the unfortunate soldiers were brought from the field, as fast as they could be found, by dint of the callings and gropings of Samaritan comrades. All night the surgeons unceasingly worked in dressing their wounds. And here Surgeon George W. Phillips, of this regiment—now brigade-surgeon, as Dr. Hazlitt had been killed during the action—and Assistant-Surgeon John C. Corbus, I believe, rendered most efficient service, the former being in charge of the amputation cases in one of the field hospitals. To those who labored so faithfully, the country owes a debt of gratitude.

The entire loss to us in the action is not known to the author; but from statistics such as he has, it is eight hundred and seventy-eight killed, two thousand eight hundred and sixty-one wounded, and two hundred and five prisoners; making a total loss of three thousand nine hundred and forty-four men. Two-thirds of this loss was in Rousseau's division alone. Such was the battle of Chaplin Hills. In it the Seventy-fifth Illinois received honorable mention. Major-General McCook says of the brigade: "Gooding's gallant attack, assisted by Pinney's Battery, drove back the enemy and re-occupied the position of Russell's house." General Mitchell says: "The Seventy-fifth Illinois, under Lieutenant-Colonel Bennett, having a reputation to gain as soldiers, nobly did the work before them." And Major-General Rousseau, speaking of the brigade which reinforced him in his hour of extreme peril, says: "The rein-forcements were from Mitchell's division, as I under-stood, and were 'Pea Ridge men.' I wish I knew who commanded the brigade, that I might do him justice; I can only say that the brigade moved directly into the fight like true soldiers, and opened a terrific fire, and drove back the enemy."

The noblest manhood and youth in the counties of Lee and Whiteside had gone forth in this regiment to battle, and how many, alas! never to return. The day is not far distant, when the pen of the historian, delving among the records of the army, and gleaning from the secret springs of action the true causes which led to the criminal neglect of McCook and Rousseau, in their direst peril, will stamp the seal of damnation upon the guilty ones.

But our individual loss is our beloved country's gain. Such is the sacrifice that a wrathful but just God demands for our Nation's boon. Then

> " Enduring Valor lifts his head
> To count the flying and the dead ;
> Returning Virtue still maintains
> The right to break unhallowed chains ;
> While sacred Justice, born of God,
> Walks regnant o'er the bleeding sod."

4

CHAPTER IV.

PURSUIT OF BRAGG—ITS ABANDONMENT, AND MARCH
UPON BOWLING GREEN AND NASHVILLE—REORGAN-
IZATION OF THE ARMY—POSITION AROUND NASH-
VILLE.

UPON the repulse of Bragg's forces, on the 8th of
October, he evacuated his position, and pushed north
to Harrodsburg, apparently to occupy a stronger
position, and again face Buell's troops; but after
making a demonstration, as if to attack us, he retired
to Camp Dick Robinson, at the junction of Dick's
and the Kentucky rivers. Heavy reconnoissances
were made to ascertain whether all the rebel forces
had crossed this river, and it proved they had; but
it was yet unknown whether the enemy intended to
offer battle in his new position. On the 12th of
October the different columns encamped on and near
the battle ground were set in motion, with the evident intention of turning his position at Camp Dick
Robinson, and compelling him to accept battle on
less favorable ground. On the night of the 13th of
October, it was ascertained beyond a doubt, that

Bragg was evacuating his stronghold, and moving southward. General Buell tardily ordered pursuit. The corps of Generals Crittenden and McCook pursued by way of Stanford and Crab Orchard, and General Gilbert's corps by way of Lancaster and Crab Orchard. The enemy's rear guard was finally overtaken and severely pressed until reaching Loudon; then all conflict ended.

At Lancaster, the thirtieth brigade engaged the enemy's cavalry in a lively skirmish, which was of short duration. During its progress, however, a battery of ours rushed to the front, to gain position on an eminence, whence it could open fire; but a force of the enemy hitherto unseen, chanced to occupy it, and opened on the artillerymen, driving them back. In their retreat, one of the guns ran foul of a tree, breaking the pole, and they abandoned it. Captain Watson, with several members of his Company, A, went forward, hauled the piece to the rear, and saved it. Captain Altman, of Company C, was severely wounded, the only one injured in the Seventy-fifth.

Having arrived at Crab Orchard, and the pursuit being now abandoned, the troops rested for four days on Logan's Creek near Hall's Gap. The rebel army had made good its escape. After a long and weary march, endured for the permanent occupation of Kentucky, after one sanguinary battle, and a repulse, Bragg distrusted his own success, was fearful of his own safety, and abandoning all his lofty resolves for the conquest and the subjugation of the

North, retreated through Cumberland Gap to Middle Tennessee. Bragg omitted the grand essential of success in his plan when at Munfordsville, as his forces were between our army and the Ohio river, that he did not attack us. Had he defeated General Buell then, his success, for a time at least, would have been insured. Had he been defeated, he still had open to him the means of retreat. He neglected to strike at the opportune moment, and from that point final victory clearly rested with our arms.

On the 19th of October, General Buell again ordered an advance. It was essential that our forces should occupy Bowling Green, Nashville, and Murfreesboro in advance of Bragg, or the safety of the garrison at Nashville, under Generals Palmer, Negley and Miller, would be jeopardized, and Middle Tennessee again be overrun with the rebel hosts. The army therefore countermarched, once more passing through Stanford, Danville and Perryville. Thence it proceeded toward Lebanon, and across the North Rolling Fork. On the 24th of October it crossed the Rolling Fork, passing through New Market, and to the vicinity of Saloma. Here, for the first time, the army trains joined the troops; and they could not have arrived more seasonably, for the next day there was a heavy fall of snow, and the weather became intensely cold. It was the first severe symptom of the coming winter. The march was now steadily southward. On the 31st of October the regiment arrived at Bowling Green.

At this place, in obedience to orders from the General-in-Chief, dated at Washington, D. C., October 21st, General Buell, on the 30th instant, turned over the command of the army to General Rosecrans. On that occasion he addressed a well-written farewell order to his troops. But the change in commanders caused no delay at Bowling Green. The army moved on to Nashville, Tennessee, reaching that city on the 7th of November. The troops mostly encamped on the Edgefield side of the river. Regiments were left along the line of the Louisville railroad to protect communications to Mitchellville, below which they had been badly damaged by John Morgan's raids. From Mitchellville to Nashville, a distance of nearly forty miles, all supplies must be hauled in wagons, until the road could be repaired, which would require at least one month. The Ninth Division remained encamped at Edgefield until the 27th of November, when it moved six miles out on the Nolensville turnpike, and established camp on the left of the road, connecting it with General McCook's Corps.

On the 7th of November, General Rosecrans issued orders for a reorganization of the army. General George H. Thomas was assigned the command of the center, composed of the Divisions of Rousseau, Negley, Dumont, Fry and Palmer.

General McCook was assigned the right wing—the Divisions of Generals Sill, Jeff. C. Davis, and Sheridan.

General Crittenden was placed in command of the left wing—the Divisions of Generals Wood and Van Cleve.

General Buell had intended to push the troops straight on to Murfreesboro, thirty miles south of Nashville, thereby compelling Bragg to fall back to his original position at Chattanooga—an object which would doubtless have been consummated had General Rosecrans moved to the same point. It is probable that the reduced condition of the army, the length of his line of communication, and the difficulties involved in the necessary transportation of supplies by wagon trains, determined him, for a time at least, to remain at Nashville. Again: the situation of the rebel army was not clearly defined. Bragg had the advantage of a powerful cavalry arm, which was ever on our front, and vigilant, and behind this cover the rebel commander manœuvred his troops and perfected his plans. Information of a positive character was soon obtained, however, and the army settled into the quietude of camp.

The front of our army was rapidly formed. A small stream, called Mill Creek, with abrupt banks, and lined with a thick growth of bushes and cane-brake, extended its entire length, and constituted a strong natural *fosse*, or intrenchment. While encamped in front of Nashville, the Federal lines were frequently assailed by the rebel cavalry, and our forage trains were often attacked, but we never lost transportation thereby. The Seventy-fifth, although often out as guard, never was engaged with the enemy.

On the 19th of December the army was again reorganized.

The NINTH DIVISION was consequently designated as the FIRST DIVISION, Right Wing, Army of the Cumberland. The brigades of the Division were thus designated:

First Brigade (old Thirtieth), Colonel P. Sidney Post.

Second Brigade (old Thirty-first), Brigadier-General William P. Carlin.

Third Brigade (old Thirty-second), Colonel W. E. Woodruff.

The soldiers, thankful for the appreciation of their services by the country, rapidly recuperated their worn-out energies, and were soon in a better condition than ever before, and only awaited the trumpet's blast to summon them to battle.

CHAPTER V.

ADVANCE ON MURFREESBORO—THE BATTLE OF STONE
RIVER—GALLANTRY OF THE SEVENTY-FIFTH—RE-
TREAT OF THE REBELS.

THE movement upon the enemy at Murfreesboro
commenced on the morning of the 26th of December, 1862. The announcement was made on Christmas night, and was greeted by the troops with a
wild, shrill clamor, which bespoke willing hearts and
the assurance of victory. The day dawned drearily.
Thick volumes of mist hugged the valleys, and dense
masses of black clouds overhung the heavens. Soon
the *reveillé* rolled through the cordon of drowsy
camps encircling Nashville, and then all was activity
and life.

Bragg did not expect Rosecrans to make a winter
campaign, but supposed he had established winter
quarters on the line of Mill Creek; and therefore
had settled his at Murfreesboro. Hugging this de-
lusion to his bosom, he had sent a large force of his
cavalry, under Forrest, into West Tennessee, to har-

rass General Grant, and another, under Morgan, into Kentucky, to destroy Rosecrans' communications. The absence of this powerful arm of the rebel service was deemed by General Rosecrans the opportune occasion for striking a blow. Positive information was had that the forces of Polk and Kirby Smith were at Murfreesboro, and that Hardee's Corps was on the Shelbyville and Nolensville pikes, between Triune and Eaglesville. The army therefore moved in three columns, to wit:

McCook, by the Nolensville pike, to Triune.

Thomas, on McCook's right, down the Franklin and Wilson pikes, threatening Hardee's right, and then to fall in by the crossroads to Nolensville.

Crittenden, down the Murfreesboro pike, to La Vergne.

With Thomas's command at Nolensville, McCook was to attack Hardee at Triune, and if the enemy reinforced Hardee, Thomas was to support McCook.

If McCook beat Hardee, or Hardee retreated, and the enemy attacked us at Stewart's Creek, Crittenden was to fight him. Thomas was to come in on the left flank, and McCook, after detaching a division to pursue or observe Hardee, if retreating southward, was to move with his two remaining divisions on his rear.

At six o'clock, General Davis's Division moved down the Edmonson pike, to Prim's blacksmith shop, and thence by a dirt road to Nolensville, with General Johnson's Division in the rear. The dirt roads

traveled by our troops, especially that taken by
Davis's Division from the blacksmith shop, were very
rugged, and almost impassable, for it rained incessantly, and in torrents, all the day; but the prospect
of meeting the foe cheered our men, and their enthusiasm increased as the barometer fell. They mani-
fested the disposition soldiers ought when going into
danger—their hearts full of confidence. The enemy
was encountered within about ten miles of Mill Creek,
but was easily driven by Davis's escort. When within a mile of Nolensville, Davis ascertained that the
town was occupied in force by rebel infantry, cavalry
and artillery. He prepared for action. His first
brigade, consisting of the Twenty-second Indiana,
Fifty-ninth, Seventy-fourth, and SEVENTY-FIFTH ILLI-
NOIS, and Pinney's Fifth Wisconsin Battery, under
command of Colonel P. Sydney Post, was immediately deployed for an advance upon the town.
The battery was posted so as to command the town,
and all approaches from the south-west. At this
time the rebel cavalry took position on a range of
hills south-west of the town, to flank Davis's position.
A rebel battery also opened fire upon Post's Brigade.
Pinney's Battery silenced the enemy's guns, and
caused his cavalry to fall back beyond the town.
Davis's second brigade, Colonel W. P. Carlin, commanding, formed its line of battle on Post's right.
His third brigade, commanded by Colonel W. E.
Woodruff, was deployed on the right of Carlin, to
check any effort to turn the right flank of his line.

They advanced in splendid style, considering the
depth of mud to be waded through the ; skirmishers
driving everything before them. Post's Brigade
pushed for Triune—Pinney's Battery on the pike,
the Twenty-second Indiana and the Seventy-fourth
Illinois on the right of the pike, and the Fifty-ninth
and SEVENTY-FIFTH ILLINOIS on the left. The enemy
was posted in a position of great natural strength,
some two miles below the town, at a place called
Knob's Gap, his line resting on the hills both to the
right and the left of the pike, with one section on the
road, and the remainder near it. The rebels opened
at long range; but our line, undaunted, moved
straight on, and soon Pinney, from a knob on the left
of the road, opened at short range with his guns,
while Post's Brigade, moving with the steadiness of
automatons, carried the heights in its front, compel-
ing the enemy to abandon one of his guns. Hotchkiss' Battery also opened a steady fire, while Carlin's
Brigade carried the heights on the right of the road,
charging the battery direct, capturing two of the
guns, and, in coöperation with Post, completely routing the enemy from his position. Woodruff's Brigade, meantime, had driven the enemy upon the extreme right, and thus maintained our line intact.
This success stimulated the men to new energy and
daring. They frequently broke out in loud cheers,
which were taken up by each regiment in turn, and
echoed in strong reverberations among the hills.

At daylight on the 26th, the corps again moved

forward, the cavalry under command of General Stanley, in the advance, followed by General Johnson's Division, Sheridan closely supporting, with Davis in the rear. A wintry fog covered the country, so that only the most prominent points could be seen, making a successful movement of troops a difficult undertaking. When a mile or so advanced, a large force of the enemy's cavalry, supported by artillery, opened on our cavalry. The skirmish growing animated, Kirk's Brigade pushed forward, and soon compelled the enemy to retire. When some half mile from Triune, the enemy was found strongly posted, and another sharp skirmish ensued, in which the Twenty-ninth Indiana and the Thirty-fourth Illinois, of General Kirk's Brigade, charged a rebel battery, but the artillerists did not stand to receive the shock.

Night coming on, the troops bivouacked one mile south of Triune. The rain had descended in torrents the greater part of the day, making marching still more tedious. Here the corps encamped during the 28th, awaiting the developments of the enemy on Thomas's and Crittenden's fronts. Meantime a reconnoissance was made by General Willich, in the direction of Shelbyville, and developed the fact that Hardee's forces had retreated to Murfreesboro. General Thomas's Divisions met no resistance, and arrived at Nolensville on the 27th. Crittenden's Corps drove the enemy from La Vergne, and charged him at Stewart's Creek, saving the bridge—a very impor-

tant one to us. Here the left wing rested during the
28th, also. Thus, on this day, the army was at rest,
while the Commanding General perfected his plans
for further movement.

On the 29th of December the army was again in
motion, the right wing on the Bulle Jack road, which
leads into the Wilkinson and Murfreesboro pike.
Davis's Division again led the advance, Sheridan at
close support. The next day the entire corps crossed
Stewart's Creek, and encamped for the night at
Overall's Creek, three and one half miles from Murfreesboro.

It was now definitely known that the rebels would
make a stand in front of Murfreesboro. The 30th
was to see our army in position, and the next day
was to become memorable in the annals of our land,
as the beginning of a combat, fearful in its intensity
and frightful in its losses, and yet ineffectually telling on the fortunes of the rival republics, under whose
banners the armies so desperately fought.

Crittenden was first in line of battle on this day.
Sturdy Thomas came in next, joining his lines on the
right of Palmer; the chivalrous Rousseau lying as reserve to Negley. General Sheridan, after stubborn
fighting, arrived opposite to Negley, and established
his line of battle on the right of the Wilkinson pike.
Woodruff's Brigade moved to the front with much
steadiness, driving the rebels out of the timber in his
front, and joining General Sill's right. Carlin steadily pressed the enemy in his front, but as he was

establishing his line, the enemy opened on his right with a terrific fire of round shot and shell, and the Twenty-first Illinois, galled into madness, charged the battery, but meeting an infantry force, and being murderously used, was compelled to fall back to the brigade. Post's Brigade, with the Seventy-fourth and SEVENTY-FIFTH ILLINOIS deployed on the skirmish line, under command of Captain Hale, acting Major of the Seventy-fifth, was still further on the right, and then constituting the extreme right of the army. They moved to the aid of the Twenty-first Illinois; but in crossing a deep ravine, were also opened on with shell and canister, and compelled, first to lie down, and then to retreat. The Twenty-second Indiana was protecting the right flank from the enemy's cavalry, while the Fifty-ninth Illinois supported Pinney's Battery. Captain Hale here displayed great gallantry, and excellent judgment. He was wounded through the fleshy part of his leg, and had a horse shot under him during this affair. Several in the Seventy-fifth were here wounded, but as their names are not designated as such on this particular day, they must come under the aggregate for the battle. Post's Brigade in line, Kirk and Willich joined him, thus completing the battle order.

Across the narrow valley which extended along our front was posted the rebel army, in order of battle; its right wing resting upon heights on the east bank of Stone river, intersecting the river parallel to our left front; the center extending along a ridge,

through cotton fields and timber, which sloped gradually toward our center; its left wing tracing the
crest of a rough and rocky ridge, partially screened
by timber, and terminating some half mile south of
the Franklin turnpike.

The 30th of December had been a dreary day.
Rain had fallen almost constantly, and the soldiers
were saturated with water. Toward night the wind
swept coldly from the north, and as no bivouac fires
were allowed on the *real* front, the aspect was truly
cheerless. At midnight the stars faintly twinkled
through the cloud-rifts which still hung heavily overhead, portentous of rain. Within half a mile of each
other lay two mighty armies, in the most perfect
silence, waiting for the morning's light, to rush together in the deadly rencontre. Peace then ruled
supreme—

> " The forests' fretted aisle,
> And leafy domes above them bent
> And solitude—
> So eloquent !"

The contest began at break of day, on Wednesday, the 31st of December, by a most audacious attack on Johnson's Division, and another almost simul-
taneously on Sheridan's; then another on Davis's.
On Johnson's front—on the devoted brigades of
Kirk and Willich—was massed more than half of the
rebel army, under McCown, Cheatham and Clai-
borne. It was a most desperate struggle, and re-

sulted in the immediate discomfiture of Johnson's men, in the death wound of the gallant and gifted Kirk, and in the capture of the brave old Willich. Captain Pinney stood by his guns in a perfect frenzy of impatience to open on the enemy as he passed in front of Davis's pickets; but as his object could not, in the dim light, be clearly discerned, he was not permitted to fire. It was a sad mistake; for as the enemy moved by the flank, within rifle shot, Pinney could have dealt death in his ranks, and aided by Post's Brigade, all of whom were anxious for the fray, the tide of battle might have been turned, and the dreadful disaster which occurred to the right wing prevented, or at least stayed until better prepared for the attack. The retreat of Johnson's Division left Post's Brigade exposed to a flank movement, which the enemy was now rapidly executing, and compelled it to fall back and partially change front. In the execution of this movement, Companies E and H, of the SEVENTY-FIFTH ILLINOIS, under command of Lieutenant Blodgett, were on the picket line, and he received instructions to contest the rebel advance as skirmishers. The tide of battle pushed back so rapidly as to leave these companies so far in the advance that some of Carlin's Brigade,—already furiously engaged by another force of the enemy, which had obliqued to the left from its attack on Johnson,—mistook it for a rebel force, dimly seen through the trees and bushes, and fired into it a terrible volley, fortunately doing but little damage.

They finally withdrew to the regiment. The brigade kept falling back, changing front three times, so that now its line of battle was perpendicular to its original formation. At last, stationed behind a fence in the edge of the timber, it awaited the rebel onset. Davis's troops resisted the terrible battle-shock of the enemy for some time; but at length they were compelled to give way. Nearly one fourth of their number lay either dead or wounded on the ensanguined field, proving how determined their resistance had been. But again and again, Johnson's troops, though stubbornly fighting, constantly give way; and as the right doubles back on the center, Davis is forced to retire also; each tree in the belt of timber furnishes a temporary shelter, and not until an enfilade fire weakened the line, would they leave their position. Again it fell back across a large cotton field, and here a most determined resistance was made. Here Captain Pinney was mortally wounded while serving his own guns, and mowing huge roadways through the rebel ranks. He was left on the field where his gallant deeds were done. Here the Fifty-ninth Illinois received magnificently a charge of the enemy, and with fixed bayonets held him at bay. During this retreat Captain Hale was wounded in the hip by a splinter from his sabre-blade, which was knocked out by a rebel bullet. This compelled him to leave the field. Here, too, dashed up a mounted officer, very near the Seventy-fifth's line, as if to give an order, and was supposed to be

5

one of our own Generals until a gust of wind blew back his overcoat, disclosing his uniform, when he was found to be a rebel. Several muskets were instantly leveled on him; he escaped unharmed, and disappeared in the cedars. The rebel tide again surged onward, and backward flow Davis's brigades. Now they near the Murfreesboro pike, which intersects the battle ground, and is the key to the position, for on it are all the Federal supply and ammunition trains. These captured, our doom would be sealed, and victory inevitably perch on the rebel banners. The enemy, thus far, had been each time repulsed on Davis's and Sheridan's front; but his heavy turning columns so completely enveloped the right, that the positions could not be maintained. They had fallen back full a mile and a half. It was now two o'clock in the afternoon, while the furious onset was commenced at a little after six in the morning. Eight hours of conflict, with a foe so overwhelming, proves of itself that there was no disgraceful panic, such as some cowardly newspaper reporters back at Nashville had stated, thereby stigmatizing with shame the fair name of our soldiers, and depriving them of their most valued jewel—*honor*. It was a serious question now, whether this position—the last one which our army could hope to take—could be held. Johnson's Division was already there, nearly in prolongation of Davis's line, and fighting with the desperation of despair. And, happily for him, his gallant division, the first to be compromised,

was now the first, aside from the pugnacious Rousseau, to hurl back the enemy with a force which demoralized him completely. Davis, seeing this, and
seeing the enemy, who had so terribly menaced his
own front, again moving upon his decimated brigades, in columns of battalion front, four battalions
deep, resolved to imitate Johnson, and crush him,
if it were a human possibility. And here, most
opportunely, other help arrived. Negley's and Rousseau's Divisions came upon the ground. Boldly the
foe marched up; short but desperately bloody was
the struggle. A 'dazzling sheet of flame burst from
the firm ranks of our heroes, which quickly shivered
their lines, and aided by several batteries which now
opened with terrific roar, shaking the very earth,
crushed into flying fragments his solid masses ; and
thus, for the right wing, ended the battle for this
day. The scene now presented was awful.. The
smoke of battle had lifted, and the field could again
be surveyed. The ground was literally covered with
the dead and wounded, friend and foe, cruelly mangled, scores of horses, broken gun carriages and caissons. Davis's troops, now exhausted in ammunition
and in strength, were relieved, and did not participate any further in the engagement until late in the
afternoon. As the division moved into position on the
right of the newly established line of battle, some
skirmishing ensued, which nightfall ended.

Thus fought General Davis's Division in that eventful Wednesday's battle. For more than eight hours

it resisted the engulfing wave of rebel prowess contesting its advance by every obstacle possible. No where, in all that extended battle front, was a firmer countenance presented; and no where, save on Rousseau's front, did the enemy charge more desperately, or meet with more disastrous receptions. And among the regiments which here distinguished themselves, none did more valiant service or is more entitled to honorable mention than the SEVENTY-FIFTH ILLINOIS. Its loss was not as heavy as that of many other commands, while it effected equally decisive results. Two were killed, twenty-five wounded, and twenty-one taken prisoners, among them Captain A. McMoore, of Company D. The gallantry of Colonel Bennett, Major Watson, and Captain Hale, elicited encomiums of praise and mention in the reports of superiors. At one time, as the regiment fell back from its position in the timber, Major Watson and Sergeant George G. Messer remained behind for several minutes, and discharged several volleys into the advancing foe.

The company commanders, Captains McMoore, Frost and Storey, Lieutenants Shaw, Sandford, Thompson and Parker, and Sergeants Elisha Bull, Frank Bingham and Augustus Johnson, commanding Companies B, H and I, respectively, did their duty well, and proved themselves gallant, discreet, and competent for the position they held. Thus, amid the glorious results of such a battle, it is a pleasing duty to mention the names of the gallant living, and it is equally painful to mention those of the heroic dead. Privates Washington Wood, of Company C, and Sydney Merriman, of K, fell in the heat of the fray, as soldiers love to fall—with their faces to the foe.

Never before was the service of the medical department so promptly executed. Surgeons braved danger nobly, and suffered captivity, that they might administer to our wounded. Among this class was Assistant-Surgeon John C. Corbus.

Wednesday night it rained, and many, during the conflict, had abandoned their knapsacks, blankets and shelter tents, so they must patiently endure their sufferings, hoping for the New Year and sunlight. At length morning came, and with it sunlight. By ten o'clock the clouds had rifted away, and a breeze swept refreshingly from the north, and dried the mud. The sky became a clear, deep blue, and Nature smiled lovingly on yesterday's field of carnage.

The results of Wednesday's battle compelled a readjustment of the Federal lines. The left wing was retired some two hundred and fifty yards from its former position, the extreme left resting on Stone river, the right on the Nashville railroad and pike; joining this was Thomas's Corps; then came Johnson, Sheridan and Davis, the whole line running nearly north-west, and refused to the right, resting along the slope of a ridge covered with a heavy cedar growth, Davis's Division extending across and to the rear of the Nashville pike. The cavalry was further down the pike to Overall's Creek.

The first of January passed without any general engagement. There were several artillery duels along the lines; skirmishing with the pickets was frequent, and reconnoissances were pushed forward to all points where it was supposed the enemy was concealed from observation. General Rosecrans made a personal inspection of every part of his lines, and directed several changes in position; and so handsomely did he arrange all things, that the designs of the enemy were defeated. The right wing threw up breastworks for defence, and in this work the Seventy-fourth and SEVENTY-FIFTH ILLINOIS were engaged. During this day, while Company F was deployed on the skirmish line, General Rosecrans rode along, and told the men they "ought to retire a little, as they were too much exposed." Captain Vorrey replied, "We were ordered, General, to hold this particular line, and mean to do it." The General rejoined, "That is right; obey orders."

Toward night General Crittenden was ordered to occupy a point opposite a ford near which his left rested. He first sent a brigade, then the division of Van Cleve, supported by another brigade of Palmer's.

About three o'clock in the afternoon—having, during the morning, opened his batteries on our center, and made strong demonstrations of attack on our right, as a feint to cover his real intentions—the enemy debouched from the woods opposite to Van

Cleve, and moved directly upon him in heavy masses
of infantry, battalion front, supported by three batteries of artillery. It was Breckenridge's command
advancing to a banquet of death. Van Cleve was
forced back, and his men rushed across the river in
great confusion, closely followed by the enemy. The
artillery of the left was now ranged to meet the foe,
when that brave and true soldier, Colonel John F.
Miller, commanding a brigade in Negley's Division,
perceiving a splendid opportunity to attack the enemy
in flank, ordered his brigade forward, charged bayonets, routed him, turned the fortune of the day, capturing four cannon and one stand of colors, besides
strewing the ground with heaps of slain. It is right,
here, that the truth should be asserted, in order that
history may be vindicated. The glory of this
grand success is universally given to General Negley.
Negley was a good soldier; but he had one failing
— that of overcautiousness. He never ventured.
At the time of the rout of Van Cleve, he was in the
rear, aiding the former general in rallying his disorganized brigades. He was not at the front when
this opportune moment presented itself, which Colonel Miller perceived and embraced. Miller inquired
for Negley, to ask leave to charge, but being informed of the mission he was then on, he assumed
the responsibility of the movement himself, and
therefore he it was who conceived, ordered and executed the crowning action of that memorable field of
carnage. Jeff. C. Davis's Division, and Willich's

(Gibbon's) Brigade of Johnson's Division, were hurried up to the support of the menaced front; but with the exception of one or two regiments, had no active participation in it; and this aid was not given where Miller operated, but on Palmer's front. It seems an injustice in Generals Rosecrans and Negley, not to give Colonel Miller the credit for this affair, as they were thoroughly conversant with the facts; and the only plea that can be made in their behalf (which does not in the least justify it), is, that its brilliancy conceded to him, would disparage too much the reputation of Negley, and deprive the Commander-in-Chief of a little of that *éclat*, which at that time surrounded him. Hence, while each of them, in their official reports, greatly complimented Colonel Miller, for his gallantry in this action, neither of them alluded to this great service, and thus, in their reports, and in all the histories of the rebellion, the credit rests upon Rosecrans and Negley. It won for the latter his second star, while Miller still wore his eagle. Finally, after the action of Liberty Gap, where he lost his left eye, the Government began to appreciate his services, and conferred upon him a Brigadier's commission, and subsequently that of Major-General by brevet rank.

When the cheers of Miller's victorious troops rolled back over the hills, commingled with the roll of musketry and the booming of cannon, all was excitement on the line of the right wing. Every one asked what it meant. Just then, up rode Colonel Post, flushed with excitement, and exclaimed, "Cheer away boys; I may take you into a fight within fifteen minutes!" and as the cheer resounded along his front, up dashed.an orderly, with orders to move to the left, as we have before mentioned. It was nearly dark when they arrived and took position upon the extreme left of our army. That night they threw up breastworks, and lay down to rest on the cold, wet ground, while the constant whiz of sharp-shooters' minies proclaimed watchfulness and auda-city on the side of the rebels. Daylight of the 3rd arrives. The rain still continues incessantly, the stream rises rapidly, necessitating a recrossing by the troops; so the position is abandoned, and Davis's troops return to their old place of bivouac. The enemy was shelled by our artillery, but no regular engagement occurred. Another great battle was then anticipated; but the rain must first cease. Du-ring that night, Bragg, despairing of success in the contest, evacuated Murfreesboro, retreating toward Tullahoma; thus furnishing the most conclusive evi-dence of his complete discomfiture and defeat. On Wednesday their success was considerable, driving our right wing back from one to two and a half miles, besides capturing twenty-eight pieces of artil-lery; but Friday's terrible repulse showed we were the final victors.

The Federal loss in this battle was fifteen hundred and thirty-three in killed, including ninety-two offi-cers, and seven thousand two hundred and forty-five wounded, besides about twenty-eight hundred prison-ers. Bragg, in his official report, admits a loss of more than ten thousand in killed and wounded; but this does not include twenty-eight hundred wounded and prisoners left in our hands.

Our army at once occupied Murfreesboro, throwing around it a cordon of camps, the position of the SEVENTY-FIFTH being some ten miles from town on the Shelbyville pike. Thus ended this fearful strife, beginning, in fact, on the 26th of December, 1862, and ending on the 3rd of January, 1863. The rebel-lion had received another blow, but at a fearful cost in life and limb. Again the nation rejoiced and mourned.

CHAPTER VI.

MURFREESBORO is situated upon high and rolling
ground, and is on the east bank of the west fork of
Stone river. It is the center of a rich agricultural
section, and cotton is a heavy staple in its trade.
From it diverge many turnpikes and roads, commu-
nicating with all the principal places in Middle Tennessee; indeed it is considered as the military key
of that country. As such, it has been in the possession either of the Union or rebel forces ever since
the outbreak of the rebellion. General Rosecrans
availed himself of its commanding heights to secure
a strong defensive position. A proportionate force
of the army was constantly detailed for the work,
and to-day every knoll of importance is crowned with
a fortification.

The rainy season had already set in, and the Cumberland river, swollen by the rains, teemed with
transports laden with supplies; and Murfreesboro
was made an intermediate depot for army stores.

The camp of the First Division was most of the time on the Shelbyville turnpike, which crossed the chain of Coffee Hills at a place known as Guy's Gap, some seven miles south of Murfreesboro. This gap was the scene of several brilliant skirmishes during the months of January and February, as McCook's Corps procured from that section the forage for its animals. Our losses were always slight, and the engagements were not of importance enough to demand special mention.

Shortly after the army moved into Murfreesboro, the War Department again remodeled it, forming it into three *corps d'armée*. The troops under Thomas were designated as the Fourteenth, those under McCook the Twentieth, and those under Crittenden the Twenty-first Army Corps.

During the month of March, the enemy appeared in heavy force along our front, and Van Dorn laid siege to Franklin. The enemy also made several demonstrations on the troops at Murfreesboro, advancing in considerable force, and attacking our outposts on the Salem and Middleton roads. Sheridan was sent to the aid of Granger at Franklin, and a reconnoissance was ordered on all the roads leading from Murfreesboro. Post's Brigade was stationed for a time at Salem, as a corps of observation. Davis's entire division shortly after moved to Franklin, but participated in no engagement, and after a week's stay, returned again, on the 11th of February, to Murfreesboro. While there, however, it built a bridge across the Harpeth river, made a ford to cross teams, and did picket duty. The weather was very rainy, and the mud almost fathomless, during the entire trip. On the 7th of March the Seventy-fifth made a recon-noissance to Triune; saw no enemy, but foraged con-siderably in the country round about, and returned again on the 10th instant.

During the severe service following the Stone river campaign, Captain Frost, of Company E, being the senior officer present, was much of the time doing duty as a field officer, and his name appears on the official records of those days of hardship as a faithful officer, ever at his post. He was especially noted for his care and attention with the picket lines.

While encamped here, Captain McMoore and Lieu-tenant Blodgett returned from their captivity in the South, having enjoyed for three months the hospita-ble attentions for which the Southern people have been so noted since the beginning of the war. Most of the men also returned, save those who fell victims to disease. The regiment here, too, shortly after the battle of Stone river, learned of the death of Lieu-tenant Ezekiel I. Kilgore, of Company I. He was a martyr to our country's cause—not a victim to the leaden hail of our enemies, but to sickness consequent upon exposure and hardships following the battle of Perryville. He died on Christmas evening, 1862.

The encampment of the Twentieth Army Corps, while at Murfreesboro, will never be forgotten by the new troops of 1862, and it will be equally remem-

bered by the friends of many a poor soldier who
there rendered his final accounts. It was unusually
rainy, even for the winter season, and lurid skies,
humid atmosphere, deep mud, miserable tents, and
inexperience in the new condition of life, all con-
spired to produce sickness and death, and convert
the camp into one great field-hospital.

Several influences were in silent operation, pro-
ducing serious disease. The chief of these were
malaria and scorbutive taint. The former displayed
itself in the different types of pneumonia, the latter
in diarrhœa. It was the process of acclimation, and
it must go on, be the process ever so fatal. Again,
the diseases produced by miasmatic influences seemed
to assume an adynamic character, and greatly per-
plexed the minds of the physicians as to the proper
mode of treatment. Measles also prevailed to a
great extent. Many died from its effects. January,
February and March of this year were dismal months
indeed to the gallant men of the North, who daily
saw comrade after comrade wasting away, unattended
by wifely care or sisterly affection, and at last followed, with solemn step and aching heart, their remains to a soldier's grave.

It was impossible to procure official documentary
evidence of the medical department of the regiment,
relative either to its monthly sickness or monthly
mortality rates; but from such data as are attain-
able, based upon the returns of Surgeon McDermot,
Medical Director of the army, the ratio of sickness

per thousand of mean strength, during the three
months named, was, on an average, 236.70 per cent.
per month. The mortality rates were higher, accordingly, the average ratio per thousand being for the
same period, 6.82 per cent. Surgeons Phillips and
Corbus worked faithfully in the discharge of their
high duties, and with marked success, considering
the stores at their command and the location of their
patients. It is the cruel fate of war, and in future
the living comrades in arms will tearfully think of
them, and the struggles they together endured. Now

> We are scattered—we are scattered;
> Yet may we meet again
> In a brighter and a purer sphere,
> Beyond the reach of pain.
> Where the shadows of this lower world
> Can never cloud the eye—
> When the mortal hath put brightly on
> Its immortality.

By the first of June the fortifications were completed, and everything in readiness for another campaign. The soldiers hailed the indications with
pleasure, and joyfully sang of the "good time coming."

By the 20th of June the location of the enemy's
army had become thoroughly understood. His main
infantry force was in position north of Duck river, its
right resting at War Trace, and its left at Shelbyville. Cavalry protected its flanks, on the right to

McMinnville, and on the left to Columbia and Spring Hill. In front of this entire position was a chain called the Coffee Hills—a spur of the Cumberland range—high, rough and rocky, with but few roads suitable for the movement of an army. These roads are, leading from Murfreesboro : by the way of McMinnville ; by the Manchester pike, which crosses the hills at Hoover's Gap ; by the War Trace road through Liberty Gap ; by a dirt road through Belle-buckle Gap, and by the Shelbyville pike, through Guy's Gap. The enemy held all these passes with a strong force, and his main position at Shelbyville was strongly intrenched. Here Bragg intended to offer battle, as he supposed General Rosecrans would attack in this direction, this pike affording most ex-cellent means for the transportation of troops and trains. Polk's Corps was at Shelbyville ; Hardee's joined him on the right, occupying the Gaps. The total effective rebel force was estimated at forty thou-sand men. Tullahoma is strongly intrenched with a redan line of rifle-pits, and a bastioned fort. It is further protected by the defiles of Duck river, a nar-row, but deep and swift stream, with a range of rocky hills intervening between it and the "barrens;" in fact, this stream constitutes the dividing line between the higher and lower lands, or basin of Middle Ten-nessee.

To expel the rebel army from this region was the object of the next campaign. The plan adopted was to menace their left and center with a heavy force of infantry and cavalry, and under cover of these feints, to turn their right, destroy the bridge across Elk river, six miles south of Tullahoma, cutting off their line of retreat, thus compelling them to offer battle on our own ground, or retreat by a circuitous and hazardous route across the Cumberland mountains and the Tennessee river.

The morning of the 24th of June—the day which was to begin the inauguration of a brilliant and enduring victory—like that of the 26th of December, the day of the advance upon Murfreesboro, opened with a dreary, dismal rain, which soon rendered the roads almost impassable for artillery and trains; but the troops were joyous, nevertheless, and indulged in all the burlesque usual to camp. General Sheridan's Division led the advance down the Shelbyville pike, proceeding on to Guy's Gap. Johnson's and Davis's Divisions followed Sheridan for six miles, and turned to the left, marching along a dirt road to Old Millersburg. The column arrived at this place about noon. Thus far, there were no signs of the enemy. General Johnson then proceeded to reconnoitre the *canon* of Liberty Gap, closely supported by General Davis. Johnson soon discovered the enemy, and right gallantly his troops proceeded to carry the hills. In two hours' time, by skillful manœuvreing, he had routed the enemy—Liddell's command—and held the entrance to the Gap. Pursuit was made for a mile, to "Liberty Meeting House." Picket lines were then established, the

6

division moved up, with Davis at the entrance of the
Gap, and there encamped for the night. Willich's
Brigade, of Johnson's Division, which did most of
the fighting on this day, sustained a loss of ninety-
two men in killed and wounded.

The men, exhausted by the weary march through
deep mud, and the excitement incident to battle,
raised their shelter-tents, rolled themselves in their
blankets, and though soaked to the skin, and lying
on the wet ground, were soon oblivious to all things
earthly. An occasional report of a sentry's gun was
all that broke the stillness of the dismal scene.

Three o'clock in the morning of the 25th found
the troops astir and in arms—a precaution against
surprise. Information, positive in character, had
been received, that Liddell's Brigade was reinforced
by Cleburne's Division, and that a stout resistance
would be made to our further progress.

The line of battle established next morning was—
for Johnson's Division, Willich and Miller in the
front, with Balderin as reserve; for Davis's Division,
Carlin and Post in the front line, with Woodruff's
Brigade as reserve. From daylight until about ten
o'clock, a desultory fire was kept up between the
forces on outpost along the entire front, at long
range, and with but few, if any, casualties. At ten,
an attack was made on Willich, and a warm skirmish
ensued. Again all was quiet, but it was the stillness
which precedes the storm. In less than half an hour
another most determined attack was made upon Wil-

lich.   This was kept up constantly until two o'clock,
when the rebel general made a furious charge upon
his front.   Willich's men stood undismayed, although
the rebel shells fell among them with fatal precision,
Four times was the rebel column repulsed.   Still it
would not yield the contest.   At last Willich's
ammunition gave out, and he determined to attempt
a decisive measure, and force the rebels from their
position at the base of the hill.   Accordingly he
ordered that splendid regiment, the Forty-ninth
Ohio, which had lain in reserve, to charge.   Its formation was in four ranks, and the order was given to
advance firing.   With the gallant Gibson at its head,
it faced steadily a perfect shower of leaden hail and
iron shell, reserving its fire until within close range
of the rebel line.   Then it opened deliberately and
unerringly.   The third volley by rank routed the
rebel brigade, and flung it back into the open field.
With a shout, Gibson's men rushed on, impatient to
use the bayonet; but the rebel retreat was too rapid,
and so the column was judiciously halted at the fence
whence the enemy had fled.

General Johnson, thinking that now the enemy,
thus pressed, could be driven from his position in the
opposite hills, ordered forward Miller's Brigade.
The Thirty-fourth Illinois formed a part of this command.   Miller deployed his regiments into line of
battle, passed to the front, and engaged the enemy
en echelons by battalions at sixty paces.   Colonel
Miller was severely wounded in the very outset of

the action, and the command fell upon Colonel Rose, of the Seventy-seventh Pennsylvania, a brave man, most gallant in battle, skillful in handling a regiment, but of too excitable a temperament to judiciously manœuvre a brigade. Hence a sad mistake was given, in an order which deprived this brigade of the full fruition of victory, by a movement in retreat, instead of by the flank. The Thirty-fourth most tenaciously held its ground, and saved the position. Carlin's Brigade moved up on the right of the Thirty-fourth, and the Thirty-eighth Illinois being directly in front, charged up the hills, thus ending the conflict. Post's Brigade did not participate in the engagement, otherwise than to maintain a prolongation of the front. ' But it was ready and willing to engage the foe, had necessity required it. Captain Hale, of the Seventy-fifth Illinois, had just received an appointment as Inspector on the Brigade Staff. Lieutenant Segur, of Company I, just promoted from sergeant, being unwell, Lieutenant Henry Parrott, of Company C, was assigned to its command. These are all the changes that seem worthy of note at this stage of the narrative.

While all this was going on, Thomas had been equally successful at Hoover's Gap, routing the foe and pushing him back on Manchester and Tullahoma. Gordon Granger had been successful in his attack upon Shelbyville, and instead of making a feint, merely, he achieved a handsome success, driving Polk across Duck river, and toward Tullahoma. Crittenden was struggling in the mud on the Manchester road, but arrived at that point with the rest of the army; and now the whole column concentered on Tullahoma, at which point the rebels had massed by the 28th. The troops marched from Liberty to Hoover's Gap, and thence to Manchester, from the 26th to the 28th instant. Here they remained until the first of July, awaiting the arrival and disposition in battle order of the other *corps d'armée*. While here, all extra baggage was sent back to Murfreesboro; but the horrible state of the roads, and the starved condition of the mules, most of whom had nothing to eat for three days, rendered it necessary to destroy most of the stuff transported.

On the night of the 30th of June the army was in order of battle, ready to engage the enemy on the morrow. Heavy reconnoissances pushed forward on the 1st of July toward Tullahoma, developed the fact that the enemy was retreating. The army was at once put in motion, but so soft and spongy was the soil from the almost incessant rain since the 24th of June, that it required eleven hours of marching for the infantry to reach Tullahoma, a distance of eleven miles. Johnson's Division remained here; but Davis and Sheridan, together with Thomas and Crittenden, pushed on across the Elk, driving the rebels into the Cumberland mountains, and capturing sixteen hundred prisoners. Davis's Division encamped at Winchester, and now that Bragg was across the Tennessee, our army established a new position, its right

resting at Winchester and Cowan, and its left at
McMinnville. Here it recruited from the exhaustion
of its weary marches. Our victory had been a brilliant, although almost a bloodless one; the losses on
our part not exceeding one thousand in killed and
wounded.

CHAPTER VII.

WINCHESTER is a very pretty town, and numbers about one thousand white population. Its streets run at right angles, and are of good width. The sidewalks are good, and the town is suburban in its aspect of green wilderness. In the center of the public square stands the Court House—a large, square, two story brick structure, but antique in its style of architecture. There are several churches, representing the leading denominations. The college is a female institution, well endowed, and bears the name of its principal donor. There are but few Unionists in this county. The voice of Freedom had no utterance during the war; it was banished like an outlaw. Three regiments of infantry, a battalion of cavalry, and one artillery company, were recruited in this county alone, to fight in the rebel cause.

Here the army rested until the 16th of August. The health of the soldiers was fine—in fact, it was never better. The orchards of the country were laden with an abundance of fast ripening fruit, and the roadways were lined with the most luscious black-berries ; of these the men ate most heartily.

On the 16th the different army corps were again in motion, soon to meet the foe on another most im-portant occasion of the war. Crittenden's Corps moved in three columns from Hillsboro, Manchester and McMinnville, over the Cumberland mountains to Thierman, Dunlap and Pikesville, in the Sequatchy valley. Thomas's Corps moved over the mountains by way of the University, to Battle Creek and Crow Creek, near the Tennessee. McCook's Corps moved as follows : Davis's Division moved to near Steven-son, Alabama, by way of Mount Top and Crow Creek. Sheridan's Division was already at Steven-son and Bridgeport, whither it had advanced upon the completion of the railroad to those points. John-son's Division moved from Tullahoma by way of Winchester, Salem and Larkin's Fork, to Bellefonte, Alabama. Cavalry moved upon both flanks of the army to protect it against the enemy's cavalry; that on the right striking the Tennessee river at Whites-burg, that on the left at Shell Mound.

By the 21st the army was encamped on the north bank of the Tennessee. And here it enjoyed a res-pite ; but it was only temporary. Meantime the Michigan Engineers, the Pioneers, and heavy details

of infantry were busy in the construction of pontoons, trestles and rafts, whereby to cross the river,
and move upon the enemy. It was evident the
ordeal of battle was not far distant, either as to time
or place.

While the SEVENTY-FIFTH lay near Stevenson,
Major Kilgore—now Lieutenant-Colonel — rejoined
the command, after an absence of about ten months,
on account of his terrible wound, received at Perryville. Possessing a very strong constitution, wiry
and vigorous, he had outlived that which would have
been the death of any one less favored by nature or
habit in health. He was now again in the field,
ready for another battle and its dreadful fortunes.
About this time, also, Sergeant-Major Silas D. Frost
passed such a creditable examination before the Military Board, that he received a Captain's commission
in one of the new organizations of colored troops.

The movement of the army across the Tennessee
commenced on the 29th of August. The crossing
was made in boats at Shell Mound, on rafts at Battle'
Creek, on a trestle bridge at Bridgeport, and on
pontoons at Copeton's Ferry, opposite Stevenson.
Thomas traversed the Sand Mountains, and concentrated near Trenton, Georgia. He then seized Frick's,
Cooper's and Stevens's Gaps on the Lookout range.
The valley along these gaps is called Le Lemore's
Cove. Crittenden moved to Wauhatchie, in Lookout valley, joining Thomas, and threatening Chattanooga across the nose of Lookout mountain. McCook

pushed his corps over the Sandy mountains, and into the valley beyond, seizing Winston's Gap at its head. The cavalry made demonstrations toward Alpine and Rome.

It was on the 30th of August Davis's Division crossed the Tennessee, and on the 4th of September it arrived at Valley Head, and encamped several days at Winston's house. While the troops were guarding this important pass, a supply train was sent to Stevenson, on which many sick men were returned to hospital, escorted in part by Company A, of the Seventy-fifth Illinois. The train returned safely on the 16th. Meantime, on the 9th, the Second and Third Brigades made a reconnoissance forward on Lookout mountain toward Alpine, and the First Brigade, Colonel P. Sidney Post, was instructed to hold all the passes to this mountain leading from Valley Head. The SEVENTY-FIFTH, during this time and for some days previous, was under the command of Lieutenant-Colonel Kilgore, Colonel Bennett being sick, although still with the regiment. He was too brave a soldier to leave the command at such a critical time, so long as he could possibly walk or ride. The brigade picketed these passes until the night of the 11th, when Colonel Post received an order from General McCook, assigning his command to the " onerous and important duty of moving all the trains of this corps and the cavalry corps to the front." The ascent over the mountain was very steep, and the task an arduous one; but by the help of seven companies of infantry, who put their shoulders to the wheels, all the trains cleared the ascent.

Colonel Post, learning from scouts and citizens, also by a letter from General McCook, that a large force of Confederate cavalry was near Lebanon, threatening his communications, and trains crossing Sand mountains, and also learning that a large cavalry supply train was moving up in his rear without a guard, he dispatched the SEVENTY-FIFTH ILLINOIS, now under command of Colonel Bennett, to protect it. The regiment returned on the 13th with the train, having made, with much endurance and commendable spirit, a march through the heat and dust of twenty-eight miles in less than twenty hours. Now, Post's Brigade being temporarily assigned to the command of General Lytle, and being informed by him that he should withdraw his command at three o'clock on the morning of the 16th, Post sent the Fifty-ninth Illinois up the mountain, to defend the approaches by the Alpine road. It reached its position near Little river about one in the morning of the 16th, and was soon after strengthened by the SEVENTY-FIFTH ILLINOIS.

On the 18th, the road being clear, Post pushed forward his trains, keeping them in constant motion until eleven that night, when he bivouacked within one mile of Stevens's Gap, having made a march of twenty-three miles over very hilly and rough mountain roads.

Meantime, developments had been made on the

centre and left. Crittenden had moved up Lookout mountain by a dangerous road called Nick-a-Jack Trace to Summertown, and developed the fact that the enemy had evacuated Chattanooga. It was now ascertained that Bragg had been ordered to fall back toward Atlanta on the Georgia State road, and await the reinforcement of Longstreet's Virginia forces, and that Breckenridge was at Rome. Crittenden occupied Chattanooga on the 9th, and moved his advance down the valley to Rossville on the 10th. Our cavalry made reconnoissances down Alpine and Broomtown valleys, and the weight of evidence now showed that the enemy was massing at Lafayette. Crittenden therefore moved to Ringgold, and reconnoitered to Gordon's Mills. Thomas moved out of the passes which he had held, pushing toward Lafayette, through Dry Gap of Pigeon mountain. Finding the enemy in heavy force, he retreated to Stevens's Gap. McCook's Corps concentrated here, and now it was further ascertained that Johnston's Mississippi army had reinforced Bragg, and that our army would soon be attacked with an overwhelming force. It was in a bad position to resist. It extended from Gordon's Mills, on Chickamauga Creek, to Alpine, a distance of fifty miles. There must be, a rapid concentration, or it would be annihilated in detail. On the 17th the concentration was effected. Crittenden remained firm at Gordon's Mills. Thomas joined him on the right. Sheridan came next, occupying Stevens's Gap; Davis's two brigades were at Dug

Gap, while Johnson was at Pond Springs, near Cat-
lett's Gap.

On the 18th the enemy made strong demonstrations toward our left, with the intention of cutting
off our communications with Chattanooga—the objec-
tive point of the campaign—and forcing it to battle
under great disadvantages and against overwhelming
odds. Rosecrans now moved his forces down the
Chickamauga, so as to cover the Chattanooga road,
and hardly were they in position, when Bragg made
a furious attack on our left. Then came the carnage
of Chickamauga, which lasted for two long September days, and far exceeded in intensity Shiloh or
Stone River. On the 21st our army arrived at Chattanooga, where it was destined to undergo a terrible
siege, which for a time seemed likely to end in our
evacuation of the place.

All in all, Chickamauga was a victory. On the
19th of September the entire army, with the exception of two brigades, was in the battle, and defeated
every attempt of the enemy to turn our left flank,
securing its own concentration, and holding the great
object of that day's strife—the approaches to Chattanooga. The battle of the 20th was equally a success,
for, after a last desperate but fruitless assault, the
enemy ceased the combat. The army then withdrew
to Rossville, and awaited attack. But the enemy,
deprived of more than nineteen thousand combatants,
felt incapable of keeping the field. The campaign
was offensive, but the battle defensive. Had we

been driven back across the Tennessee, it would have been a sore defeat for our cause; but as we occupied, fully and securely, the great point which we sought to gain—Chattanooga—the impartial mind can but say we secured the substantial fruits of a victory. Our side, too, sustained a fearful loss of more than fifteen thousand men, in killed, wounded and prisoners.

We will now return to ascertain the fate of Post's brave command, which, in that hour of extreme peril, had been left so isolated from the protection of the main army. At two o'clock on the morning of the 19th, Post received a letter of instruction from Department Headquarters, to remain at Stevens's Gap, and "to hold that point at all hazard; but if compelled to abandon the Gap, to retire along the mountain road to Chattanooga, contesting the ground inch by inch." Dispositions were made accordingly. At four o'clock, on the morning of the 20th, General McCook directed him to send the trains by the mountain road to Chattanooga, and to hasten his brigade to the battle-field by way of Crawfish Springs. With the train were sent sixty-seven rebel prisoners, captured during the march and the stay at Winston's and Stevens's Gaps. As the brigade advanced, the cannonading grew more and more distinct, telling, too truly, that a tremendous contest was waging, in which they were not participating, yet suffering all the disquietude incident to separation and exposure. At the Ringgold road the enemy was found in considerable force, but a heavy line of skirmishers, under command of Captain Robert Hale, dispersed him, though constantly annoyed until the command reached the Springs, which was one o'clock that afternoon. Here Post reported to General R. B. Mitchell, commanding a cavalry division, who was posted to partially cover the right flank of our army. Mitchell informed Post that all communication with McCook was cut off, and that it would be madness to attempt to join him with a single brigade. Mitchell therefore directed Post to form his brigade in line of battle to repel an attack which he greatly feared would be made upon him. This disposition was made; but Post, having received orders from McCook to join the army, felt extremely anxious to do so, or at least to inform him of his arrival at Crawfish Springs, and ascertain what further should be done. Mitchell's cavalry had made several ineffectual attempts to communicate with McCook, but each horseman sent was either captured or yielded the mission. Captain Hale, ambitious to serve the cause in any way honorable to himself, and as full of intrepidity and daring as ever was Israel Putnam, of the "olden time," stepped forth, and volunteered to act as a courier. It was deemed rashness by Mitchell, and was considered doubtful by Post; but so earnest was Hale to venture the experiment, that both consented, and mounting one of the swiftest cavalry horses in the command, he started, safely reached McCook, although environed with perils, and several

times narrowly escaping death or capture; and not
only did he this, but he returned, bearing a dispatch
from McCook. Later in the day he repeated the
adventure as satisfactorily as before, and received the
official compliments of Post, Mitchell, Davis and
McCook.

Captain Hale's reports fully satisfying Post and
Mitchell that it would be unwise to attempt joining
the main army, the two forces remained together,
moving down Chattanooga Creek into Lookout valley, resting for the night at McCulloch's house. On
the 21st orders were received from Department Headquarters, directing Colonel Post to remain with
Mitchell. Accordingly, position was taken beside
Crook's Division. The enemy passed in heavy force
within gun-shot range, but did not attack them. At
one o'clock in the morning of the 22d, Post stationed
his command at the cross-road leading to Rossville,
the order now being received to retire to Chattanooga. The battle of Chickamauga had ended, our
forces were already in Chattanooga, and the enemy was
fast taking possession of Lookout mountain and Missionary Ridge. Hence it was of the most vital importance that the immense wagon trains should safely
reach the army, or Chattanooga would have to be
abandoned for want of immediate transportation and
supplies. While Post was in this position, the cavalry all passed to the rear. He then resumed the
line of march, but had not proceeded far before he
came upon the enemy in force, who now had posses-

sion of the road, and defended it with a battery of artillery. He formed line of battle on the side of the road, and prepared to contest its occupancy. Gardner's (Pinney's) Battery opened with all six guns with such good effect, that the rebel battery retired, yielding the right of way. The command then moved by the left flank on the right of the road, Gardner's artillery in it, thus being able to reform his line of battle instantly, if occasion required. The enemy's artillery soon opened again, but its shell and shot passed harmlessly overhead, and the troops safely crossed the bridge over Chattanooga creek, rejoining the division at one o'clock that afternoon.

Upon reporting to General Davis, the brigade was ordered to relieve the third brigade of his division, doing duty upon the skirmish line, and that afternoon and night thoroughly intrenched itself. While doing this a rebel battery sought to drive it away, but McKnight's section of artillery caused it to withdraw.

The army was now safely established in its new position, and the campaign completed. The troops whose course we have traced, although they did not rush into the fore-front of battle, nevertheless did a most important duty. And their willing hearts, valor, and endurance of fatigue, in this long and perilous march, were entitled to, and did receive, the thanks of the Commanding General. Had the enemy presumed to attack them while they were holding

7

the mountain passes, their conduct throughout the campaign justifies the assertion that they would have made a Spartan defence.

CHAPTER VIII.

CHATTANOOGA AND ITS SCENERY—REORGANIZATION OF
THE ARMY—POST'S FAREWELL ADDRESS—REMOVAL
TO WHITESIDES.

CHATTANOOGA is not a beautiful, but evidently a very
pleasant little place "in the piping time of peace;"
in time of war the town itself certainly possesses
no great charm. Its main street is nearly a mile in
length, and constitutes the business portion of the
place. Its population is about two thousand, and its
citizens ordinarily are inspired with a goodly degree
of activity and spirit. The center of almost the
entire system of Southern railroads, it could not fail
to derive importance from that fact. Besides, it is
the great *entrepôt* of vast mines of coal and nitre.

It nestles lovingly beside the broad and beautiful
Tennessee, and among mountains famous for the
grandeur of their scenery. Three miles away rises
Lookout mountain, mighty in its frowning battle-
ments, studded with the foliage of the cedar and oak,
whose shadows sometimes hang heavily across it,
deepening its beauty, like the veil of a nun. To the

eastward is Missionary Ridge, not so lofty, but no less pleasing in its charms. Across the Tennessee are the spurs—the ground-swells of that great mountain range, whose grim, black walls rise upon the vision away in the distance—the Cumberland. Such scenery seen in autumn, as it was now by our soldiers, could but lift the soul of him who possessed an ideal nature and refined culture far above the mere dross of worldly things, and fill him with something akin to inspiration. Indian summer was indeed existent, "in reality as in name," and scarce a morning passed but a vaporous veil of mist overhung mountain and stream, reflecting the rich and fervid hues of the forest leaves, giving them the brilliancy and glare of stained glass in some grand old cathedral of Nature's building. There is a sublimity and awe in this grand landscape which can seldom be surpassed anywhere in the wide world; and old Lookout strengthens this feeling, as, towering through the mist, and fog, and clouds, like Hawthorne's great stone face, it looks down so fatherly and benignantly upon us. And could it be possible, that ere long a deadly conflict would rage upon its fore-front, its forests be lurid with lightening fires, the rebel host, which so ignobled it, be routed from its resting-place, and the sacred banner of *E Pluribus Unum*, the hallowed emblem of Freedom, float proudly from its topmost peak?

Practically, Chattanooga was in a state of siege. The enemy extended his lines from the Tennessee

river, east of Chattanooga, to the river at and below
the bold promontory of Lookout, west of Chattanooga. His main force rested principally on Missionary Ridge and Lookout mountain, with extended
lines of fortifications at their base in Chattanooga
valley. In Lookout valley, west of the mountain, a
brigade was posted, and securely intrenched. His
pickets also extended along the river, through Whiteside, Shell Mound, and almost to Bridgeport, thus
holding nearly thirty miles of the Memphis and
Charleston railroad, compelling our army to rely for
its supplies on wagon trains moving from Stevenson
through the Sequatchy valley, and over the Cumberland mountains. The most strenuous exertions of
the Quartermaster's Department could not furnish
the army with quarter rations, and the animals, over-
worked, and actually starved, died by hundreds.
Trains were frequently twenty days on the route
from Stevenson, a distance of sixty miles, so bad
were the roads; and as each must be accompanied
with a guard, the instances were frequent when all
the provisions on the train were consumed ere its
arrival at Chattanooga, and the men compelled to
draw rations out of the meagre stock in the commis-
sary depots. Indeed, by the 1st of November, so
reduced were the public animals, that they could not
be relied upon to haul the empty wagons, and more
than ten thousand of them strewed the road from
Chattanooga to Stevenson. Scores dropped dead
daily in the streets of the town. The soldiers, too,

suffered severely, especially those who chanced to be there unassigned to any command. Day after day they consumed the pittance furnished them, and hundreds could be seen following the track of the wagons, and picking out of the mud the kernels of coffee and rice which scattered from broken sacks and barrels. Hard bread, grown moldy and rotten from exposure to the rain while *in transitu*, and which had been condemned by the commissaries, was seized by the half-famished soldiers, and eaten with avidity. A squad of the SEVENTY-FIFTH were reduced to even greater extremity than this. The regiment had moved down the river, and these men, unable to march, were left behind. Not requiring medical treatment, they were not admitted to hospital, and for some reason the commissaries, who were very fearful lest they should issue a starving soldier a ration without strictly *red tape* authority, would not recognize the provision returns made out for them, and they were compelled to rely upon their own wits for a subsistence. So they gathered around the slaughter yards, and when the cattle were killed for the troops, they secured the tails from the hides, and gleaned all other eatable bits that were left with the offal. The Orderly Sergeant of Company G was one of the squad, and by force of circumstances learned to prepare an excellent article of *ox-tail soup*, without the facilities of a first-class restaurant.

The evacuation of Chattanooga seemed a " military necessity," and more than once it was seriously contemplated. Happily, the dogged tenacity of our beloved Rosecrans butted against fate, and sustained the siege. His successor, that "tower of strength," the noble George H. Thomas, was equally persistent; and when General Grant, on the 19th of October, telegraphed him to "hold Chattanooga at all hazards," his reply was, "I will hold the town until we starve!" Most noble language, and grand augury of a transcendent victory.

But highly important changes were destined soon to occur—no less than a reorganization of the Army of the Cumberland, the destruction of two corps and several division organizations—commands which on the field of battle had won imperishable glory for the National arms.

On the 10th of October, 1863, General Rosecrans, under orders from the War Department, published an order discontinuing the Twentieth and Twenty-first Army Corps, relieving Generals McCook and Crittenden from their commands, and consolidating these divisions, brigades and regiments into a new organization, entitled the Fourth Army Corps, Major General Gordon Granger commanding. It was the misfortune of the FIRST DIVISION to be included in this humiliating order. It was much to be regretted. But the chivalrous men whose career we have thus far traced, could not and would not fail to prove equally as daring in glorious deeds, when the opportunity should present, no matter what the organization under which they were known.

Colonel Post's Brigade was completely disorganized. The SEVENTY-FIFTH ILLINOIS was assigned to the Third Brigade, First Division, Fourth Army Corps, Brigadier-General William Grose commanding; General John M. Palmer in command of the division.

We possess no copy of General Davis's farewell address, if he issued one; but Colonel Post, who was greatly esteemed by his brigade, issued the following. It expresses true sentiments and lofty patriotism, and touched a tender chord in the hearts of his men; and he retired to his new field of duty with the hearty "God bless you!" of all who ever knew him:

"HEADQUARTERS FIRST BRIGADE,
    FIRST DIVISION, 20TH ARMY CORPS.
        CHATTANOOGA, Oct. 16, 1863.

" *General Order* No. 51.

"In the reorganization of the army, this brigade will lose its identity, and be transferred to another division and corps.

"Organized on the banks of the Ohio more than a year ago, it has traversed Kentucky and Tennessee, scaled the mountains of Northern Alabama and Georgia, and now terminates its existence on the south bank of the Tennessee. The year during which it has remained intact will ever be remembered as that in which the gallant armies of the West rolled back the advancing hosts of rebellion, and extinguished the Confederacy in the valley of the Mississippi.

"In accomplishing this glorious achievement, you—soldiers of the First Brigade—have performed no mean part. On the laborious march you have been patient and energetic, and in battle and skirmish second to none in stubborn valor and success. In one year you lost upon the battle-field eight hundred and fifty heroic comrades.

"Baptized in blood at Perryville, this brigade led the army in pursuit of the retreating foe, and again attacked him at Lancaster, whence he fled from Kentucky. In the mid-winter campaign it opened the battle of Stone river by attacking and driving the enemy from Nolensville, and on the memorable 31st of December, together with the rest of the Twentieth Army Corps, valiantly met the attack of the concentrated opposing army. At Liberty Gap, and in the late battle of Chickamauga, it performed well the part assigned to it, and finishes its honorable career weaker in numbers, but strong in the confidence and discipline of veterans.

"For the able and hearty coöperations its commander has received from the officers, and for the cheerful support yielded by its gallant men, he returns his sincere thanks. No. petty jealousies, no intrigue or disorganizing influences, have ever disgraced and paralyzed our efforts for the country's cause ; and the commander unites in the just pride which all feel in the history of, and in their connection with, the First Brigade, First Division, Twentieth Army Corps.

"P. Sidney Post,

"Colonel Commanding Brigade."

The new brigade to which the Seventy-fifth was assigned was composed of the Ninth, Thirtieth, and Thirty-sixth Indiana, the Fifty-ninth, Seventy-fifth, Eightieth and Eighty-fourth Illinois, and the Seventy-seventh Pennsylvania.

On the 25th of October the entire division moved across the river, over Walden's ridge, thence across the river again, one brigade securing lodgment at Shell Mound, another at Bridgeport, while the third brigade occupied Whiteside. During this trip, General Rosecrans was relieved from the command of the army by General Thomas, and General Palmer assumed command of the Fourteenth Army Corps. General Charles Cruft was temporarily placed in command of the division.

Whiteside is the name of a small station on the Memphis and Charleston railroad, fourteen miles west of Chattanooga. The object of the movement hither was to hold the different points along this road so far as practicable, and to cover the movement of General Joseph Hooker's command (the Eleventh and Twelfth Corps of the Potomac Army) whose duty it was to dislodge the rebels from Lookout mountain, thus aiding in raising the siege of Chattanooga ; also to reinforce Hooker in his movements, should battle ensue and help be needed.

Whiteside is a very romantic place—in reality no town, but a succession of very high hills with narrow gorges, through which a small stream flows, called "Running Waters." It is a bleak, dreary region, but its hills abound in mines of coal and nitre, several of which were partially worked before the rebellion; also considerably during its progress. Now the war is ended, the indications of petroleum are found to be very strong, and much excitement prevails in that locality. Several mining companies have been organized to experiment for this valuable oil. But only in a military point of view was it held by our forces. As such, General Grose's Brigade remained here, awaiting the hour for a new call to arms, and the *éclat* of another enduring success.

CHAPTER IX.

THE BATTLES OF LOOKOUT MOUNTAIN AND MISSIONARY RIDGE — RINGGOLD — HEART-SICKENING SCENES ON THE OLD CHICKAMAUGA BATTLE-GROUND—THE WINTER ENCAMPMENT AT WHITESIDE.

Most memorable among the many grand events of this war is the series of brilliant successes achieved by Major General U. S. Grant and his able corps of subordinate generals, around Chattanooga, in October and November, 1863.

General John M. Palmer, with a portion of his command, moved down the north bank of the river to Whiteside, crossed over to the south bank, holding the ground passed over by Hooker's command in its march to Whiteside and Wauhatchie, thus at the same time practicing a feint upon the enemy, and guarding against any attack he might make on our communications, owing to Hooker's advance from Bridgeport.

In the meantime a force under the direction of General W. F. Smith, Chief Engineer, was thrown across the river below Moccasin Point, and at or near Brown's Ferry, to seize the range of hills at the mouth of Lookout valley. The seizure of these hills was of the highest importance to us, as they covered the Brown's Ferry road to Wauhatchie and Whiteside, and would enable us to draw supplies by a much safer and shorter route than the mountain roads over Walden's ridge. It also afforded a shorter line by which to reinforce our troops in Lookout valley, in case an engagement ensued.

The expedition under General Smith, on the night of the 27th of October, was most brilliant in character. It consisted of a force of eighteen hundred men, under General W. B. Hazen, which, in sixty pontoon boats, containing thirty armed men each, floated from Chattanooga quietly down the river, past the grim-visaged heights of Lookout and its armed sentries, landed on the bank below the foot of the mountain, seized the enemy's pickets stationed there, and the adjacent hills; and all this was accomplished with the loss of only four or five men wounded. Twenty-two hundred more, under General Turchin, with the materials for a bridge, moved down to Moccasin Point, thence to Brown's Ferry, unobserved by the enemy, and before daylight were ferried to the south bank, and effected a lodgment, securing great advantages, and completely astounding the enemy at the audacity and success of the enterprise.

On the 28th of October, Hooker advanced to the position assigned him, and Bragg found himself foiled in his scheme of starving out the Army of the Cum-

berland. He saw in this achievement a foreshadow-
ing of defeat. To regain the lost ground and retrieve
his own good name, were now the foremost things to
be accomplished. The very night after Hooker's
arrival in the valley, Longstreet's forces attacked
Geary's Division; but Geary's men displayed great
heroism, and repulsed the enemy. But this was not
all. General Howard directed a bayonet charge up
the heights west of Lookout creek. The hill was
more than two hundred feet high, and defended by
two lines of barricades. Right gallantly our heroes
drove the enemy out of his defences, off the hill and
down into Lookout valley. And it is well here to
mention that the mules of Geary's command contributed much to that night's success. A large number
of them, affrighted by the noise of battle, dashed
into the ranks of Hampton's rebel legion, causing
much dismay, compelling them to fall back under a
supposed charge of cavalry. Thus handsomely was
accomplished the beginning of the end in this fearful crisis. The signs were auspicious, foretelling a
glorious victory.

  Finally, on the 23rd of November, General W. T.
Sherman's Fifteenth Army Corps having arrived in
its designated position, the main action commenced.
Sherman, aided by Davis's Division of the Fourteenth Corps, safely effected a lodgment on the south
bank of the Tennessee, above Chattanooga, and near
the northern terminus of Mission Ridge. Thence, by
a skillful movement, he established himself securely

on a very important chain of hills, the first of the series leading to Mission Ridge—the main point in contest. Here he fortified, and awaited the next day to resume operations. Thomas, meantime, was alert, awaiting the developments made on his right and left, under Hooker and Sherman.

With this general outline of the situation, we will now turn to recount the operations under the indomitable Hooker, whose mission it was to carry the steep and wooded heights of cloud-capped Lookout.

It being feared that the enemy had discovered Sherman's intention, and that he would withdraw his forces on Lookout to Mission Ridge, and thus endeavor to crush him, Hooker was directed to take Osterhaus's and Geary's Divisions, and Whittaker's and Grose's Brigades, and make a strong demonstration on the northern slope of Lookout, thus attracting the enemy's attention, leading him to suppose this to be the real point of attack, and thereby preventing the massing against Sherman. Hooker was instructed, that in making this demonstration, if he found the position and strength of the enemy favorable to carrying the mountain, he should do so.

By four o'clock on the morning of the 24th of November, Hooker reported all ready for an advance. Lookout creek, swollen by the rains, was found to be impassable; so Geary's Division, supported by Whittaker's and Grose's Brigades, under General Cruft, moved down to Wauhatchie to cross the creek, while the balance of his forces constructed a temporary bridge across the creek on the main road.

In this eventful affair it is our duty to particular.
ize the part taken by the gallant brigade under that
true and tried soldier, "Old Billy Grose," as the soldiers familiarly called him.

Grose's effective force in the affair was sixteen hundred and ninety-three officers and men.   This force
moved from Whiteside to Lookout valley on the 23rd
instant, and bivouacked near Hooker's headquarters.
At daylight on the 24th, Grose was ordered by
Hooker to drive the enemy from a crossing at a
destroyed bridge on Lookout creek, near the railroad
crossing, and close to the base of the mountain.
Grose, nothing doubting, ordered up the Eighty-
fourth Illinois, closely supported by the SEVENTY-
FIFTH ILLINOIS, the former in line, with skirmishers
in front, and advanced them through a bayou, or
pond, which they waded, waist deep, driving the
enemy under cover, and gaining a foothold on the
west bank.   Captain Chambers, with a detail of the
Thirty-sixth Indiana, undertook to repair the bridge,
the two advance regiments sharply skirmishing with
the rebels.   It soon became evident that the good to
be effected would not compensate for the loss of life
and limb which would ensue in maintaining the position, so it was abandoned.

Hooker then directed Grose to proceed up the
creek, where Wood's command was preparing to
cross by constructing a pole bridge, which was nearly
completed.   Some poles were thrown lengthwise
over the gap, on which the SEVENTY-FIFTH and the

Eighty-fourth Illinois crossed. These regiments deployed into line of battle, the SEVENTY-FIFTH with Company E on the skirmish line. Two other regiments of the brigade followed, prolonging the line of battle on Wood's right. Grose formed his command in double lines, with the Thirty-sixth Indiana and the Fifty-ninth Illinois in advance, filling up the interval between the brigades of Whittaker and Geary.

The line thus formed moved obliquely up the mountain slope in most splendid style, full of spirit, and resolved to conquer. What cared they for the enemy's fierce cannonade and musketry hail? The mountain was before them, and there also the foe. Theirs the task to scale its precipitous side, to pierce through the thick veil of fog and mist which hung heavily upon it, and behind and beyond which other forces of the enemy lay in ominous silence, waiting the moment when they should illume it with the lightning flashes from thousands of muskets and "deep-mouthed dogs of war." It was veteran against veteran. The day was full of peril; nay, the very air was charged with it, and ere night victory must surely settle on Union or rebel banner.

But our heroes felt that God was with them, and like Godfrey de Bouillon, in the contest of the Crusades, they emblazoned "God wills it," on their standards, and staked all in the issue.

Never was presented a nobler sight. Onward they went, and upward, sweeping everything before them,

through rebel camps and over rebel pits, still press-
ing the foe, who, now that Geary had extended his
line so as to flank their last line of pits, surprised at
the unthought-of occurrence—the " Yankee trick,"—
became dismayed, disheartened, and in their panic
threw away their arms and ran, or instantly surrendered. Nearly, if not quite two thousand men were
thus entrapped, and made prisoners of war.

Then the SEVENTY-FIFTH and Eighty-fourth Illinois moved forward to the left, covering and advancing on the main Chattanooga road, over the mountain slope, opening communication with Thomas's
forces in Chattanooga valley, and enabling him to
send reinforcements when necessary.

So full of enthusiasm were the brave men of the
SEVENTY-FIFTH, and so ardent in the accomplishment
of great deeds were Colonel Bennet and his officers,
that they only halted when imperatively ordered to
do so. But it was well they did, for isolated as they
were, a serious fate might have awaited them. Near
nightfall Colonel Grose sent the Ninth Indiana and
the Fifty-ninth Illinois to relieve two other regiments who were immediately under the high ledge
of rocks at the top of the mountain. These two regiments were engaged in an active but desultory fire
until they exhausted their ammunition, when the
Thirty-sixth Indiana and the Twenty-fourth Ohio
relieved them. The enemy ceased his efforts at dis-
lodgment at midnight, and silence the most profound
reigned every where. .

8

Thus gallantly served Grose's Brigade. The confidence reposed in it is exemplified in the fact that ere the day's battle had ended, all its regiments were in the front line, ready for danger and duty.

At daylight, next morning, the SEVENTY-FIFTH and Eighty-fourth Illinois pushed forward on a reconnoissance, to develop the position and strength of the enemy. They captured a few guards, considerable abandoned camp equipage, and several boxes of ammunition; but the enemy had evacuated the mountain, and crossed Chattanooga valley to Mission Ridge. This fact was at once reported to Hooker, and at ten o'clock all his troops started for Rossville, five miles distant, at the base of Mission Ridge, and constituting the outlet of Chattanooga valley.

Meantime the "Stars and Stripes" were raised upon old Lookout's highest peak, proclaiming far and wide the completeness of the victory won. Cheer ascended upon cheer. The troops at Chattanooga, seeing the "old flag" proudly floating where but yesterday the rebel banner was displayed, renewed the wild acclaim, thrilling all true soldiers with joy, and filling traitor hearts, too, with ill omens, as it swept over to Mission Ridge in utterance clear and sonorous.

Yes, Lookout is won. Our heroes triumph.

"They have conquered! God's own legions! Well their foes
        might be dismayed,
Standing in his mountain temple, 'gainst the terrors of his aid;
And the clouds might fitly echo pæan loud and parting gun,
When, from upper light and glory, sank the traitor host, undone."

There was a definite object in Hooker's moving to Rossville. Sherman had been stubbornly fighting at the north end of Mission Ridge, and by noon had carried its summit, so he could overlook Chattanooga, and view Thomas's force as it lay in the valley. As soon as Hooker should arrive at Rossville he was to change direction, and with his left in Chattanooga valley, his center and right covering Mission Ridge, move northward, striking the enemy in flank and rear, until meeting the center of our lines, or advance as near as possible. Then, Sherman having by his persistent attacks caused Bragg to weaken his center, Thomas, with strong columns, was to assault and carry the ridge in his front, thus breaking the rebel center, and hurling Bragg's shattered columns back upon Sherman and Hooker, making the capture of his entire army almost a certainty. Hooker's column, after working for four hours in rebuilding the crossing over Chattanooga creek, arrived at the designated point about three o'clock. Osterhaus was in the advance, and engaged the enemy as he reached the gorge. The rebels were soon routed, and the passage made. Coming to Mission Ridge proper, Cruft's command changed direction, and moved at a right angle with the road. The ridge ascended, a volley of musketry announced that the enemy had again made a stand, and Cruft's cavalry escort fled precipitately to the rear. Grose's Brigade advanced in three lines, the Ninth Indiana and the Fifty-ninth Illinois in the advance, and the SEVENTY-

FIFTH ILLINOIS in the third line. The advance, full of courage, charged the enemy with the bayonet, driving him from two lines of barricades, inflicting severe loss and taking many prisoners. Soon Hooker's whole column was in motion northward, and the advance was rapid. The rebels, though stoutly resisting, were forced back constantly, until at nightfall, Hooker's and Thomas's right Division—General R. W. Johnson's—were within eight hundred yards of each other. A force of near four thousand rebels now found themselves in a terrible dilemma, and, graciously as possible, surrendered.

The battle was now ended, and the troops bivouacked for the night. The prisoners were disposed of, the wounded cared for, the dead buried.

The victory was complete; one of the grandest in the war. Two formidable mountains had been carried by assault, and the enemy routed. His losses were severe, although in killed and wounded not as heavy as our own. He had lost more than six thousand prisoners, forty cannon, sixty-nine artillery carriages and caissons, and seven thousand stand of small arms. The balance of his forces, greatly demoralized, withdrew during the night toward Ringgold, Georgia.

On the morning of the 26th, Granger's Corps was ordered to the relief of Burnside, at Knoxville, who was besieged by Longstreet, while Sherman and Thomas pursued Bragg—the former by way of Chickamauga, the latter by way of Grayville.

Sunset found our troops in Pea-vine valley. The deep mud and dense underbrush of this region demanded slow movement. Grose had closely supported the advance all day, and skirmishing with the enemy's rear guard was frequent. That night the brigade bivouacked in battle order, with a heavy skirmish line in front, three companies of the SEVENTY-FIFTH aiding in this duty.

While here, on guard, a rebel soldier and some citizens were groping about in the dark for abandoned forage, and unconsciously ran into the picket line of Company A. They were captured, and feeling very sore at this discomfiture, revealed the fact that many more soldiers were at their houses, half a mile distant. Colonel Bennett pushed Company A forward cautiously through the brush, and directed Corporal George G. Messer, a most trusty soldier, to move a few paces in advance, to draw the fire of the enemy, should there be a concealed force awaiting them. They soon reached the houses, and captured the soldiers there without harm to a single one of our own men. The night was intensely dark, and the mission perilous; but handsomely accomplished.

On the 27th the troops moved to Ringgold. Here the rebels were found strongly posted, and Osterhaus's Division became seriously engaged. The battle lasted for four hours, and was desperately fought. At last the enemy were flanked and forced to retreat, but we lost many valuable men. Here the Thirteenth Illinois distinguished itself for bravery. Here, too, the noble Major Bushnell, a fine soldier and popular officer, fell, a sacrifice upon our country's altar. That night Grose's command lay in the town of Ringgold. On the morning of the 28th, by request of General Osterhaus, Company A, Captain Parker,. was sent off to the right of his position, to watch the enemy, lest he should pass through a gorge in the mountains, and turn his flank. The rebels were plainly visible a greater part of the day, but no effort was made in that direction. The company returned at night. On the 29th Grose's Brigade moved in advance of the column, pursuing and skirmishing with the enemy to Tunnel Hill, where a division was found strongly posted, and prepared to contest the ground.

The pressure upon Burnside being very great, and the necessity urgent for more troops to be sent to his aid, General Grant ordered Sherman to move toward Knoxville, and directed Hooker to push the enemy, but not to risk a general engagement.

The campaign was now ended. Hooker's troops remained at Ringgold until the evening of November 30th, when they were ordered back to their old encampments, as before the battle. On the return, Grose crossed the memorable field of Chickamauga, and halted there a day, to bury the dead of that carnage field.

The marks of that fearful strife were still visible. Here and there were lines of barricades hastily constructed; the ground was strewed with knapsacks,

haversacks, pieces of clothing, fragments of harness,
canteens, tin plates bullet-pierced, round shot and
unexploded shell. Here, too, were straps, buckles,
cartridge-boxes, old socks and old shoes, rotting let-
ters—all sad signs, and all telling their sad but silent
story of the great fight at Chickamauga. What a
crowd of sorrowful memories press upon the mind
and sicken the heart at their contemplation! Then,
indeed, can be felt the wing of the Death-angel as
the gloom shadow flits over the soul. Where is the
brave soldier who wore that mud-stained belt?
Where the one who wore those shoes? Is he cold
in death? If so, what eyes have been bedimmed at
his sad fate! What hopes have been destroyed,
what affections crushed, what hearts wrung with
anguish, never more to brighten!

But sadder sights than these greeted our brave
boys as they passed over the field of battle. Sadder
thoughts, too, filled their minds—the unburied remains of hundreds of Union soldiers. Here, full-
length skeletons lay side by side; there, skulls
"touched each other like the cheeks of sleepers."
In some places the head and feet were visible; in
other, the trunks only, of human bodies. Others,
again, had been covered so slightly that the swine
had rooted them out, and the remains lay scattered
about in promiscuous heaps.

The rebels remained masters of the field, and it
was their duty to have given a decent interment to
our dead. Their own were generally well interred;

but on our right and right center they had neglected the burial of their own as well as our dead. What shameful negligence! What awful guilt must weigh down the necks of those who could thus cruelly leave the mangled bodies of human beings, friend and foe alike, to decompose in the hot sun and the chill night air, and their bones to bleach upon the plain! God pity and have mercy upon them! Justice will be done. And you, fathers, mothers, brothers, sisters, sweethearts, what think you? And my country, how beats thy great heart? Oh remember thy fallen braves!

> " Lay the laurel on their cold brows,
> Honored martyrs to their Union vows—
> The brave soldiers whose lives on their country's shrine were
> given ;
> Bow the head and drop the tear,
> As you plant banners o'er the bier
> Of the patriot whose spirit soars with angel wings to heaven."

This last sad task ended, the command returned to Whiteside, where it arrived on the 2d of December. On the return, Companies C and H were detached, and under command of Lieutenant Bannister, gathered up the abandoned rebel property—stores, caissons, ammunition, etc.—taking it to Chattanooga. Here it enjoyed a respite for a season.

In the battle the brigade captured seven hundred and seventy-seven prisoners. Its loss was surprisingly small, and can only be accounted for in the fact that the audacity of our men in charging what were considered impregnable defences, astonished and demoralized the enemy. Four were killed and sixty wounded. The loss of the SEVENTY-FIFTH was but two wounded. With a full consciousness of having done their whole duty in this hour of peril, the soldiers now quietly performed their accustomed camp duties, biding the time when they should again be called forth to meet the foe, and strike another blow for the Constitution and the Union.

CHAPTER X.

WHITESIDE is situated on the Charleston and Memphis railroad, and is equi-distant from Chattanooga
and Bridgeport. It is not really a village, although
there are, perhaps, in the vicinity of the depot, one
hundred inhabitants. It is a wild, romantic spot,
environed by high, cone-shaped hills, well wooded,
which yield abundant coal. Mines have been started,
but they are only nominally worked. Northern
enterprise will yet develop their rich resources.
Through the valley at the base of these hills winds a
stream called Running Waters. Where the railroad
crosses it is a deep gorge, more than one hundred
feet deep, and the bridge which spanned it had been
destroyed by order of General Rosecrans, during the
Chickamauga campaign. It was a serious task now
to rebuild it, so as to facilitate supplies to the main

army at Chattanooga. This work was intrusted to the energetic bridge-builders, Boomer and Company, of Chicago, and many of the men in the regiments had opportunity to aid the work, not by detail and compulsory labor, but voluntarily and with compensation. The soldiers of the brigade engaged in its 'construction were under the charge of Major James A. Watson, of the SEVENTY-FIFTH ILLINOIS, a man selected by Colonel William Grose expressly for his competency and energy in work of this character. It was completed about the first of February, and since then the trains have traversed the road unimpeded, and the troops have never since seen Point Starvation quite so plainly as before. All the timber for this bridge of such great height and length (being nearly four hundred feet), was cut from the adjacent forests, hewed and fitted to its place mostly by the exertions of this brigade. It is worthy of commendation. While here, the non-veterans of the Fifty-ninth Illinois infantry, a detachment of seventy-four men, were assigned to the SEVENTY-FIFTH, remaining with it from January 29th to April 16th, proving themselves worthy peers in morality, bravery and fidelity to duty. They were under command of Lieutenant Blodgett, of Company E.

.This completed, another field of duty lay before them. The construction of other bridges was necessary. To guard those engaged in rebuilding these, the First Division was moved up to Charleston, arriving there on the 3rd of February. Two days after the command returned to Blue Springs, four miles south of Cleveland, where it remained until the 3rd of May.

While lying here, the second and third brigades of the division aided in making a most important recon- noissance near Dalton, Georgia. The object of this was simply to ascertain the precise locality of the enemy's forces, and the nature of his defences. The second and third brigades of the Fourth Corps par- ticipated in it. The third brigade, under Colonel Grose, left Blue Springs on the morning of the 22d of February, with the additional strength of the Eightieth Illinois, under Lieutenant-Colonel Kilgore, of the Seventy-fifth Illinois, and Battery H, Fourth United States Artillery, Lieutenant Heilman com- manding. The former had been placed temporarily with the brigade. It had been captured the spring before, in the famous Streight raid to Rome, and the officers had not yet been exchanged. The total force of the brigade in this affair numbered seventeen hun- dred and ninety-six officers and men. The brigade was in the advance, the Thirty-sixth Indiana in front. It arrived at Red Clay, or "Council Ground," at 12.30 p.m.; thence it moved toward Dalton, to feel the enemy. At Wade's house, three miles beyond, the enemy's pickets were found. These were driven back, and a company of the Fourth Michigan Cav- alry, by order of Colonel Grose, pursued them rapidly a mile and a half. It being near night, the com- mand then withdrew to Red Clay, and bivouacked.

On the 23rd the reconnoissance was pushed in another direction.   The two brigades moved twelve miles westward, near Catoosa Springs, to form a junction with the Fourteenth Army Corps, arriving there about nine o'clock at night.

The next morning the two brigades countermarched some six miles to Lee's house; thence moved south-east, toward Dalton.   To move upon Dalton in front was impracticable, as it is covered by an inaccessible ridge, presenting one continued line of rock epaulments, and known as Rocky Face. Through this ridge there is a *canon*, or pass, called Buzzard's Roost, lying between Tunnel Hill and Dalton.   North of Tunnel Hill the ridge is passable, and here Grose passed his command.   The country is very mountainous, it being little less than a constant succession of hills and narrow ravines or valleys.   Having crossed two of these hills, Grose pushed down a road running south, and at Neal's house joined Colonel Long with six hundred cavalry. Neal's farm is six miles north-west of Dalton, and three miles from the Dalton and Chattanooga railroad. Both advanced on the wagon road until beyond Davis's house, where it crosses to the west side of the ridge. Some five hundred yards from its western base, a deep gorge, through which Mill Creek flows, separates it from another, beyond which is the valley which farther on forms Buzzard's Roost.   The column steadily advanced along this ridge, with Long in front, driving the enemy from all the ground north of the creek. Arriving in the valley, Long deployed to the right, along the base of the hills to the west, while the SEVENTY-FIFTH and Eighty-fourth Illinois moved down the valley on the left of the cavalry, covering the slope of the eastern ridge with skirmishers, thus protecting the right flank of the line. The Twenty-fourth Ohio supported the cavalry. Sharp skirmishing ensued, the rebels constantly falling back, until they were forced out of their camps at the railroad. This advanced line was firmly maintained for some time, when the enemy, realizing Grose's intention, began to move his infantry upon him. The engagement now became lively; but the skirmishers evinced so much pluck that with the aid of the artillery they were halted and forced under cover. It was now ascertained that Stewart's rebel division was posted in their front, with Stevenson's near at hand. Reinforcements were not within quick supporting distance; night, too, was again throwing its sable mantle over the weary combatants, so it was deemed prudent to retire.

Kilgore, with the Eightieth Illinois and the cavalry, was left at Neal's farm; the remainder halting further back, at the widow Burke's. Here the facts were reported to the commanding general, and orders awaited.

Early on the 25th, General Cruft joined Colonel Grose with the balance of the division, and the advance commenced. Kilgore had ascertained that the rebels occupied the ridge beyond Davis's house, and that his line extended a full mile to the north. Nearing this point, the division formed in battle order—Grose's Brigade on the ridge to the right, covering the summit and the greater part of the eastern slope, with the Thirtieth Indiana, the Seventy-fifth and Eightieth Illinois in the front line, and the Eighty-fourth Illinois, Twenty-fourth Ohio and Thirty-sixth Indiana in the second line. The second brigade, Colonel Champion, deployed on his left, with Long's cavalry extending his left, while the first brigade, Colonel Dickerman, served as a reserve. It was now nine in the morning, when General Palmer appeared on the field and requested Colonel Grose to meet him. They met and consulted, *in front of the skirmish line*. At eleven o'clock Baird's Division joined Grose on the right, and the bugles sounded Forward ! Then was presented one of the finest and most imposing scenes ever witnessed by man. The SEVENTY-FIFTH ILLINOIS was the " battalion of direction," and the movement left oblique, treading the crest of the ridge. Far to the right and the left, over the hills and through the valleys, were the long lines of blue coats, their bayonets and sabres glistening with the sunbeams ; while in the valley beyond, and on its background of hills, were the hosts of the enemy, prepared to try titles to the passage.

Hardly was the line in motion, when the fire of musketry began, constantly growing sharper and heavier, intermingled, too, with the thunder of artillery ; clouds of smoke ascended toward heaven from either side, as if invoking aid from the great God of battles. This affair did not assume the dignity of a battle, but was, nevertheless, quite decisive in its results. The enemy could not withstand the prowess of the Federal heroes, and were constantly forced from one position to another, for at least a mile and a half. During the action Major Watson was severely hurt by the falling of a limb which a cannon ball had struck down, and several were wounded. Ere the conflict ceased night again set in, and General Palmer reporting that the object of the reconnoissance was gained, the entire force withdrew to the west of Tunnel Hill, and rested for the night. Once during this day's affair, Companies A, F and D were on the skirmish line, and elated with their success, charged the rebel lines, scattering them pell-mell, Company F capturing two prisoners. Companies C, H and I were also on the skirmish line, and behaved nobly. On this day, Sergeant Oscar A. Seely, of Company C, who is noted for his cool bravery, was struck in the back by a musket ball, which passed through his body, coming out just above the groin, and then through his right arm near the wrist. In this condition he walked back to the rear unsupported, bearing with him his gun and accoutrements. On the 26th, the Surgeon of the regiment, a Frenchman, Octave P. F. Ravenot, a genial man and a good doctor, but quite eccentric in his manners, was sent to look after a man wounded the day before, and on his return was captured by Wheeler's cavalry. He rejoined the command on the 13th of September, 1864.

On the 26th Grose's Brigade moved south a mile on the ridge, encountering some rebel cavalry, and drove them out of sight and hearing. That night Grose moved to the old "Stone Church," near Catoosa Springs. On the 27th the brigade started for Blue Springs, where it arrived on the 28th, and settled quietly down in its olden routine of duties.

In this affair the SEVENTY-FIFTH displayed the heroism and endurance which ever have character-ized it, and received mention in the reports of supe-rior officers. Its casualties were seven wounded, in-cluding Major Watson, beside the surgeon captured. From this time until the first of May nothing of importance transpired. The army was slowly recruit-ing its strength for another and grander campaign than had ever yet been attempted during this war; one which, in fact, has never been surpassed, if ever equaled, in the annals of European warfare.

CHAPTER XI.

On the 14th of March, 1864, General W. T. Sherman received notice from General Grant that he had been appointed as commander of the Department of the Mississippi. Sherman immediately proceeded to Nashville and held a conference with General Grant, at which a full understanding was had of the policy and plans of the ensuing campaigns, Sherman's part of which extended from Chattanooga to Vicksburg.

The troops destined to operate in this campaign were designated as the Army of the Tennessee, General McPherson; the Army of the Cumberland, General Thomas; and the Army of the Ohio, General Schofield. These commanders were visited, and the lines of operation explained to them; garrisons were appointed to guard the lines of railroad; Chattanooga was established as a secondary base, and the storehouses were filled with supplies to overflowing.

Finally, in the last days of April, Sherman received a letter from Grant, announcing that on the 5th of May he should move upon the enemy from his camp near Culpepper, Virginia, and desired him to do the same. Accordingly, on the 29th of April, Sherman had all the troops of the Armies of the Ohio and Tennessee *en route* for Chattanooga, and on the 6th day of May the campaign was fairly commenced.

There was now upon the line of march to Dalton a force of 98,797 men, and 254 cannon, all under the orders of General W. T. Sherman.

This army, now prepared to advance South, was the largest, and by far the best appointed force that our Government had ever yet placed under the command of a single general officer, to undertake either regular operations or an adventure.

For an army whose object is to withstand the march of invaders who came from the north, the position in and about Dalton is happily formed by nature, and capable, of being made very strong by art.

I have before mentioned that Dalton was protected in front by a high, inaccessible ridge, whose summit is faced by a steep ledge of rocky epaulments known as Rocky Face. The only pass at or near this point is Buzzard's Roost, through which passes the rail and wagon roads. Mill Creek also flows through it, and was now of great service to the rebels. The valley itself being narrow, was thoroughly obstructed by abattis, and was flooded by dams built across this stream. It was thoroughly commanded by batteries located upon the hills and acclivities, whose fire could penetrate its entire length, and into all its narrow ravines and winding gullies. A skillful engineer had doubtless exhausted his contrivances for the defence of a ground having all this natural strength of feature. So much in favor of its defence. It was undeniably safe against any attack that could be made in front or immediately in flank. Johnston's forces consisted of three corps of infantry and artillery, viz: Hardee's, Hood's and Polk's, together with Wheeler's Cavalry Corps, making a total strength of 55,000 men. I have no data by which to estimate the number of his guns. This was the force to be overcome or destroyed. Sherman was too wise a general to mass his army for an attack against such a position, where defeat would be an inevitable consequence, and the hills and valleys in contest run red with brave men's blood.

Against Johnston's plan of occupying this range of hills, covering Dalton with the forces at his command, there were two cogent reasons : one was, that the Federal troops greatly outnumbered his own : the other, that the position which, in consequence of this, he would be required to cover, was too extended for the number he had to defend it.

Understanding the physical obstacles to this front movement, Sherman resolved upon turning the enemy's flank. Accordingly, McPherson was ordered to move from his position at Gordon's Mill, *via* Ship's

Gap, Villanow and Snake Creek Gap, directly on Resaca, or to any point below Dalton on the line of railroad, and meeting the enemy, make a bold attack; or failing in this, to destroy the road for a good distance, and then fall back to a strong defensive position near Snake Creek, there to strike the enemy in flank if he should be forced to retreat. Meantime, Thomas was to make a strong feint of attack in front, while Schofield pressed down from the north upon the enemy's right flank.

It is proper here, in compliance with the requirements of this book, to go back to Blue Springs, where the First Division lay encamped up to noon on the 3d of May, and trace out briefly its line of march, and the part which it, or a portion of it, had in the demonstrations in front of Dalton.

Another thing must be mentioned. By order of General Sherman, issued previous to the campaign, each regiment in the army was directed to organize a pioneer company, composed of twenty men, by details of two men from each company in the regiment, the whole to be under the command of a Lieutenant and two non-commissioned officers, trustworthy and energetic. The detail of the SEVENTY-FIFTH ILLINOIS was commanded by Lieutenant John L. Newton, with sub-officers Sergeant R. D. Talbot and Corporal Isaac Barr. These men had frequently a double duty to perform, for while they carried the musket and cartridge-box, they also were armed with an axe, hatchet, pick or spade. It was their duty to construct corduroys for the passage of artillery and trains, rifle-pits and breastworks to protect the troops, pontoons to cross streams, and, in fact, everything requiring the use of implements. It will be seen hereafter, that the pioneer organization of the SEV-ENTY-FIFTH ILLINOIS won for itself a good name, and rendered most efficient and praiseworthy service. Lieutenant Newton also retained command of Company H.

The regiment, together with Grose's Brigade and the Division, left camp at Blue Springs at noon on the 3rd of May, *via* Red Clay, for Catoosa Springs, the point of concentration for the army, where it arrived on the 4th and rested until the 7th instant. On the morning of the 7th, the Fourth and Fourteenth Corps advanced upon Tunnel Hill. This day the SEVENTY-FIFTH was in the second line of battle. The advance regiments drove the enemy from his intrenchments, and camped on the ground they had won. On the 8th the command advanced upon Rocky Face. On this occasion the SEVENTY-FIFTH ILLINOIS, and the Ninth and Thirtieth Indiana, were in the front line. Grose's position was on the left of the rail and wagon roads leading through Buzzard's Roost. As in February, this position was found strongly fortified. And although impregnable in front, yet in obedience to Sherman's orders to Thomas to threaten heavily, Grose frequently made assaults upon the enemy in heavy skirmish line, and in these affairs his loss was some forty killed and wounded. The brigade lay close under the ridge, firmly holding the ground, and occasionally worrying the enemy with shot and shell, until, on the 9th, Davis's Division, in line on the right of the Fourth Corps, being severely engaged, it moved to his support. Finally, on the 11th, the foremost battalions of Davis's Corps carried the ridge in his front, and pursued the retreating columns. The Fourth Corps occupied the ground vacated by it.

On the 7th instant, while the brigade lay close under Rocky Face, the pioneer company was ordered forward to build breastworks for cover. The enemy, divining the purpose, made a vigorous assault upon our lines, temporarily driving them in, and resulting in the capture of a good many tools, and very nearly that of many of the men. While here, too, on the 7th, Company D was detailed for picket duty, and in conjunction with the details of the brigade did constant skirmishing, and was not relieved until the 9th instant. Once it charged up to within fifty yards of the enemy's main line.

By the 12th, the entire army, save the Fourth Corps and some cavalry, left to watch Dalton, were in motion, west of Rocky Face Ridge, for Resaca. These columns fairly passed through Snake Creek Gap, the Fourth Corps pushed through Dalton, soon coming upon the rebel rear guard. These were steadily driven back, until, three miles south of the town, the rebels were found posted upon a high wooded hill ready for battle. When in cannon-shot range, his artillery opened, and ours replied. A heavy duel now progressed for some time, only an open farm with a low valley intervening. During the advance here, the SEVENTY-FIFTH was on the skirmish line, and captured a rebel captain, and Company A was the first to occupy the town of Dalton.

The enemy's guns becoming very annoying, and passive, enduring courage not suiting the pride of Grose, he ordered the Ninth and Thirty-sixth Indiana, supported on the right by the Eighty-fourth Illinois, to form into line and carry the position by assault. Grandly these regiments traversed the open field under a shower of fire, scaled the hill, encountered the rebels, almost hand to hand, drove them from their barricades, and remained masters of the position. This ended the contest for that day. The troops now moved to the west, on the Dalton and Rome road, passing into Sugar Creek valley, and encamped there for the night, nine miles from Dalton.

During the night of the 13th, the enemy fell back to his works around Resaca. Our army closely pressed him. McPherson's Corps first struck his infantry pickets, advancing from Snake Creek Gap, drove them within their fortified lines, and occupied a ridge of "bald hills," his right on the river Oostanaula, and his left abreast the town. Thomas, with the Fourteenth Corps, moved up on McPherson's left, while Schofield, after hard and tedious toil, gained his left. Two things saved Johnston's army at Dalton. One, the topographical nature of the country; and the other, the foresight of the rebel chieftain.

At Resaca the Fourth Corps joined the Fourteenth on the left, and the First Division lay upon the right bank of the Oostanaula. About 12 o'clock, noon, on the 14th, Colonel Grose was directed to conform his movements to those of General Wood, of the Third Division. The other two brigades of the First Division were to have formed on Grose's left, but they failed to be in position. So, when at two o'clock the advance was made, Grose found himself at the extreme left of the line. His brigade was formed in double lines, with the Seventy-seventh Pennsylvania, Seventy-fifth and Eightieth Illinois, and the Thirtieth Indiana in the advance. Of the SEVENTY-FIFTH, the Pioneers and Company A were on the skirmish line, and behaved well. Private Thomas Wood was wounded. The ground over which the troops must march to attack the enemy's main line, was very rough in its configuration—hilly, ledgy, and heavily wooded for the most part, with here and there an opening of some small farm. Thus, it was difficult, on a rapid advance over such ground, to maintain much military coherence, yet the formation was kept remarkably well, under the circumstances.

The enemy opened a terrific fire of round shot and shell, which continued some forty minutes; but when the command "Forward!" was given, our brave battalions moved right on, through the iron shower, none wavering, none falling back, save those whom fate there destined to fall dead or wounded. Where Grose faced the enemy, it was impracticable to move artillery, and thus our men were without that valuable arm. Nevertheless, by dint of active, fiery courage, the assault was made, the enemy driven from the woodland, through the valley, and over a hill beyond it, to his interior line of works.

Then, for a time, the fighting ceased. The command bivouacked for the night. Taking advantage of the darkness, the pioneers, ever faithful, constructed barricades for defense. Late that afternoon, the other two brigades of the Division advanced and formed line of battle on Grose's left. Just at nightfall, these regiments were destined to suffer assault. The enemy, maddened at the advantage we had gained, charged upon these two brigades most furiously, hurling them back, threatening Grose's left flank, and endangering the safety of the army.

In the midst of danger, and unforewarned, to form a line so as to answer for the safety of an army, is a work of great moment, and requires sound judgment, a quick eye, and steady nerve.

These Grose possessed to an eminent degree. Soon as the enemy struck the brigades on his left, and drove them in, thereby compromising his own command, Grose formed his rear regiments in a line facing his left, and perpendicular to his rear. This formation was made on the double-quick, by the Fifty-ninth Illinois, the Thirty-sixth Indiana, and one company of the Eighty-fourth Illinois.

Hooker's column chanced to be coming into position on the left and to the rear of the two discomfited brigades, and the routed troops passing it, his men gave the exultant rebels a terrible welcome, piling the ground with dead and wounded, and forcing them back under cover. Grose's men only participated in this bloody contest at long musket range. His Battery, "B," Second Pennsylvania, however, which had now arrived, dealt an effective fire upon the enemy's flank and rear.

This day witnessed the loss of many brave and noble men. Captain Davis, of the Seventy-seventh Pennsylvania, Assistant Inspector-General, a most faithful officer, here fell, struck by a cannon-shot in the thigh. He was thought to be mortally wounded, but he finally recovered, although a cripple for life. Here, too, Sergeant Jacob Rhodehamel, of the Seventy-fifth, was killed. And he deserves special mention. At the call of patriotism, and although too old to be liable to the draft, he left a large family, to volunteer for the defence of his adopted country. From his enlistment, in 1862, up to the hour he was struck by the fatal missile—a fragment of shell—he was never away from the command, nor off duty an hour. He was a noble, whole-souled man and patriot, and his loss is mourned by his brave compatriots in arms. A piece of the same shell struck Norman Brooks, of Company I, breaking his leg, and disabling him for life. Another shell burst over the right of Company F, and a fragment of it tore through the folded blanket of Ernest Wernick, unstrapping it from his back. The blanket doubtless saved his life, and that of Sergeant James D. Place.

On the afternoon and evening of the 15th, Schofield and Hooker, on the left of the First Division, engaged the enemy in a heavy battle, driving him from several strongly fortified hills, and capturing a four gun battery and many prisoners. The First Division swung around its left, to conform with Hooker's advantage. Later at night, the rebels charged Hazen's Brigade, on the right of Grose, and the Third Brigade went to his assistance. The assault was repulsed with heavy loss.

That night Johnston escaped, retreating across the Oostanaula, and the next morning our forces entered Resaca. Early on the 16th, the whole army started in pursuit, with the Fourth and Fourteenth Corps close on his heels. McPherson guarded well the right flank, crossing the river at Lay's Ferry, while Schofield pushed forward by obscure roads to the left. In Resaca another four gun battery was found abandoned, also a large supply of stores, showing with what rapidity the rebel chief had been compelled to act.

The pursuit was continued without remission until the 19th, the enemy only making a short stand at Adairsville; but General Newton engaged him there handsomely, and he withdrew. Johnston passed through Kingston, and four miles south to Cassville. Here the ground was comparatively open, and well adapted for a grand battle. Hence, proper dispositions were made. Schofield closed in upon Cassville on the north, followed by Hooker on his right, with the Fourth Corps still further to the right. McPherson remained at Kingston, as a reserve. While moving into position, the Fourth Corps did heavy skirmishing, Grose routing the foe in his front, capturing hospitals, property, etc. Skirmish and artillery firing was very heavy until nightfall, and among the wounded was Sergeant A. S. Christopher.

Again the Pioneers and other details constructed trenches for protection, and that night the enemy again retreated, across the Etowah, and south to Cartersville and Allatoona Pass. Here the army rested until the 23rd. For sixteen days it had been one constant battle of greater or less intensity, and prudence dictated a respite for the men. Besides, thus far our army might be likened to an engine drawing its supplies, by means of long pipes, from a river, and it must be thoroughly replenished by drawing fresh supplies from its base ere it could hope to move on 'successfully and satisfactorily. This was quickly accomplished, however, and by the time above indicated, all was ready for another forward movement.

Meantime, Jeff. C. Davis's Division, which had made a diversion to Rome, down the west bank of the Oostanaula, from Resaca, returned from this expedition, having achieved great success. He had captured Rome, with its forts, eight or ten guns of heavy calibre, its valuable mills and foundries. He also secured intact two good bridges across the Etowah, near Kingston, affording the army a speedy crossing towards the South.

General Sherman, satisfied from his maps, and the knowledge gained from others who were familiar with the locality, that Johnston could and would hold Allatoona Pass, resolved, without even making a feint in front, to flank it on the right; and having supplied his wagon trains with twenty days' provisions, cut loose from the railroad, leaving only a garrison force at Rome and Kingston, and pushed his columns on to Dallas.

McPherson crossed the Etowah at the mouth of Conasene Creek, near Kingston, and marched to the position assigned him, south of Dallas, *via* Van Wirt. Davis's Division moved directly from Rome to Dallas, *via* Van Wirt. Thomas, with the Fourth, and the other divisions of the Fourteenth Corps, proceeded to Dallas *via* Euharlee and Burnt Hickory, while Schofield moved by other roads to the east, aiming to form line of battle on Thomas's left.

This movement of Sherman's was one seldom performed; yet there are many precedents in history. It was what is called in military parlance, a "movable column," in contradistinction to "regular operations." As will readily be seen, the difference is broad. In the former, the commander purposely places himself in those very circumstances which would ruin an army carrying on regular operations. He yields the road to his resources, yields the defence of everything but himself. If in such an adventure he meets with success, all is well; otherwise he is placed in jeopardy, in danger of ruin—aye, extermination. It remains to be seen how Sherman succeeded.

The head of Thomas's column reached Burnt Hickory on the 23rd of May, and captured a rebel courier, bearing a letter of Johnston, showing that he detected Sherman's move, and was prepared to meet him at Dallas. Still the army pushed on. The country through which it passed is very rugged, mountainous, and densely wooded; the roads few and obscure.

On the 25th, while Thomas's command was moving across Pumpkin-vine Creek, on the main Dallas road, his advance was encountered by cavalry. A fight ensued, the cavalry were driven, but not until they had set fire to the bridge. But our men rushed through the flames to the other bank, and finally saved it. Two miles further on, the rebel infantry were encountered, and Geary's Division had a sharp rencontre. Hooker's other divisions came up at last (they were moving on different roads), and he deployed two divisions into line, and, by order of General Sherman, made a bold push to secure possession of a position designated as "New Hope Church," a point where three roads meet—from Ackworth,

Marietta, and Dallas.   Here the battle grew fierce, the men on either side fighting with desperation. Night setting in, dark and stormy, and the rebels having constructed temporary barricades, Hooker was compelled to cease his efforts.   Hearing heavy firing in the advance, the First Division of the Fourth Corps moved up to within close support of Hooker, Grose's Brigade forming line of battle, the SEVENTY-FIFTH ILLINOIS in the second line.   None of the Fourth Corps, however, became engaged.

On the morning of the 26th, the enemy was found strongly intrenched, and prepared to dispute our further progress.   This compelled a new disposition of our army.   McPherson was moved up to Dallas, Thomas was deployed in front of New Hope Church, while Schofield was directed to move well upon our left, to turn the enemy's right.   One cavalry division, under Garrard, operated with McPherson ; another, under Stoneman, with Schofield.   McCook guarded the rear.

The country being so rugged, and so densely timbered, several days were occupied in deploying into position.   Finally our lines were placed in close contact with the enemy.   This accomplished, Sherman resolved to extend his line eastwardly, and strike for the railroad east of Allatoona.   In making this development before the enemy, several sharp skirmishes ensued, in some of which Grose's command participated.   On the 27th of May the SEVENTY-FIFTH was engaged, losing one man wounded—Elisha

Drew, of Company D.   The skirmishing lasted all
day; and at night, in conformity with Sherman's plan
of extending his left, the First Division moved into
the position held by Wood's Division, he in turn
occupying the ground held by Hooker. This position was held by the army until the 1st of June.
And here the pioneers of the regiments were again
brought into important use.   With daring unex-
celled—those of the Seventy-fifth, especially—felled
trees, cut them into logs, and then rolled them to
within four hundred yards of the enemy's line of
breast-works, secured them in position, and constructed a formidable barricade, the rebels all the
time pouring into the boys a terrific plunging fire,
but to no purpose.   After shifting about from one
part of the line to another, enduring night and day
a heavy fire, holding themselves in readiness to reinforce McPherson, on the one hand, when he was so
furiously attacked, and Hooker, on the other, when
he with equal persistence repulsed the foe, they were
gladdened with the intelligence that one more stronghold was yielded, and another stride made towards
Atlanta, the goal so eagerly sought for.

The movement of our army to the left, thereby
occupying all the roads leading back to Ackworth
and Allatoona, while Stoneman and Garrard occupied Allatoona and the west end of the pass, turned
this famous position of the enemy.

The operations of the "movable column" were
now at an end.   Its mission was fully and satisfac-

10

torily accomplished. *Eclat* was won from the bold enterprise. Sherman now ordered the railroad bridge to be rebuilt across the Etowah, and examining the Allatoona Pass, and finding it served an excellent purpose as a depot for supplies, he established it as a secondary base. It was duly fortified and garrisoned, and by the 9th of June communication with Chattanooga was re-established. Again the army rested for a time; but it was only for a mere breathing spell.

The fortunes of the rebels had, indeed, thus far, been checkered, and it might be safely said that at this moment their prospects were a good deal overcast. Nevertheless, they were enlisted in a bad cause—one of anarchy and ruin—and that madness, which it is said the gods inspire men with whom they wish to destroy, possessed them, and they rushed on to a gloomy and tragical fate.

CHAPTER XI.

As our grand army was moved upon the enemy, on the 10th of June, they faced a drenching rain, which soon made them very uncomfortable, but did not in the least depress their spirits—these were as buoy-ant as ever. In their front lay Kenesaw, the bold and striking Twin Mountain, as it is called, with a long and high range of chestnut covered hills, trend-ing away to the north-east, and terminating in a knob designated as Brushy Mountain. On its right was a smaller hill, Pine Mountain, and further on, Lost Mountain. These hills are so arranged as to form, one with another, a continuous chain of em-bankments, the most commanding heights presenting a conical peak. On these the enemy was posted, and his position was admirably chosen, with one exception—his line was too long. Kenesaw, Pine,

and Lost Mountains constitute a triangle, in which
Pine Mountain is the apex, the other two the base.
The natural rampart thus formed, securely protected
the town of Marietta in its rear, and the railroad
back to the Chattahoochie.

Johnston rested his hopes now upon the assump-
tion that he could hold this position against repeated
assaults; and he prepared the ground for a great
defense. Extensive lines of breast-works threaded
along the base of these hills, signal stations turreted
each conical peak, and all along the summit were
placed his batteries. It were a wonder, indeed, if
our army could soon overcome these obstacles, and a
wonder still greater if it were done without immense
loss of life. But the Chattahoochie and Atlanta, the
enemy's great magazine and workshop, lay beyond;
these must be reached. Therefore these defenses
must be encountered, and the foe routed. So willed
the chief.

To accomplish this task, McPherson moved toward
Marietta, his right resting on the railroad; Thomas
on Kenesaw and Pine Mountains; Schofield to Lost
Mountain; while the three divisions of cavalry looked
to either flank and the rear. The depot of supplies
was Big Shanty.

On the 10th, Grose's brigade is in the advance,
and after moving some three miles, meets the enemy.
Skirmishing begins; the foe is found in force, and
the line halts. That night earth-works are constructed, and the position maintained. At daylight

the works were strengthened from the inside, to resist a heavy artillery fire, which the rebels directed
upon them. That night the SEVENTY-FIFTH ILLINOIS
and the Thirty-sixth Indiana moved into the front
line, and were soon pushed forward some three hundred yards, to erect a new line of works—the enemy
looking down upon us, and thoroughly commanding
the ground—this could not be done in the day time.
Two more days' labor strengthened these lines won-
derfully, and made them proof against any force of
cannon shot. During this time the SEVENTY-FIFTH
lost one man wounded.

: Finally, Sherman's dispositions to break the enemy's line between Kenesaw and Pine Mountains succeeded, and during the night of the 13th he evacuated his first line of intrenchments. On the 14th a
severe demonstration was made upon the enemy both
along the Fourth Corps, and Howard's front. Our
lines had advanced on to the mountain early that
morning, and there was but little disposition to skirmish on the rebel side. The artillery fire, however,
was constant and terrific. Havoc was made, and
among the lives lost was that of the rebel ex-Bishop
and Lieutenant-General, Leonidas Polk. He fell by
a shot from Simonson's Fifth Indiana Battery, which
was under Grose's command, and was in position to
the right and front of his brigade.

Again, under cover of the darkness, the enemy,
huge and grey, valiant, yet half discouraged, crept

gliding down the inner slope of the hill, retiring to Lost Mountain.

Two miles of pursuit, and he was again confronted in fortified lines. As ever, field-works were built. The presence of the enemy was immediate, and at such times this kind of fortification is of infinite value, even though it be a mere rudiment, as it inspires confidence in the men, gives greater security, and forms a basis for that coherence, or unity of purpose, demanded of men when regular formations are endangered.

On the 16th the trenches were advanced, but by dint of hard skirmishing. Every inch of ground was fought for, and several valuable lives were lost, among them that of the brave and gallant Captain Simonson. His men swore to avenge his death.

Daylight of the 17th showed that Lost Mountain, too, was abandoned, and pursuit was next in order. The enemy retired, sullen and morose, doggedly contesting our advance with his rear guard. Of the Fourth Corps, Wood's Division led, closely supported by the First Division. Our army pressed the enemy at all points, on all fronts—Hooker's, Howard's, Davis's, McPherson's, and Schofield's. Over hills, through ravines and dense forests, it slowly fought its way, until the bold front of Kenesaw towered above them. Here evidently was to be an herculean struggle. Johnston's position was strongly intrenched, with Kenesaw as his salient, his right wing thrown back, covering Marietta, while his left ex-

tended across Nose's Creek, protecting his communications with the Chattahoochie. Thus had he cor-
rected his first mistake of defending too long a line
—fully two miles in extent—and now his lines were
contracted, and strengthened accordingly.

From the time of coming into this position until
the 19th, Grose's Brigade was held in reserve, and
was not under fire. The men thus gained rest, for
they sorely needed it.

But even this position of the rebel chief could not
be held against the pressure Sherman brought to
bear upon it. So, during the night of the 18th, he
fell back three miles further, locating himself more
directly on Kenesaw. Our army kept close upon
his heels, Grose's Brigade leading the First Division.

Two miles out shots were exchanged, and soon a
battle became imminent. Grose formed his brigade
in two lines—the Ninth and Thirty-sixth Indiana,
the Eightieth and Eighty-fourth Illinois, in the front
line, the Fifty-ninth and SEVENTY-FIFTH Illinois,
Thirtieth Indiana and Seventy-seventh Pennsylvania
in the second line. Then he advanced, driving the
enemy from his position—mostly an open field farm
—and into his fortifications at the base of Kenesaw
and the adjacent hills. The men fought splendidly,
and Grose's loss was severe in officers and men. It
was here that gallant soldier, Lieutenant Bowman,
was shot down and killed.

Whilst Grose's advance battalions stormed the
rebel works, a little squad of men, a mere handful of

braves, consisting of Company B, and five men from
Company A, Seventy-fifth Illinois, under command
of Captain Charles R. Richards, distinguished itself
equally as well; for being sent out on the flank as a
skirmish line, it fought constantly and with accuracy.
Finally, being hard pressed, the balls raining into
the ground around them, and being firm, proud men,
they resolved to chastise the foe. On they went,
forcing him into a run, scattering him over the field
and into the belts or clusters of timber, capturing
several prisoners. But this was done under so thick
a flight of balls, that several were struck down,
killed and wounded. Among the latter were two of
Company A, Joseph Crawford and Anthony Zimmer. I regret that I am unable to give the
names of those in Company B. They were heroes,
and deserve mention; but the record of casualties
does not specify clearly the precise time of the incident.

The contest continued all of the 20th, the enemy
trying to hold, and our forces to drive him from, a
swamp between the main trenches. In this the brigade succeeded; but it was not all a permanent advantage, for a portion of the works had to be abandoned, owing to a destructive artillery fire which the
enemy directed upon them from batteries located at
three different points. It was a flanking fire, and
particularly affected the SEVENTY-FIFTH ILLINOIS,
severely wounding four men.

As near as I can judge, it was here that a blanket

wrapped around Edwin E. Faunce, of Company F, saved his life. A four-pound cannon shot struck him in the chest. Its power of resistance prevented its crushing in.

The night of the 20th was villainously bad—the rain descending copiously, and the scene black as Cimmerian gloom. Yet on this night there sprang up in one of the rebel columns a warlike spirit, and it resolved to spend its fitful ire on some portion of the First Division front.

This warlike mass came on. It moved slowly, as if in awe or doubt. But it moved, and fired not a shot; for the orders were not to fire, but to charge with the bayonet. The dirty, grey mass moved upon Whittaker's Brigade, conjoining with Grose. Whittaker's men were alert, and lay with their rifles leveled across the parapet, and with their eyes just peering above its top, were face to face with the front rank of the surging mass. Arriving within fifty yards of the works, the order was given, "Charge!" and on the rebels rushed with unearthly whoops and yells. It was an awful shock, and for some moments the issue seemed doubtful. It was a hand to hand encounter, and the slaughter was cruel. But the Fortieth Ohio seemed endowed with superhuman strength and will, and did much to repulse the assault. Again and again it was repeated, but failure crowned each rebel effort. Grose, realizing the vigor of the attack, promptly dispatched the Ninth Indiana and the 59th Illinois to Whittaker's aid, and they, too, participated with great honor in this bloody affray. On the 21st, the balance of the brigade moved over to Whittaker's position, and he withdrew, aiding the Fourteenth Corps in flanking the rebel position in front of Kenesaw, further to the right. Here they strengthened the breast-works already commenced, but their possession was one of doubtful tenure, for the rebels directed a fearful artillery fire upon them, which penetrated through, wounding several men. They were Sergeant L. H. Burkett, Corporal W. A. Howland, Calvin DeFrain, of Company A, Sergeant Oscar Seeley and Private William Squires, of Company C, and Private Charles Reynolds, of Company I.

The brigade remained here on the 22d, and strengthened the position; but the men were terribly annoyed with the enemy's shells, and the SEVENTY-FIFTH lost one man killed, and one wounded. That night the brigade moved two miles to the right, and occupied a portion of the position vacated by the Twentieth Army Corps.

On the 23rd, a series of demonstrations were made upon the enemy's lines around Kenesaw, mostly resulting in a repulse of our forces.

In obedience to orders, Grose deployed a heavy skirmish line, and under the brave Captain Hale, charged the enemy, capturing the rebel outer works; but was unable to hold them against such superior numbers. Company I, of the Seventy-fifth Illinois, was in this affair, and did gallant service. When

assailed in the rebel works, it made stubborn resistance, and lost, as prisoner, Sergeant Samuel Orcutt.

The position of Grose's command was substantially
the same from this date until the 3rd of July. The
troops lay in the intrenchments, and within four
hundred yards of the enemy's works. They suffered
all this while a most annoying fire from artillery off
Kenesaw, and many were the victims.

On the 24th of June, the SEVENTY-FIFTH was on
the front line, with one company on picket. Here
Lieutenant R. L. Mangum, of Company D, was
wounded, losing a leg. Two were killed and three
wounded.

Some time had elapsed, and still our army fronted
Kenesaw. Heavy demonstrations had not convinced
the rebel general of the policy of yielding it. He
considered the task a difficult one to outflank it, and
he did not believe Sherman would venture an assault
on fortified lines, like those he now held. Our own
men were of the latter opinion, and looked for the
commander to outflank.

Sherman seemed to appreciate the reasoning both
of friend and foe, and therefore resolved to test the
moral power of an assault. But he had a policy to
execute, as well as a moral force to achieve. He
selected the left centre as the point of attack, as, to
use his own language, if he could "thrust a strong
head of column through at that point, by pushing it
boldly and rapidly two and one half miles, it would
reach the railroad below Marietta, cut off the ene-

my's right and centre from its line of retreat, and then, by turning on either part, it could be overwhelmed and destroyed."

The 27th of June was the day appointed, and the assault was to be made at two points, south of Kenesaw—one near Little Kenesaw, by General McPherson, and the other a mile further south, by General Thomas. The hour was fixed, and the details given in Field Orders No. 28, of June 24th, and the assaults were made at the hour and in the manner prescribed; but both were signal failures, and cost us dearly, losing Generals Harker and McCook—in fact, an aggregate of three thousand men.

Of Thomas's troops, Jeff. C. Davis's and Newton's Divisions made the assault; and it was here the gallant Thirty-fourth Illinois displayed such bravery, and lost so heavily. The assault was made upon Grose's immediate front, and the assaulting columns passed over his brigade. Some of these troops becoming terribly demoralized at the failure, rushed back in a panic, and were halted by Grose's men at the point of the bayonet. The First Division took no active part in this affair; but lay as a reserve for any emergency.

Sherman has been severely criticised for ordering these assaults—and with some degree of justice. He assumes, however, the whole responsibility of it, and claims that although a failure, it " proved to General Johnston that he would assault, and that boldly." One thing certainly was gained—ground so close to the enemy's parapets that he dared not show a head above them. It is but justice, however, here to state, that the assault was made strongly against the opinions of Generals Thomas and McPherson, both of whom predicted its failure; yet each did his best to make it a success.

General Sherman understood the nature of his soldiers too well to lie long in idleness after such a failure; accordingly, Schofield was ordered to push strongly on the rebel left; and on the first of July, Garrard's cavalry occupied the position held by McPherson, while he prepared to throw his corps by the right, down to Nick-a-jack Creek and Turner's Ferry, across the Chattahoochie. The effect was instantaneous. Hardly had McPherson commenced moving, ere Johnston comprehended the movement, and feeling that he could not prevent its success, hastened to save himself.

Consequently, on the night of the 2d of July, he evacuated Kenesaw, and made good his retreat to the Chattahoochie. Pursuit was immediately made. McPherson and Schofield pushed forward to attack him in flank as he crossed the river; but Johnston had covered his movement too well. He had intrenched a *tete-de-pont* at the Chattahoochie, with a strong intrenched advance line at Smyrna camp-meeting ground, five miles south of Marietta, and four north of the river.

Thomas's column moved forward to the railroad, and turned south in pursuit. Arrived at Smyrna,

Thomas found him, his front covered by a formidable parapet, his flanks behind the Nick-a-jack and Rotten-wood creeks.

Grose's Brigade led the advance of the First Division, and at nightfall of the 3rd, commenced skirmishing with the enemy. The brigade halts, and the pioneers construct works in an exposed position, losing three men wounded. The Fifty-ninth Illinois, of Grose's Brigade, has the honor of being the first to enter Marietta.

The 4th of July was made memorable by pushing a strong skirmish line down the main road to Smyrna camp ground, capturing the entire line of the enemy's pits, and making strong demonstrations along Nick-a-jack Creek and Turner's Ferry.

. In this affair Grose was heavily engaged. His brigade made a charge across a large corn farm, carrying the enemy's outer works, and capturing many prisoners; but at the sacrifice of eighty-nine in killed, besides the wounded. This position was held until night, when the enemy withdrew to the heights along the Chattahoochie.

And here I must go into details. When the skirmish line was formed which must charge these rifle-pits, Company E, of the SEVENTY-FIFTH ILLINOIS, under command of Lieutenant James H. Blodgett, was moved to its support. After advancing a half mile, it halted in a ravine to re-form, and charge anew. It was now in close proximity to the rebel works. When the order was given to advance again, for some reason it stood still. Captain Hale, who was in command of the whole line—a body of some two hundred men—seeing this, proceeded to Lieutenant Blodgett, whose Company lay as reserve still, and asked him to lead in the charge. Blodgett and his brave boys advanced to the front line, and on the double quick, charged the pits, killing or capturing nearly every soul in them. This company crowned itself with honor. 'Not a member left the ranks save one, and he to conduct the prisoners to the rear. I do not know to what other Companies of the Seventy-fifth the details in the skirmish line belonged, except Company C; but the regiment lost seven men wounded, and the accomplished soldier, Captain Hale, killed. He was struck by a random shot, while drinking from his canteen, after his task was accomplished. Corporal Lyman Chase, of Company C, was also shot down in the act of taking the Captain off the field. He suffered intensely for a few moments, and he remarked to his comrades, "Well, boys, I guess I'll go with the Captain."

The regiment, now under command of Major Watson, maintained its lines firmly, and in unison with the brigade, fought splendidly. Watson, in particular, was distinguished for great gallantry. I regret that I have no details of the affair.

Daylight of July 5th, found the works of the enemy abandoned. He had yielded all of the country north of the Chattahoochie, and was now massed to cover his pontoons. Again Sherman resorted to

a flank movement. He transferred nearly all his
army from the right to the left, built three bridges
across the river above Johnston's position, one at the
mouth of Soap's Creek, one at Power's Ferry, and
one at Roswell's Ford. These were secured by the
9th of July, and preparations made for a movement.
That night Johnston abandoned his *tete-de-pont*,
destroyed his bridges, and fell back upon Peach
Tree Creek. Thus was gained the chief object of
the campaign, namely, the advancement of our lines
from the Tennessee to the Chattahoochie. The
army had rested quietly from the 5th to the 10th,
doing nothing but picket duty. But another prize
lay before them—one worthy of the gain—Atlanta,
with its magazines, stores, arsenals, workshops, and
foundries. Here, too, converged the Southern system of railroads, which not only supplied Johnston's,
but Lee's forces, away in Virginia.

Meantime, General Sherman ordered a raid upon
the enemy's communications. General Rousseau was
placed in command of the expedition. It consisted
of two thousand cavalry. There is but one stem of
completed railway connecting the channels of trade
between Georgia, Alabama and Mississippi, running
from Montgomery to Opelika. To destroy this road
was Rousseau's object. He left Decatur, Alabama,
on the 10th of July; crossed the Coosa at the Ten
Islands on the 14th instant, whipping the rebel General Clanton's Brigade, passing thence through Tal-
ledaga, striking the railroad at Loachapoka, and

destroyed it from Chehaw Station (whipping the
rebels again at this point) to Opelika ; thence out
three miles on the Columbus and West Point road—
about thirty-two miles in all. He then moved north,
arriving at Marietta on the 22d, having sustained a
loss of less than thirty men.

This was one of the most successful raids of the
war. Its results were splendid, and it added greatly
to Rousseau's already brilliant reputation as a bold,
daring, and skillful chieftain.

During this time, supplies were collected at Allatoona, Marietta, and Vining's Station. Finally, on
the 17th, all being ready, a general advance was
ordered. Grose's command, however, had crossed
the river on the 12th, at Roswell Ford. Here Major
Watson superintended the building of a bridge.
Thomas crossed at Power's and Price's Ferries, and
moved to Buckhead; Schofield crossed at Soap's
Creek, and marched by Cross Keys ; McPherson
moved straight against the Augusta road, near Stone
Mountain, continuing by a general right wheel. The
whole army was now in a line along Peach Tree road.
On the 18th, the several columns were in motion ;
moved six miles to Peach Tree Creek. The next
day the SEVENTY-FIFTH ILLINOIS made a reconnoissance up to and across Peach Tree Creek. Two
companies, under command of Lieutenants Isaac L.
Hunt, of Company K, and Frank Bingham, of Company C, went in advance of the regiment, and took
a position on the creek, sending two sentinels across

11

to the opposite bank. No enemy was discovered; but two mounted men, wearing the uniform of Federal soldiers, rode up, and, wheeling away when ordered to halt, were fired at and wounded. The regiment was suddenly left without support, the reconnoitering force of the Second Division having become frightened at the supposed presence of the enemy, and retired. Company A, Captain William Parker, was placed on picket, and soon discovered the rebels throwing up works, south of the creek. Shots were exchanged, but no advance was made. The brigade soon came up, and the position was intrenched. On the 20th, the brigade moved to the left, taking a new position, and fortifying it. One man was killed.

The enemy's position was carried by assault on the 21st, very handsomely, by our troops, our loss being slight, the SEVENTY-FIFTH having one man wounded. Forty-three prisoners were taken. On the 20th, all the armies had closed in, closely converging upon Atlanta. But a gap existed between the Corps of General Thomas and that of Schofield, and two divisions of General Howard's Corps were transferred to the left to fill it, thereby leaving Newton's Division resting on the Buckhead road, and somewhat in air. About four p.m., the enemy sallied out in heavy force, and attacked Newton, swinging around upon Hooker's Corps, next south, and upon General R. W. Johnson's Division, of Palmer's Corps. Newton's defence was a line of rails, hastily piled up. Hooker was entirely uncovered, and was compelled to fight desperately; Johnson was well intrenched, and held his position with ease. The enemy's loss was nearly five thousand men, besides seven stands of colors, and many prisoners. This engagement is called the battle of Peach Tree Creek.

On the morning of the 22d of July, the enemy's lines were found abandoned, and it was thought Atlanta would fall without further contest; but it was a mistake. General Johnston had been relieved from the command of the rebel army, and General J. B. Hood substituted. Johnson was removed because he did not contest the ground desperately, even to the sacrifice of his army. Hence, with a knowledge of this, Hood was bound to fight, even against his better judgment, in order to still the clamors of the Southern people, grown desperate at their constant reverses. Poor man! he was doomed to be sacrificed, let him choose either horn of the dilemma. Did he fall back at Sherman's flanking movements, he would be denounced as incompetent in generalship, and afraid of hazard. Did he meet the Federal troops at every point when pressed, hurl his columns against them, and suffer defeat and great loss, then the stigma of rashness and butchery would attach to him. As an index of his policy take Peach Tree Creek.

Again the order was forward. At three a.m., on the 22d, the army was in motion, and at sunrise the city of Atlanta was in sight. When within three miles of the centre of the city, the enemy was encountered, with a bold front, and behind well-finished parapets. Our advancing ranks charged them with great enthusiasm, sweeping over them, routing or capturing all in them.

The skirmishers of the SEVENTY-FIFTH were under command of Lieutenant Prentiss L. Bannister, of Company C. His men did bravely, driving the enemy back into his main works, within two miles of the centre of the city. Sergeant Martin L. Johnston, of Company I, was killed, and Mark S. Plant, of Company D, badly wounded, by a shell from one. of our own batteries. Lieutenant-Colonel Kilgore says of the former, in his official report of the campaign, that "his soldierly conduct and bravery, all through these series of battles and skirmishes, is deserving of all praise."

The regiment lay here in nearly the same position until the 25th of August. Picket duty was regularly performed, and a few men were wounded. On the 23d of July, Captain William Frost, of Company E, was wounded seriously.

On the 27th of July, General Stanley assumed command of the Fourth Army Corps, and Colonel Grose that of the First Division. This placed Colonel P. Sidney Post, of the Fifty-ninth Illinois, in command of the brigade. On the 5th of August, Grose returned to his brigade wearing the "star," having, during his absence, received his well-merited commission as Brigadier-General.

During the investment of Atlanta, there were several sharp battles on the fronts of the different corps. No attempt was made to carry the enemy's defences around the city. It was surrounded with strong redoubts, built a year previous, and these were now connected with curtains, making a continued line of fortifications, and well strengthened by rifle trenches, abattis, and *chevaux-de-frise*. On the 22d of July, the Army of the Tennessee had a terrible engagement with the enemy, lasting for several hours, losing very heavily; and among others was the gifted and noble Major-General McPherson. Our loss was more than three thousand in killed, wounded, and missing; the enemy's loss was frightful. His dead alone were 3,200, and in aggregate, more than 8,000 men.

Finally, the expeditions sent out under Generals Garrard and Stoneman having destroyed the Augusta and Macon roads, but not as effectually as desired, owing to the failure of General Stoneman to concentrate his forces at Lovejoy's (he having been captured), General Sherman resolved to move his army by a grand right flank movement, and thus obtain possession of the Macon road, over which the enemy still brought his supplies. Meantime he ordered down from Chattanooga four four and a half inch rifled guns, to try their effect upon the city. From the 10th to the 16th of August these guns were kept in constant use, night and day, doing much execution, destroying many buildings, and creating great confusion; but the enemy seemed determined to hold his works, though the city were destroyed. Sherman did not desire this, so, on the 16th of August, he issued orders for the march. Learning, just then, that the rebel General Wheeler, with a large force of cavalry, had attacked his communications at Adairsville, and broken the road at Calhoun, he countermanded the orders, and again attempted the destruction of the Macon road. Kilpatrick was selected this time; he, too, failed to do sufficient damage, owing to meeting superior forces of the enemy, and returned on the 22d of August. Then Sherman re-issued his orders. This was a most important movement. Of necessity, it raised the siege of Atlanta, and compelled an attack upon the enemy's communications, instead of upon himself. The sick and all surplus baggage was sent back to the Chattahoochie, and the Twentieth Corps with it.

On the night of the 25th, the Army of the Cumberland drew out of its lines on the extreme left, and moved to a position below Proctor's Creek. The next night the Army of the Tennessee moved circutiously to Sandtown, and across Camp Creek, the Army of the Cumberland moving, meantime, to Utoy Creek, Schofield remaining in position. The third movement by the flank placed the Army of the Tennessee on the West Point railroad above Fairborn, the Army of the Cumberland about Red Oak, and Schofield at Digs and Mins. Then commenced the destruction of the railroad. And it was effectually broken up. For twelve miles the ties were burned, the rails heated and bent, the cuts filled up with trees, rock and earth intermingled, while loaded shell, prepared like torpedoes, were placed all through them, to explode in the event of an attempt to clear them out. This task performed to General Sherman's satisfaction, the army pushed eastward—Howard on the right, toward Jonesboro, Thomas on the centre, by Shoal Creek Church to Couch's, and Schofield on the left, about Morrow's Mills.

On the 31st of August, Howard found himself within a mile of Jonesboro, and in presence of a large force of the enemy. He at once formed line of battle, and the men covered their front with a parapet. Fighting soon commenced. Schofield at once moved on Rough and Ready, Stanley's Corps supporting. Davis's Corps struck for the railroad. While these movements were progressing, the enemy sallied out of his fortifications at Jonesboro, and attacked Howard, *en masse*. He met with a dreadful reception, and after a contest of two hours, withdrew, leaving four hundred dead on the field. Schofield soon met opposition, and Stanley's Corps deployed to the front, Grose in advance of the First Division. His advance line, the Ninth and Eighty-fourth Indiana, and the Eighty-fourth Illinois, drove the rebel cavalry from the east bank of Flint river, and advanced, striking the Macon road about 4 p.m. on the 31st instant. Grose now formed line on the right of the division, Newton's Division joining his right, the whole line fronting south. Here the troops rested for the night.

September 1st, the troops were all in motion for Jonesboro, moving down the railroad, and destroying it as they advanced.

Towards night the First Division joined the left of the Fourteenth Corps, two miles north of Jones-boro. Line of battle was established, Grose forming on the left of the First Brigade. Grose was much troubled while getting into line, as he was checked by a thick bramble, or underbrush, through which it was almost impossible to move. Besides, a heavy skirmish line of the rebels, supported by artillery, which played upon him, did not help the difficulty; however, he forced his way through. Emerging from the brush, he found a long interval between the first and his brigade. He moved by the right oblique, swinging around his left, until suddenly he came upon the rebel barricades. It was now near night, yet the Ninth Indiana, the Eighty-fourth Illinois, and the Seventy-seventh Pennsylvania, charged up under a perfect hailstorm of bullets, to within three hundred yards of the barricades. The position was maintained, and during the night, the rebels fled. The fighting had been continuous along the entire line, Davis's Corps, in particular, having distinguished itself. The Thirty-fourth Illinois here did important service.

Jonesboro evacuated, the rebels moved south to Lovejoy's. During the night of the 1st, heavy explosions were heard in the direction of Atlanta, twenty miles north, succeeded by minor explosions, which seemed to the troops around Jonesboro like a battle raging fiercely at or near Atlanta. · No one knew the cause, but evidently it was one of two things—either General Slocum had made a night attack on the city, or the enemy was blowing up his magazines, preparatory to an evacuation.

The rebels were pushed rapidly into Lovejoy's Station, Thomas moving down on the left of the road, Howard on the right, Schofield two miles to the east.

As usual, the rebels were found strongly in-trenched; with flanks well protected behind a branch of Walnut Creek, to the right, and a confluent of the Flint River to the left. On this march of six miles, the First Division was the rearmost of the corps. About 2 p.m., the advance division came upon the enemy, and the deployment of the column was ordered. Grose moved to the left of the railroad, and formed in battle order—the SEVENTY-FIFTH and Eighty-fourth Illinois, and the Eighty-fourth Indiana in front, in a corn-field to the left of Wood's Division. Soon the whole army was in line of battle, and an advance ordered. The configuration of the ground was very rough and hilly, and rapid movement difficult. They were soon upon the enemy in his rifle pits, charg-ing upon him with a shout, routing or capturing all his forces. Nearly in front of Grose rose a hill, one which the enemy held, and the key to their position, for it commanded their main works, still to the rear. Colonel Bennett was directed to take this position.

Generals and others gathered to witness the assault. Off started the command, the skirmish line in advance under command of Lieutenant James H. Blodgett. A terrific fire of artillery and musketry greeted them as they neared the crest. Nothing daunted, they moved straight on with precision and alacrity, none falling behind save the dead and the maimed. The summit reached, a shout, long, and clear, and wild, arose upon the air, and the issue was made—the works were scaled, the victory won. The sulphurous canopy lifted from the earth, and disclosed how complete the success. In this charge, Sergeant Draper Angel, of Company H, and Corporal John Nass, of Company E, captured and took to the rear eight prisoners.

The rest of the brigade performed its part well, carrying the parapet in its front, sustaining heavy loss. The skirmishers advanced some distance toward the main works; but the contest was too unequal, and they retired suffering severely.

The position gained was fortified, and the troops to the right and left conjoined, intrenching. Here the army rested until the 5th, skirmishing at intervals with the enemy, who presented a firm front, as if still determined to contest obstinately.

On the 4th of September, Colonel Bennett assumed command of the brigade; and that night a courier arrived from General Slocum, reporting that the enemy had evacuated Atlanta, blown up his magazines and seven trains of cars, and retreated by the McDonough road.

The object of the campaign was accomplished—the Gate City was in Federal possession—and as it was useless to chase a demoralized army through the wooded country below them, Sherman ordered a concentration of the army near Atlanta. Therefore, on the 5th, the countermarch was commenced; on the 8th, the armies were encamped—Thomas's around Atlanta, Howard's about East Point, and Schofield's at Decatur.

Thus closed one of the most eventful and successful campaigns in the history of modern warfare. For four months the contest was waged steadily, and for full one hundred days were the armies under fire. For endurance of the men, severity of fighting, and tenaciousness of purpose in attaining its object, the campaign is without a historical parallel.

The soldiers who fought its battles need no eulogium. Their record is their country's; their laurels constitute the nation's wreath of glory. General Grose, in his official report, says this of the brave men constituting his command:—"It is due to the officers and men to notice, in terms of gratification to myself, and commendation to them, that better soldiers I NEVER WISH nor expect to command." Lieutenant-Colonel Kilgore, in his report, says of Major James A. Watson, that "he did credit to himself for his bravery and readiness at all times, and ably performed his part as commanding officer of the regiment in the battle of Smyrna Camp Ground, on the 4th of July."

To Captain Hale he pays a high tribute of respect.
Of him he says: "The regiment has lost one of its
best officers, the country a valiant and patriotic soldier. He died as he had lived, a Christian soldier
and gentleman." The loss of the SEVENTY-FIFTH
during the campaign was, in officers, one killed and
four wounded; in enlisted men, ten killed and fifty-
three wounded—a total of 68. The loss of the brigade was, in killed, ninety-six; in wounded, six hundred and one—a total of six hundred and ninety-
seven men. These, as General Grose—that true-
hearted and noble soldier—feelingly says in conclu-
ding his official report, "present the bitter fruit of
such a brilliant campaign, and leave many aching
hearts; not only with families and friends at home,
but these fallen heroes will ever be remembered and
lamented by their comrades in arms, as the jewels
sacrificed upon the altar of our country."

The Atlanta campaign seemed to clear the prospects of the war. It confirmed to the Union armies
that military ascendancy over the Confederate forces,
which had been more than half gained already by
the valor of our men, displayed on former battle
fields. It lent the sanction of a victory to the hazardous enterprise of an invasion. It more than ever
pronounced the war a rebellion. It did more. It
proved that the prize for which we contended—the
restoration of the Union—was within our grasp, were
the opportunity pressed, and that speedily.

CHAPTER XIII.

THE RETREAT OF THE UNION FORCES—THE DECOY OF
HOOD — SKIRMISHES AT COLUMBIA — BATTLE OF
FRANKLIN—ARRIVAL AT NASHVILLE.

THE preceding chapter left the Union army encamped around Atlanta, West Point and Decatur;
the rebel army at Lovejoy's Station.

Our army rested quietly in its camps until the 3rd
of October. Meantime, it underwent a thorough
reorganization. The time of service of the original
three years' troops, except those who veteranized,
had now expired, and they mustered out. The veteran organizations, new regiments, and recruits, were
consolidated, the entire army re-clothed and equipped,
and great preparations made for another campaign.

During September, the rebel army under Hood
moved westward from Lovejoy's toward the Chattahoochie, and despatched its cavalry forces in the
direction of Carrollton and Powder Springs. The
spirits of the rebel soldiery were at a low ebb; and
they despaired of ever achieving success. To prevent the utter and voluntary disbandment of their

armies, Jefferson Davis, the so-called President of the rebellious States, proceeded to Macon, Georgia, and harangued them, saying an active campaign would at once be inaugurated, and that ere it ended, the Union forces would be hurled back across the Tennessee, and the rebel banner firmly planted as far north as Kentucky soil. Thus encouraged, their armies started northward, with Cheatham, S. D. Lee, and Stewart, as corps commanders. Wheeler had command of the cavalry. The fact of this movement became definitely known to General Sherman on the 28th of September. General Thomas was sent to Nashville, to organize the new troops expected there (volunteers and drafted men), and to make preparations to meet Hood from the north.

About the first of October, Wheeler's cavalry crossed the Chattahoochie, and the infantry forces were closely following. Sherman immediately ordered the Twentieth Corps to hold Atlanta and the Chattahoochie bridges, and on the 4th of October, the Fourth, Fourteenth, Fifteenth, Seventeenth, and Twenty-third Corps, moved to Smyrna Camp Ground, and on the 5th, arrived at Kenesaw. Wheeler had already destroyed the railroad at Big Shanty, and French's Division of infantry had moved against Allatoona, where were stored a large amount of Government supplies. Its redoubts were held by a force of three small regiments, under Colonel Tourtellotte, of the Fourth Minnesota. General Corse reinforced him during the night of the 4th of Octo-

ber, and met the attack of the enemy on the 5th instant. After a very severe fight, lasting all day, the
rebels were repulsed with great slaughter. Hearing
the sound of the battle at Kenesaw, Sherman ordered
the Twenty-third Corps toward Dallas, threatening
the enemy's rear. This caused his withdrawal to
Dallas.

Hood's army was now well concentrated and
pushed westward, feigning on Rome, but striking at
Resaca. Here he demanded a surrender. But Colonel Weaver was a plucky soldier, and refused. Being reinforced by Raum's Brigade, he repulsed the
assaults made upon him, and Hood then employed
his time in destroying the railroad from Tilton to
Dalton.

Our troops pushed on rapidly, moving through
Allatoona Pass to Kingston, thence to Rome, Calhoun, and Resaca, reaching this point on the 14th of
October. Here Sherman determined to strike Hood
in flank, or force him to battle. The enemy held
Snake Creek Gap. The Army of the Tennessee
moved upon this position. The Fourth and Fourteenth Corps moved by Tilton to the rear of the Gap
near Villanow. Howard engaged the rebels in front,
but Hood, divining the trap set for him, retreated
before Stanley could get to his rear. Our armies
now pushed for Lafayette, desiring to cut off Hood's
retreat. He was now stationed at Ship's Gap. On
the 17th, the march was in the beautiful valley of
the Chattooga. Howard pursued by way of Lafay-

ette and Alpine, Stanley by Summerville to Gaylesville, and Cox from Villanow by Glover's Gap to
Gaylesville. Hood, however, marched light, unen-
cumbered by long trains, and when arrived at Gaylesville, Sherman found the enemy was near Gadsden,
where the Lookout range abuts on the Coosa river.

The Chattooga valley is very rich in soil, and at
this time it abounded in a plentiful harvest, yet un-
garnered. And as General Sherman did not yet
fully know what course Hood would pursue, he
determined to rest a few days, subsist off the country, and watch the rebel leader's movements. It
was evident to Sherman that Hood wished to avoid
a battle; and it was further evident, by the strategic
game Hood was playing, that he had a sufficient
force to give Sherman much trouble, by endangering
his communications, but insufficient to meet him in
armed conflict. In view of these facts, Sherman reasoned this way:

" To remain on the defensive would be bad policy
for an army of so great value as he commanded; and
to follow Hood would simply amount to being de-
coyed away from Georgia, with little prospect of
overtaking and overwhelming him."

He therefore submitted a plan to General Grant,
which involved the destruction of Atlanta, the railroad to Chattanooga, and a march from Atlanta
through the heart of Georgia, to one or more of the
great Atlantic seaports. Sherman's plan having received the sanction of the Commander-in-chief, he
prepared for the march.

The Fourth Corps was ordered to Chattanooga on the 26th of October, and on the 30th instant the Twenty-third Corps proceeded to the same place—both under orders to report to General Thomas at Nashville, who had full powers of command over all the troops in his Military Division, excepting the four corps which were to move southward. This gave Thomas the Fourth and Twenty-third Corps; also the Sixteenth Corps, A. J. Smith's, then in West Tennessee; also all the troops in the various garrisons, and the cavalry forces of Kentucky and Tennessee, under Generals Wilson and Johnson. This aggregate force Sherman deemed sufficient for Thomas to repel any invasion Hood might attempt.

Sherman now turned his attention southward. Rome and Atlanta were destroyed. All garrisons, muniments of war and supplies were sent to Chattanooga, fortifications razed, and the country, so far as possible, desolated. By the 14th of November all was in readiness, and the campaign commenced. It does not belong to this book to detail these movements. Sherman's "Great March to the Sea," is as familiar as Dickens' "Household Words;" and to its "Story," published by several ambitious writers, I refer.

By the 1st of November Hood's army had moved westward from Gadsden, made a feint upon Decatur, passed Tuscumbia, and laid a pontoon at Florence, Alabama. It was plain, now, that Hood was carrying out the invasion announced by Davis in his

12

speech at Macon, and that its aim was the occupation of Western Kentucky.

This necessitated a rapid movement of the Fourth and Twenty-third Corps to Pulaski, to intercept the onward march of the rebel horde. Consequently the Fourth Corps was embarked as speedily as possible in cars, and pushed forward to Athens, Alabama. The First Division was in advance, and the Third Brigade, Colonel L. H. Waters, Eighty-fourth Illinois, now commanding, was the first to reach this point, disembarking at 2 a. m., on the first of November. The fort was found abandoned, the regiments (new ones) which held it had been terribly frightened at the mere *report* of an enemy in their vicinity, and ignominiously retreated. The ground was strewed with camp and garrison equipage, clothing, blankets and rations. The Pioneer Company was the first inside the fort, and made their choice in the spoils. A reconnoissance was made, but no enemy was found. A squad of rebel cavalry had ventured into the vicinity, but attempted no harm, not even displacing a rail on the road. Information was gathered that Hood had crossed the Tennessee near Florence, and was moving north by the old military road, the one which General Jackson used when, in 1812, he marched to New Orleans. The corps having all arrived at Athens, daylight of the 2d instant found the troops *en route* for Pulaski, wading Elk river, and camping at Pulaski on the evening of the 3rd of November. While here, all

the hills around the town were fortified, and an extensive line of rifle pits constructed, the enemy being
expected to attack that point, as until near the 20th,
it was defended by the Fourth Corps only. About
this time a small portion of the Twenty-third Corps
arrived, the larger part of it remaining at Columbia,
thirty-four miles north, that place being also threatened by the enemy's cavalry. On the 23rd of
November, General Thomas ascertained, beyond a
doubt, that Hood was striving to outflank him by
passing some distance westward, and crossing the
defile of Duck river, thence moving rapidly on Nashville and its defences, unguarded save by the force
under Major-General L. H. Rousseau, District
Commander, and his subordinate, the Post Commandant, General John F. Miller. . The Fourth
Corps fell back upon Columbia during the night
of the 23rd, arriving there in the afternoon
of the 24th, making a forced march of thirty-four
miles over a hard pike in less than twelve hours.
By the time they reached Columbia, the men were
tired nearly to death, yet there was no rest for them.
The presence of the enemy was immediate. Indeed,
the rear of the column had skirmished briskly the
last five miles out. Here the pioneers, and, in fact,
all of the troops, as at Pulaski, were engaged in
throwing up breastworks facing south and west, and
in a semi-circular line, about a mile from town.

When Pulaski was evacuated, the SEVENTY-FIFTH
ILLINOIS was left behind to destroy all stores and

ammunition which the trains were unable to trans-
port north. A large amount of supplies, principally
sanitary, was consigned to the flames—more, in fact,
than had ever been issued to the Fourth Corps during its entire existence. Yet the corps had lain at
Pulaski full twenty days, and sorely needed much of
what was destroyed. The Sanitary Commission
knew full well that the tenure of the place was extremely doubtful; still they preferred their whole-
sale destruction to their speedy issue, although well
deserved.

This fact excited much bitter comment among the
soldiers—and justly. Nor is it the first instance in
this army where a similar scene has transpired. This
work was accomplished by midnight, and the SEV-
ENTY-FIFTH joined the brigade two miles from town,
and hastened north, serving as the infantry rear
guard of the retreating column. A small force of
cavalry covered their movement. They arrived at
Pulaski at 8 p. m., on the 24th, having marched
constantly, and without stopping to cook rations.

The troops remained in position on the defences
around Columbia until the night of the 28th of
November. They then withdrew to the north bank
of Duck River, and intrenched, the Pioneers doing
the principal work. It is well here to add a word
concerning that little force of the SEVENTY-FIFTH
ILLINOIS. After the close of the Atlanta campaign,
Lieutenant Newton was relieved, being placed in
charge of a transportation train, and Sergeant Tal-

bot went home on furlough. Sergeant George M. Houck, of Company E, was then placed in command, and thenceforward discharged the duties of commanding officer faithfully and well, constructing embrasures and bridges across the Elk and Duck Rivers. On the 29th instant, the position was abandoned, and the whole army retreated north to Spring Hill. While on this march, General Grose, who had been absent home, returned, and assumed command of the Third Brigade.

Let us now, in order to a full understanding of these movements, examine the designs and operations of Hood, the rebel chief. His aim was, if possible, to reach Kentucky without offering or being forced into a battle. The reason of this was, that he expected the rebellious portion of her people would flock to his standard, and that his army would thus be increased to at least 80,000 or 90,000 effective men. This, he judged, would enable him to defeat any force Thomas could bring against him. Hood commenced his campaign by moving from Florence, Alabama, on the 21st of November. The want of a good map of the country, and the deep mud through which his army marched (for it had rained almost constantly for three weeks previous) prevented him from appearing in front of Columbia within three days' march of the time he intended. Thus General Thomas ascertained his locality, and checkmated the game by falling back upon Columbia on the 23rd instant. During the 29th, his army was all in posi-

tion in front of our defences at Columbia. And here
he sought again to outflank and cut off. With this
view, on the night of the 28th, he crossed Forrest's
cavalry to the north bank of Duck River, a few miles
above the town, and during the 29th, followed with
Stewart's and Cheatham's Corps, and Johnson's
Division of Lee's Corps, leaving Lee's other divisions
to make a show of front at Columbia, and hold
Thomas's forces in position. His troops marched
light, with only one battery to a corps, his object
being to turn Thomas's flank by moving on roads
running parallel to the Columbia and Franklin pikes,
intersecting at Spring Hill, and thus cut off that portion of our army at Columbia. But again Thomas
discovered Hood's intention, and retreated to Spring
Hill. His cavalry engaged our forces in charge of
the trains, which stretched fully ten miles, about
mid-day, but they were so strongly guarded that no
impression was made, nor damage done, save in a
few killed and wounded. Here our army had a narrow escape. Cheatham's Corps had formed in line
two miles south of Spring Hill, and he was ordered
to attack the column in charge of the trains vigorously, destroy the trains, and get possession of the
pike. But for some reason, Cheatham made but a
feeble and partial attack, failing, in consequence, to
reach the pike. Stewart's Corps and Johnson's
Division were hastening to Cheatham's support; but
night had now come on, and it was one of pitchy
blackness; and Stewart, who was instructed to form

his line on Cheatham's right, failed to find it, and after groping about until near 11 p. m., went into bivouac., It was about midnight that the greater part of our forces pushed through Spring Hill, moving in great confusion—artillery, wagon and ammunition trains, and troops, all intermixed. Not a mile to the right were seen the camp fires of Stewart's Corps, brightly burning, and all along the line of flankers were heard the exchanged shots with the rebel pickets. This made matters worse. All of our men expected capture and rout. Hood was informed of this fact, and ordered Cheatham to attack him with a heavy force of skirmishers, and still further confuse the march. Again Cheatham failed to accomplish the duty assigned him, and all passed safely, reaching Franklin on the morning of the 30th of November. It cannot be questioned that had Cheatham deployed a skirmish line, and pressed it firmly, there would have been an abandonment of our entire trains, and a perfect temporary rout of our army. The only reason that can be assigned for Cheatham's non-compliance with Hood's order is, that he was himself unfamiliar with the country around him, and was afraid to attack in the night, lest his own corps should, in the confusion, become demoralized, and be as badly off as the Union forces. Again, he doubtless thought our troops would make a stouter resistance than they were really capable of doing, for they were stretched along the pike by brigades, for miles. Thus was the golden opportu-

nity lost to Hood to bring disaster upon our arms.
Now there was no chance of cutting our army off
from its depot of supplies and defences at Nashville.

Our troops, now under command of General Schofield, of the Twenty-third Corps, fell back upon
Franklin, making a feint as if to give battle on the
hills some four miles south of Franklin; but upon
the appearance of Stewart's Corps, which immediately deployed for attack, and sought again to
flank by the left, Schofield ordered them to retire
slowly but obstinately to Franklin. Hood now
ascertained, by dispatches from Thomas to Schofield
(and which were captured at Spring Hill), that the
latter was directed to hold that place until the position at Franklin could be fortified, indicating that
Thomas would hold his old line of defences from
Franklin to Murfreesboro. Hood, therefore, judged
it all-important to attack Schofield and Stanley before this position was secured.

Schofield established his line of battle in the south-
erly limits of the town, with its flanks resting upon
the Harpeth River, which here makes a very abrupt
bend, half encircling the place. The First Division
of the Fourth Corps formed on the extreme right, its
left resting on the extension of the main street. Its
general direction was east and west, with a portion
of Grose's Brigade refused to the right. Joining
this division was the Second Division of the Twenty-
third Corps, prolonging the line in a north-east direction. The First Division of this corps completed the

line, its direction being due north. A reserve force rested in the rear centre of each division. Seven hundred yards of this front was an advanced fortified line extending across the Columbia Pike, and defended by the Second and Third Brigades of the Second Division, Fourth Corps. The Third Division of the Fourth Corps was placed in position on the north bank of the river, to protect the trains, and serve as an auxiliary force, if the emergency required. The men were very tired, worn out by the tedious marches and fatigues, and many of them fell asleep while constructing their hastily-formed barricades. It was near three o'clock, p. m., when our troops were all in position, and they were immediately confronted by Hood, whose front line was formed by deploying Stewart's column to the right, and Cheatham's to the left, of the Columbia Pike, his right stretching across the Nashville and Decatur railroad, reaching well to Carter's Creek Pike. Wheeler's cavalry guarded well his flanks, and Johnson's Division lay in rear, as reserve. At 4 p. m., Hood's line advanced, with orders to drive our forces, at the point of the bayonet, into or across the Harpeth River, while Forrest, if the charge should be successful, was to cross the river, attack and destroy the trains and broken columns. It was a fearful moment when the rebels advanced to the charge. With an iron steadiness they marched up to the outer works. Our soldiery for a time held their ground, fighting most desperately, and dealing fearful execution on the assailants. But they were overpowered and forced to retreat to the main line. The rebels had indeed handsomely carried the position, and captured many prisoners.

Emboldened by this success, they advanced against our interior lines, and succeeded in this also, in some places. And here, too, the battle was of the fiercest possible character. The main assaults were directed upon the divisions of the Twenty-third Corps, and lapping partially on the front of the First Division of the Fourth Corps.

The enemy advanced but once upon the front of Grose's Brigade, and then he met with a disastrous reception. This charging column, as it swept over the open field, was directed full upon the front of the Ninth and Thirtieth Indiana, and the SEVENTY-FIFTH ILLINOIS. As he approached within easy musket range, General Grose ordered his men to fire. The effect was terrible, and the rebels fled precipitately. They made no lodgment on Grose's front; but on the left of the First Division their success was more encouraging. Never did brave but deluded men fight more earnestly, or with more infatuation of madness. The rebels were for some distance on the outer side of the parapet, our heroes on the inner side. Muskets were clubbed, the bayonets freely used, and in many instances the pioneers fought with their spades and axes.

I regret that I am unable to particularize more of what occurred with Grose, although I am satisfied I have, in the brief statement made, done the command justice.* Such, in brief, was the battle of Franklin. It was terrible; the rebels held out, constantly, though vainly, hoping to break our centre; till, after suffering unparalleled loss, night came on, which the rebels had the melancholy honor of passing on the field of battle. General Stanley, who was ever present, and distinguished himself by his daring bravery, was wounded. Among the rebels killed were Major-General P. R. Cleburn, Brigadiers Gist, John Adams, Strahl, and Granbury. Among the wounded were Major-General Brown, Brigadiers Carter, Cockrell, Manigault, and Scott. General Gordon was captured.

Each party claimed the victory; Schofield and Thomas exhibiting, as proof of their success, twelve rebel banners, which their corps, admitted to be inferior in numbers, bore off the field; and the heavy loss which they had inflicted upon the rebels: Hood, that he kept possession of the field, while our forces retired, the very night of the battle, from Franklin to Nashville. Five of our flags were in rebel hands, and the ground between was strewed with six thousand killed and wounded; but five-sixths of them were gray-coats.

About 9 p. m. the troops commenced falling back upon Nashville. General Grose's Brigade, under

* In writing this chapter, I find that what purported to be General Grose's report of the battle of Franklin was only a duplicate of the battle of Nashville; and I have no time nor opportunity to obtain it.

command of Colonel Bennett, moved as rear guard, covering the retreat until after passing Wood's Division, still in bivouac on the north side of the river. The brigade marched all night, arriving at Nashville in the forenoon of December 1, 1864. During that day the entire army was in position around the city, and awaited Hood's advance.

CHAPTER XIV.

THE position around Nashville was quickly taken, and rapidly fortified with a redan line of pits, connecting the forts, which had been previously erected.

Major-General Steedman, commanding the colored troops, formed and intrenched on the extreme left of the line, his left flank resting on the Cumberland River above the city, and one mile from its outskirts. The Twenty-third Army Corps, General Schofield commanding, joined Steedman on the right, extending to the Granny White Pike. The Fourth Army Corps, General Thomas J. Wood, joined Schofield, his right stretching across the Hillsboro Pike, and nearly to the Hardin Pike. The Sixteenth Army Corps, General A. J. Smith, having arrived from Memphis, extended Wood's line to the river below the town. General Wilson's cavalry corps rested near the river, and behind Smith's right wing. The forces of General John F. Miller, Post Commandant, occupied the inner line of intrenchments, from the Murfreesboro Pike to Fort Negley. The Quartermaster's forces, consisting of all Government employees, numbering thousands, guarded the line from the Granny White to the Charlotte Pike.

On the 2d of December, the enemy made his appearance, deploying along our entire front, and threw up a line of works, varying in distance from 700 to 1,500 yards of ours. On the 3d he advanced upon the front of the Fourth Corps, and attacked the skirmish line. He was repulsed, and our men occupied the position lost by him. On the 6th it was ascertained that Hood was calling for volunteers to storm our works; in consequence of which, unusual vigilance was kept up, and extra dispositions made to meet the attack; but nothing came of it. On the 8th, the enemy attacked the outposts in front of the First Division, drove in the pickets, and occupied the line of works; but by rallying the skirmishers and charging the enemy, they were repulsed and the line retaken and held. From this time until the 14th, heavy details were constantly engaged strengthening the works, and preparing both for offence and defence. On the 14th, General Grose received orders to march at 6 a.m., on the 15th, this being the day set by General Thomas for attacking the enemy in his fortified position.

The plan of the battle was this: General Steedman attacked the enemy's advanced position on his right, as a demonstration, and Wilson's cavalry made a wide detour, to attain the enemy's left and rear. Smith's Corps moved *en echelon*, to strike the rebel left, in conjunction with the cavalry movement. Wood's Corps held its intrenched line, connecting with Smith's right. The intrenchments and forts were held by new troops. Schofield's Corps lay in reserve. Steedman's demonstration was successful. Johnson's cavalry, on the extreme left, drove the rebel General Chalmers's cavalry from his position on the river, capturing his artillery, and pursued him down the Charlotte Pike. Smith's Corps swung around to conform with the cavalry advance. At 1 p.m., Wood's Corps assaulted and carried Montgomery Hill. Then Smith's Corps and Hatch's cavalry advanced and seized the rebel positions in their fronts. This was at 2 p.m. Schofield's then moved rapidly to the right of Smith, and formed line of battle, extending his right.

Then the whole line swept forward. Wood's Corps forced every rebel position in his front, routing the enemy from three fortified hills. Smith, Schofield, and the dismounted cavalry, pressed back the rebel left, and drove them a mile among the Brentwood Hills. It was now night, and darkness ended the conflict. The conflict was bloody, the battle desperate—the spoils, thirty cannon and 2,000 prisoners. Such was the outline of the battle on the 15th of December.

It is proper now to particularize the operations of Grose's command. His effective force was seven regiments—in all, 2,190 men. The order of battle, when the corps advanced from its works, was *en eche-lon*, by divisions forward on the right. His brigade was formed on the right of the Hillsboro Pike, and directly in front of the enemy's fortifications, which, in fact, extended around the city. The Second Division of the corps was on his right; the First Brigade of the First Division on his left. The Ninth Indiana, Eightieth and Eighty-fourth Illinois, were in the front line; the SEVENTY-FIFTH ILLINOIS, Thirtieth and Eighty-fourth Indiana in the second line; the Seventy-seventh Pennsylvania in reserve. The enemy's line of works ran at right angles with the Franklin and Granny White Pikes, and continued until it reached a high hill to the left of the Hillsboro Pike. Then it made an angle obliquely to the rear, fronting near the left of that pike, covering well the left flank of his main line of battle.

Grose's brigade was formed directly in front of this angle. It was noon when Smith's Corps and the cavalry had swung around, they having much farther to move, before the Fourth Corps could advance in a general and effective line of battle. Meantime, a furious musketry fire was kept up, and the guns from Forts Negley, Confiscation, and Morton, thundered away with ominous mutterings, filling the air with screaming shells, which exploded in the enemy's line frequently, dispersing his moving columns, and disorganizing his order of battle. When Smith's Corps had attained its proper alignment, the Fourth

Corps moved forward in grand style, driving the enemy's outposts—Grose's men, especially, capturing many prisoners, and sustaining some loss, occasioned mostly by artillery fire.

The hill was carried, the rebels falling back to their works. Skirmishers were then thrown well down the acclivity. While resting here, General Grose suggested to the corps commander that if another intervening ridge, to the left of his command, and in front of Kirby's Brigade, was carried, he could advance across the valley, and carry by assault the enemy's main line, where was posted the artillery which had done him so much damage. General Wood promptly replied that it should be done. Soon after, he advanced, in conjunction with Kirby's Brigade. Away went the line, through hedges and over stone walls, and across the narrow valley, until it reached a long stone wall at the base of the enemy's hill, and about four hundred yards from his main works and battery at the angle before mentioned. Much time was spent here, under the protection of this wall, in preparing for the assault, and awaiting the advance of the division on the right, to preserve intact the line. Meantime, Grose's and Kirby's skirmishers gradually crept up the hill. The loss at this time was not great; but the next movement seemed to the soldiers pregnant with danger. A thick storm of shot and shell crashed through the air above them, but it seems that these missiles of war sound far more dangerous than they are. Near

13

four o'clock all was in readiness, the bugle sounded "forward," and the whole line, from right to left, was instantly in motion. The Eightieth Illinois, Grose's centre regiment, struck the enemy right at the angle of his works, the Eighty-fourth Illinois to the right, and the Ninth Indiana to the left. Up the hill they rushed, like the surging of a tidal wave, stark on, full against the rebel stronghold, over his works, fighting hand to hand, routing the host, killing many and capturing many. And, strange to say, the loss to us was trifling. Thus do dangers shrink before the advance of brave men. The struggle was very short—scarce ten minutes. A four gun battery was among the trophies. Grose's advance was now all excitement; eager for pursuit, his two left regiments, without support, followed the enemy some six hundred yards beyond the works, and halted only under imperative orders. It was now near dusk. The sun was already setting, and fighting must soon cease.

This grand triumph had necessarily broken the line formation. This was now re-adjusted, and pursuit attempted. The brigade crossed the Granny White pike, moving along the enemy's works to the east, feeling for the rebel outposts ; but night settled down heavily, and the pursuit was abandoned. The pioneers threw up a hasty line of defence on the brigade front, and the command rested for the night.

Thus ended the first day's battle. The morrow was to witness a deadlier strife. On the 16th of

December, the operations were as follows: Wood's
Corps pushed the enemy's advanced lines backward
across the Franklin Pike into his intrenchments on
the Overton Hills. Smith's Corps, connecting with
Wood and Schofield, pressed the enemy closely. A
furious assault was made upon the enemy at Overton Hills; but the rebels fought with frightful madness, and the attack was repulsed. Meantime, Wilson's cavalry, under Hatch and Croxton, made a detour to the Granny White Pike, and attacked the
enemy's left and rear vigorously. Smith then assailed
and carried the key point to the enemy's position, on
the Brentwood Hills, and to the right of the Granny
White Pike. This success was followed by an
advance of the whole line to the extreme left, resulting in the capture of every part of the rebel intrenchments, twenty-five guns, and 3,000 prisoners. The
enemy, routed at all points, retreated toward Franklin, pursued by cavalry, under Hatch and Johnson.

Again to detail Grose's movements. At daylight,
on the 16th, he advanced, crossed a creek, and occupied the abandoned works of the enemy, on the right
of the Franklin Pike, skirmishing going briskly on.
Beyond this was discovered another abandoned position of the enemy, and the brigade occupied it.
There was much moving about at this time, to ascertain the precise locality of the enemy's main line.
It was near noon when this was discovered, and
orders issued for an advance. Grose formed in three
lines: the SEVENTY-FIFTH ILLINOIS, Eighty-fourth

Indiana, and Seventy-seventh Pennsylvania in the front line; the Eighty-fourth Illinois and Ninth Indiana in the second line; the Eightieth Illinois and the Thirtieth Indiana in the third line.

Advancing a little, the rebel lines were in plain view. Sharpshooters were busy, and the irruptions of artillery frequent. The ground in Grose's front was open—mostly tillage land, with a ravine. running obliquely across his front to the left, and which he must cross before reaching the enemy's line. Soon after noon the advance was ordered, and the Fourth Corps moved to battle. The rebel skirmishers rapidly withdrew to their advanced line of works. These were assaulted and carried with inconsiderable loss. At this juncture, Grose discovered the Third Division moving on the enemy's main works, some four hundred yards on his front; and, anxious to be as forward as the most daring, he ordered an advance. Hardly was his line in motion before he discovered that the Second Division, on his right, had not moved. Not wishing to expose his right flank to a decimating enfilade fire, he directed his two right battalions to halt. The left battalion, Seventy-seventh Pennsylvania, moved forward on the right of the Third Division, to within a few paces of the redoubt. A terrific fire of round shot, canister and grape, caused the Third Division to fall back, and Rose retired with it. In this charge, the gallant Lieutenant A. T. Baldwin fell dead. Grose now directed the line of parapets which he held to be strengthened. And here he rested securely. About 4 p. m. Smith made his assault upon the key point of the rebel defences, and after a heavy slaughter it was carried. Then the rebels began to "roll up" the flank back upon its centre, and the Fourth Corps desired to aid in the good work. Soon as the Second Division started, Grose moved, keeping the alignment, and close upon him followed Wood, the line striking the rebel parapet at an angle. Steedman, beyond Wood, continued the assault with mixed troops, white and colored, and the engagement became general. It was magnificent, grand—if, indeed, a scene of war can be grand—grand in its awfulness and power for evil. As our lines neared the parapet, first one gun, then another, then more, vomited fire and iron hail. From west to east the parapet grew white, and so enfolded it in a bank of silver smoke, that the guns could no longer be seen except at the moment when they were pouring a blaze through the cloud. Yet our men were within three hundred yards of what may be termed its glacis; and when one is that close, the lightning, the thunder, and the bolt, are hardly a second in time apart. Death loves havoc, and on such occasions as this he reaps his harvest. Our men fell rapidly; but fortunately the exposure was only temporary, for the advance never ceased, and in less than five minutes, the works were ours. Then ensued a scene of rout such as is seldom witnessed. Most of the enemy in Grose's front, as indeed on some other fronts, were captured. Grose's men claimed three guns now as trophies. The rebel trenches were strewn with arms, accoutrements, camp equipage, etc., and officers and men vied with each other making captures, and still further discomfiting the foe. Colonels Bennett and Kilgore, and Major Watson—in fact, all the company officers, with their men—sought to outstrip each other in the chase. There were no cowards there; none who loved safety more than honor. And among the heroic actions displayed on this day—and they were numberless—was the capture of five armed rebel soldiers by private Joseph Watson, of Company A, and of another stalwart Irishman, who was in the act of firing, by Patrick Dailey, of Company D. It was here, too, that Lientenant Henry Parrott, of Company C, aide-de-camp to General Grose, a most gallant young officer, fell, dangerously wounded in the hip.

Grose now advanced his command several hundred yards beyond the right of our line of battle, throwing his skirmishers into Brentwood Pass, and bivouacked for the night.

Early on the 17th pursuit was continued, Grose in advance of the First Division. Our forces persistently pressed the enemy, until the remainder—those not killed, wounded, or captured, had crossed the Tennessee River, one hundred and ten miles south of Nashville. The weather was villainously bad, the mud very deep, and the marches made with great labor and fatigue.

In brief, Grose's command routed the rebels from every position attacked, captured seven pieces of

artillery, a large number of small arms, twelve captains, twenty-three lieutenants, and six hundred and
six enlisted men. The loss of the SEVENTY-FIFTH
ILLINOIS was two officers wounded, Lieutenants Parrott and Erwin, and enlisted men wounded, privates
Byron, Willilon, Talcott, Haley, and Whalen — a
total of six. It is wonderful that the loss was so
small, considering the nature of the assaults. The
loss of the brigade was proportionately as small,
there being but four killed and seventy-six wounded.
General Grose extended his "grateful thanks to his
officers and men for their willing obedience to orders,
their brave and efficient execution of every duty, on
the battle-field, and during the campaign." The
army quietly settled in its new camping grounds.
Major General Thomas issued the following congrat-
ulatory order to his army:

HEADQUARTERS DEPARTMENT OF THE CUMBERLAND,
PULASKI, Tenn., Dec. 29, 1864.

General Orders, No. 169.

SOLDIERS:—The Major-General Commanding announces to
you that the rear guard of the flying and dispirited enemy was
driven across the Tennessee River on the night of the 27th instant. The impassable state of the roads, and consequent im-
possibility to supply the army, compels a closing of the campaign
for the present.

Although short, it has been brilliant in its achievements, and
unsurpassed in its results by any other of this war, and is one of
which all who participated therein may be justly proud. That
veteran rebel army, which, though driven from position to position, opposed a stubborn resistance to much superior numbers
during the whole of the Atlanta campaign, taking advantage of
the absence of the largest portion of the army which had been

opposed to it in Georgia, invaded Tennessee, buoyant with hope, expecting Nashville, Murfreesboro, and the whole of Tennessee and Kentucky, to fall into its power an easy prey, and scarcely fixing a limit to its conquests, after having received the most terrible check at Franklin, on the 30th of November, that any army has received during this war, and later, met with a signal repulse from the brave garrison of Murfreesboro, in its attempt to capture that place, was finally attacked at Nashville, and, although your forces were inferior to it in numbers, it was hurled back from the coveted prize, upon which it had only been permitted to look from a distance, and finally sent flying, dismayed and disordered, whence it came, impelled by the instinct of self-preservation, and thinking only how it could relieve itself for short intervals from your persistent and harrassing pursuit, by burning the bridges over the swollen streams as it passed them, until finally it had placed the broad waters of the Tennessee River between you and its shattered, diminished, and discomfited columns, leaving its artillery and battle flags in your victorious hands, lasting trophies of your noble daring, and lasting mementoes of the enemy's disgrace and defeat.

You have diminished the forces of the rebel army, since it crossed the Tennessee River to invade the State, at the least estimate, fifteen thousand men, among whom were killed, wounded, or captured, eighteen General Officers.

Your captures from the enemy, as far as reported, amount to sixty-eight pieces of artillery, ten thousand prisoners, as many stand of small arms—several thousand of which have been gathered in, and the remainder strew the route of the enemy's retreat—and between thirty and forty flags, besides compelling him to destroy much ammunition, and abandon many wagons, and unless he is mad, he must forever relinquish all hope of bringing Tennessee again within the lines of the accursed rebellion.

A short time will now be given you to prepare to continue the work so nobly begun.

By command of Major General GEO. H. THOMAS:

WILLIAM D. WHIPPLE,

Assistant Adjutant General.

CHAPTER XV.

MOVEMENT TO EAST TENNESSEE—RETURN TO NASH-
VILLE — MUSTER OUT — CLOSING EPISODES — FINAL
PAYMENT AND FAREWELL.

THE pursuit of Hood's broken and demoralized columns having ceased, the army settled into the quiet
of camp life, stretched along from Chattanooga to
Florence. The First Division encamped at Hunts-
ville on the 5th of January, 1866, and remained there
until the 13th of March. While here, another change
occurred in the command of the Pioneers. Sergeant
Houck having been promoted to Orderly Sergeant
of Company E, was relieved, and Lieutenant Joseph
Dexter, of the same company, was placed in command, with non-commissioned officers Sergeant
George G. Messer, and Corporal Samuel Snyder.
These, too, fulfilled their duty, and merit mention.
Meantime, it was ascertained that the rebel army,
reorganized, and under the command of Dick Taylor,
had moved easterly through Alabama and Georgia,
hoping to pass through East Tennessee, and thence
into Virginia, to reinforce Lee's army, who was now

struggling in death throes with the indomitable and
never yielding Grant. The Fourth Corps was
rapidly transported to Knoxville by cars, and on the
17th instant reached Strawberry Plains, memorable
for the defeat of Longstreet's Corps by Burnside in
December, 1863. The First Division, on the 25th
of March, moved to Mossy Creek, then to Bull's Gap,
and five miles beyond. The army was now so disposed as to prevent the rebel forces from entering
into the long mountain defiles through which alone
Virginia could be reached; and here it remained
until about the middle of April. It was on the 18th
instant that the First Division started for Nashville,
where it arrived on the 24th. The grand drama of
war had ended. Lee had surrendered to Grant,
Johnston to Sherman, and Taylor to Canby. There
was now no armed force against the Union, save in
Texas, where a force of some 20,000, under Kirby
Smith, still renounced the terms of capitulation. But
the Government made active preparations to meet
this refractory force, by sending a large corps to New
Orleans, to prepare for an active campaign against
him. With this view, the Fourth Army Corps was
recalled to Nashville. And here it lay, awaiting
developments, expecting each day to be ordered to
Texas. Finally, the order came for the payment of
the veteran troops, and the muster out of all the
three years' regiments and detachments whose term
of service would expire by the 1st of September ensuing. This order included the SEVENTY-FIFTH ILLI-

NOIS, save about eighty men—recruits. These men —hard seemed their fate—were organized into a company, and placed as guard to Corps headquarters, General Stanley's, to share the fortunes of the veterans, be it good or ill. On the 10th of June, Colonel Bennett, now Brigadier-General by brevet— a reward for his gallantry in action, and soldierly conduct—received the welcome order to prepare their muster out rolls. The intelligence was received with a wild clamor of cheers, and the old forest in which they were encamped echoed them back wildly. Soon the Eightieth and Eighty-fourth Illinois, and the Eighty-fourth Indiana, received similar orders, and the brigade was ablaze with joyful glee.

The work rapidly progressed, and was soon consummated; and on the 13th day of June the SEV-ENTY-FIFTH ILLINOIS was *en route* for Chicago, there to be paid off, doff the soldier's blue, and don the toga of a citizen. And who could be more entitled to the rights of American citizenship, than those brave men, who for two years and nine months had risked their lives in their country's defence.

While lying at Nashville, several episodes occurred worthy of mention. On the 25th of May, General Grose, who had been absent at home for some time (there being no necessity for his presence in the field), returned and resumed command. Every soldier's heart was glad, for he had become endeared to them as few officers do, and they resolved to give him a glorious welcome. A torch-light procession was improvised, by mounting candles in the sockets of their bayonets, and at 8 p. m., they marched to the General's headquarters. The blaze and flicker of thousands of torches, as the men moved through the timber, presented a pleasing scene. And the joyous acclaim which rang out on the evening air, proved that the demonstration was spontaneous, and from the heart—a tribute to their gallant commander. And, indeed, it was fitting that hearts thus united in defence of a common cause, should, now that the strife was ended, and the great victory won, unite in the expression of mutual confidence and love. When considering the progress of events for the past four years, and more especially for the last year and a half—the great marches made, the sanguinary contests waged, the presence of the living, and the memories of the fallen brave—the scene was touching, and could not fail to swell with emotion, akin to commingled joy and grief, the heart of every patriot soldier or citizen who witnessed it. The band first discoursed a few stirring airs, and the general presented himself. After the enthusiastic cheers which greeted him had subsided, he proceeded to make a speech, earnest, feeling, and common-sense.

He thanked them for the welcome they had extended him; reviewed briefly the struggles through which they had passed; the progress of humanity and civilization which the war had engendered; the triumph of our cause, of liberty and a constitutional

Government; and referred with emphasis to the fact, that now our land was free in reality as in name, and that the humblest citizen could now utter his sentiments in favor of human rights and democratic doctrines every where within our borders.   He then spoke glowingly of the feelings of the northern people in regard to her patriot men in the field, and said they would be hailed gladly by the great northern heart when they should return home.   He gave them sound advice as to the manner in which they should conduct themselves upon resuming the peaceful avocations of life, remarking, feelingly: "Oh! never let it be said that one of my comrades in arms, who for four long years has risked his life in his country's defence, and then battle-stained and battle-worn, triumphantly returns home, and disgraces himself by violating the laws of the land he has fought to maintain, or so conduct himself as to tarnish the bright reputation he has won."   Finally, thanking his true and tried men for their great kindness toward him since his connection with them, he bade them good night.

Never did a brave soldier, a tried and skillful general, a pure, patriotic man, utter sounder sentiments, or give utterance to nobler ideas, than did General Grose on this occasion.   There was no effort at rhetorical flourish, but the plain expression of manly duty, and the practical interests of life.   There was not one unsatisfied heart—not one but who went away feeling a better man, and proud that his cause was maintained by so good a man.

The brigade then called for Brevet Brigadier-General Bennett, Colonel of the SEVENTY-FIFTH ILLINOIS, another soldier who had won the love of the entire brigade. Reluctantly he appeared upon the stand. He too, made a stirring speech, replete with olden memories, historical allusions, and lofty sentiment. The attentiveness which was given him proved how great the effect of his remarks, which, although purely extempore, exhibited the elegance in diction of a finished orator. Colonel Suman, of the Ninth Indiana, being called for, said that "it would not do for him to discharge pop-guns after the firing of such heavy guns. It was all he could do to keep up in the field. It was sufficient for him to attempt to talk to plebeians at home, not to such veterans as those before him. Therefore, as it was ten o'clock, he would propose three cheers for Generals Grose and Bennett, and a return home." The Colonel's remarks were applauded, the cheers given with a will which showed that they were meant, the band played "The Star-Spangled Banner," and each regiment again wended its way to camp, rejoiced at the success of their endeavor to please, and the appreciation it had met.

And somewhat earlier than this occurred another scene, equally touching, but confined to the regiment. This was the sending home of the regimental and national flags—colors which had been carried through the war. I can not better portray the feelings of the soldiers of the regiment than by giving, in full, the letter of General Bennett, given to the Color Sergeants, who bore the colors, and addressed to His Excellency, Governor Oglesby.

HEADQUARTERS SEVENTY-FIFTH ILLINOIS VOLUNTEERS,
CAMP HARKER, NASHVILLE, TENN.,
May 6th, 1865.

HIS EXCELLENCY RICHARD J. OGLESBY,

Governor of the State of Illinois.

HONORED SIR :—I have the honor to present you, as the Chief Executive of the State of Illinois, by the hands of David R. Bryson, and John W. Weldon, Color Sergeants of this regiment, our Regimental and National Colors, to be placed in the archives of the State.

In doing so, allow me to say that these colors were the first ever received by us from the hands of the Government, and have been borne the most of the time by these brave Sergeants. They also contain upon their folds the record of the many engagements we have been in with the enemies of our glorious Union, with the exception of the Atlanta campaign, and the battles of Franklin and Nashville.

Beneath their starry folds, many of our brave comrades have fallen, and now sleep their last sleep upon the field of their glory. These old banners, though tattered and torn, are sacred mementoes of the past; and in parting with them, we do so with sadness, mingled with pride and pleasure; with sadness, at the thoughts of those who left their happy homes in 1862, who went nobly forth to battle for their country, but now fill honorable soldiers' graves; with pride and pleasure—that we can send to you, and the State of Illinois, who sent us forth, so honorable a record.

And now that the Angel of Peace is about to spread her wings over our once prosperous country, we know of no more appropriate place to deposit these sacred relics.

Hoping that we may all soon have the pleasure of returning to our quiet homes in Illinois, and that the nation may learn the art of war no more, I am,
        Very respectfully,
           Your obedient servant.
             JOHN E. BENNETT,
      Col. Seventy-fifth Ill., and Brevet Brig. Gen. U. S. V.

Nor was this all. As the day drew near when the brigade was to be reorganized—the veterans now being ordered to Texas—the staff officers of General Grose, two of whom were from the SEVENTY-FIFTH ILLINOIS—Captain Frank Bingham, and Lieutenant Henry Parrott—addressed the General a farewell letter, as follows:

          CAMP HARKER, NEAR NASHVILLE, TENN. }
    HEADQUARTERS THIRD BRIGADE FIRST DIVISION, }
        FOURTH ARMY CORPS, June 10th, 1865. }

BRIGADIER-GENERAL WILLIAM GROSE.

DEAR GENERAL:—The storm-clouds of war have now been rifted by the calm sunlight of peace, and the hour has come when we must separate. You, and others of us, who have been honored with positions as your staff officers, hail with pleasure this gladsome time, as we are enabled to return again to the duties of civil life. Others of us must still remain for a season ; not to breast the surges of a stormy warfare, but to aid our misguided countrymen in restoring order out of chaos, tranquillity out of anarchy. This accomplished, we, too, who remain, trust a kind Providence will permit us to enjoy the fruits of our labor and our sacrifice.

In parting with you, General, we feel that we lose a good friend, a true counselor, yea, the presence of an earnest, upright, honest, and high-minded man. You came into this conflict of war against treason, determined to lend your helping hand in our country's defence, and most bravely, ably, have you performed your mission. God be thanked that your life has been spared to witness the glorious consummation of your highest hopes—the maintenance of our liberties and our nationality.

It is with pride that, in the future, when the history of our struggles shall have been written, we can read of the battles in which you have borne so conspicuous a part; and on the bright Roll of Honor which our noble *Alma Mater* shall inscribe for the perpetuation of the memories of her heroes, yours will be far from the least worthy, in generous devotion to duty, sacrifice of self, or in the accomplishment of grand results.

We have endeavored to do faithfully our humble part in the positions assigned us. We trust our services have met your approval. Your generous confidence is all we ask, and in the future, as in the past, we desire to have your sympathy and friendship. Twenty battles have done somewhat to cement our attachment; and, whether as soldiers or citizens, their dark forefront can never be forgotten.

General, we bid you farewell. God bless you and yours, spare you to a good old age, deal gently with you, make you an honor and an example to our young men at home, and finally accept you to a life eternal, within the portals of never-ending joy.

Captain FRANK BINGHAM, A.A.A.G.

" —— GRUBBS, A.P.M.

Lieutenant HENRY PARROTT, A.A.D.C.

Crowning all, and paramount to all, is the farewell address of General Grose to his comrades in arms.

HEADQUARTERS THIRD BRIG., FIRST DIV., FOURTH A. C., }
CAMP HARKER, TENN., June 6th, 1865. }

SOLDIERS OF THE THIRD BRIGADE :—The object for which we have been associated together having been accomplished, we are now about to separate, and most of us join our families and

14

friends at home, while some of us continue for duty. You have acted well your part, faithfully and bravely, in the great struggle of your country, for the maintenance of right and justice, over wrong and oppression. You will feel better that you have done your part for your country than to have stood an idle spectator. Since we are compelled to separate, I feel thankful that I leave you in the enjoyment of an enviable reputation, a reputation of which your friends can boast, and you feel proud. Your toils, hardships, and perils will be attended with the perpetuation of the National Government, with greater power and glory than ever before.

Treasure up for our fallen comrades a kind remembrance as heroes of their age, in a great and good cause. Take home, and into the future with you, the heartfelt gratitude of your humble Commander, for his lot having been cast with such gallant soldiers and kind-hearted gentlemen. God bless and take care of you. Good-bye.

WILLIAM GROSE,
Brigadier-General Volunteers.

The Seventy-fifth arrived at Chicago on the 17th day of June, and was paid off and finally discharged on the 1st day of July. Then came the last farewell as soldiers, and each proceeded to his home, where they were welcomed by their immediate relations, friends and neighbors.

Thus ends the history of the Seventy-fifth Illinois. I have aimed to trace its career truthfully, and as fully as the material gathered would permit. And among the many thousands who have rallied to the defence of our republican institutions, none have

rendered more signal service, or aided in the achievement of more enduring victories, than those patriotic
men comprising the regiment whose glorious career
is herein presented. Fearlessly they went forth to
battle for the right. Many, alas! fell upon fields
deeply crimsoned with human gore; many, too, suffering most intensely from wounds and disease, have
gone to that "bourne whence no traveler returns."
Its casualties in battle have not been so heavy as in
many regiments, yet they were in bloody battles and
desperate charges. A kind Providence seemed to
watch over them. Still, the loss is great. Sixty-four
were killed, thirty-one died of wounds, and ninety-
one of disease. Besides, two hundred and sixteen
were discharged on account of disability; and the
total of wounded men during its term of service
numbers one hundred and eighty-four, making a
grand total of casualties of all kinds, of five hundred
and eighty-six, or 56.94 per cent.

Such heroism and such devotion is its grandest
monument of glory. In their loss, the hopes and
joys—all that is most dear to thousands of immortal
beings, were crushed; but their deepest pangs of pain
are merged into the glorious realization of national
triumph, and the unity of the republic—a temple of
Liberty grander far than Ephesian dome; and the
nation, whom we love, and whose great heart pul-
sates with paternal interest in the weal or woe of
each patriot son, will inscribe their names in the
grand Roll of Honor, which shall be cherished as one

of the most sacred jewels in the casket of her fame. Yes,

> " Enough of merit has each honored name
> To shine untarnished on the rolls of fame;
> To stand the example of each distant age,
> And add new lustre to the historic page;
> For soon their deeds illustrious shall be shown
> In breathing bronze, or animated stone;
> Or where the canvas, starting into life,
> Revives the glories of the crimson strife."

And for the no less honored living—heroes amid trumpet pealing, joyous cannon, foeman's sabre, and leaden death-shots, rattling fast—

> " Let the bugle swell the note of triumph!
> Sound, trumpets! praise our bravest and our best!
> Thousands of voices bid each hero welcome;
> Rest! soldier, rest!"

THE END.

OFFICERS OF THE SEVENTY-FIFTH ILLINOIS.

BREVET BRIGADIER-GENERAL AND COLONEL JOHN E. BENNETT
was born in the town of Bethany, Genesee County, N. Y. At
the age of thirteen he was sent to the Genesee Wesleyan Sem-
inary, where he remained for three terms. When sixteen, he
taught school. His father's health failing, he managed his business until twenty-one, displaying excellent mercantile qualifica-
tions for one so young. In 1854 he entered the employ of C. J.
Baldwin, a merchant of Cleveland, Ohio, as cashier and book-
keeper. Towards the close of 1855, wishing to engage in business for himself, he made a tour westward. Through the influence of W. H. Van Epps, Esq., of Dixon, Illinois, he settled in
the neighboring town of Morrison, as a merchant, and proprietor
of the "Bennett House." While engaged in business there, he
made several trips across the plains to the Pacific coast. He
was always somewhat of a politician, participating actively in all
local matters. He was ever a staunch Democrat of the Jefferson, Jackson, and Douglas school. He entertained, with the
leaders of that party, their particular sensitiveness concerning
the slavery question; but the developments of the character of
that institution, made during the progress of the war, materially
changed the complexion of his views, and he saw, as every other
patriot did, that the national safety depended upon its destruction, and he lent efficient aid towards its consummation. He
was among the first to enter warmly into the national cause, and
aided in sending troops to the war. In the summer of 1862,
when the call was made for " 600,000 more," he applied to the
Adjutant-General of the State for permission to recruit a company. On the 29th of July it was granted, and on the 5th of
August he had enlisted 118 men. He was elected Captain unan-

imously, repaired with his company to Dixon, and on the organization of the SEVENTY-FIFTH ILLINOIS, was elected its Lieutenant-Colonel. When Colonel Ryon resigned, he was promoted
Colonel, and as such served with great gallantry through the
war. Near its close he was brevetted General. He was in
every battle in which the regiment was engaged, save that of the
4th of July, 1864. Then he was back for three days in hospital,
the only time he was ever compelled to leave the command. He
was frequently in command of a brigade, which he handled with
great skill, showing perfect competency for the position of a full
Brigadier. And it is a pity that one so competent as he, should
not have graced a "star," long ago, instead of the many who disgraced it.

General Bennett is tall, and rather commanding in person, of
strong constitution and an active mind. Quick to comprehend,
and prompt to execute; like the lamented General E. N. Kirk,
he seemed born for a soldier. He was a strict disciplinarian,
firm in his administration, yet ever kind and just. Like all truly
good officers, he was at first disliked by many of his men; but at
last he conquered all prejudices, and became highly popular.
And what must ever be pleasing to him, he retired from the war
with the kindest regards of every soldier in his command. During the present summer he has accepted a lieutenancy in the
Regular Army. The country has gained thereby the services of
a valuable soldier.

LIEUTENANT-COLONEL, BREVET COLONEL, AND BREVET BRIGA-
DIER-GENERAL WILLIAM MATHERS KILGOUR was born in Cumberland County, Pennsylvania, and was still a youth when, in
1836, his parents removed to Whiteside County, Illinois. For
a time after his arrival, he carried the mail, on horseback, from
Rock River to Fulton, on the Mississippi, a distance of some
forty miles.

He is emphatically a self-educated man. He read law at
Sterling, Illinois, and was admitted to practice in 1855, having
license as Attorney at Law, Solicitor in Chancery, and Proctor
in Admiralty, in the State Courts, and in the District and Circuit Courts for the Northern District of Illinois.

Like Colonel Bennett, he is something of a politician, but of
an opposite party—the old Whig—and he makes it his boast
that he never voted a Democratic ticket in his life. He was a
representative from his county in the mass convention held at
Bloomington, which organized the Republican party in Illinois,
and nominated Colonel Bissell for Governor. And when, in
1861, Abraham Lincoln, duly elected President of the United
States, proceeded to Washington to take his seat, he was one of

about eight hundred, who, of their own accord, went to that city, to see that no harm happened him, as assassination had been threatened. Immediately after, the war bugles roused the nation to arms, and Kilgour was among the very first to respond, volunteering as a private in Company B, Thirteenth Illinois Infantry. Upon its organization he was elected Second Lieutenant, and served with that regiment for a year in Missouri, participating in the affairs of Wet Glaze, Lynn Creek, Springfield, and Salem. While here, he served as Judge Advocate, hearing many important causes.

In the early summer of 1862, he was taken sick with camp fever, and resigned. But his respite from army service was short, for he had hardly recovered from his illness, ere another call was made for troops, and again he volunteered. He was commissioned as Captain of Company I, and upon the organization of the regiment, was made a Major. Scarcely in the service, he encountered the ordeal of Perryville, where he was supposed to be mortally wounded, but a tough constitution enabled him to withstand the blow, and in August, 1863, he rejoined the command. His services through the war have been fully described in the preceding pages. Suffice it to say, he was in every battle fought by the regiment, from the time he rejoined it until its muster-out, save that of Culp's Farm, and, during a greater part of the Atlanta campaign, he was in command of the Eightieth Illinois. The record of his gallantry is that of nearly every battle fought in the Department of the Cumberland.

Colonel Kilgour is a very tall man, a brave and kind-hearted soldier. He is genial yet eccentric in his manners. He is lately married, and lives upon a fine homestead in Sterling, Illinois, with his mother and sister. He keeps open house, and all are welcome. Of a highly sociable disposition, he enjoys most heartily a good story, a good joke, and a good laugh. He was ever the friend of his soldiers, and greatly enjoyed their esteem. He has now resumed the practice of his profession, and quietly moves in the social circles of life.

MAJOR AND BREVET LIEUTENANT-COLONEL JAMES A. WATSON was born in the State of New York, on the 21st of April, 1815. He was a farmer's boy, and worked at home until eighteen years of age. He then learned the carpenter's and joiner's trade. He then went to Canada, where he remained for six years, witnessing many important scenes in the Canadian Rebellion. While here, he contracted for and built many of the bridges across the Welland Canal. Leaving Canada in 1838, he proceeded to Michigan, and worked at his trade. In 1843, he removed to Illinois, and for three years was engaged in constructing bridges on the

Illinois and Michigan canal. Afterwards, he secured the first contract for bridging on the old Galena road, when that was building. This completed, he entered into a contract with the Illinois Central Road, for eight miles of grading, running south from Dixon, on Rock River. When the SEVENTY-FIFTH ILLINOIS was raised, he recruited Company A, and was commissioned Captain. When Kilgour was promoted Lieutenant-Colonel, he succeeded him as Major. He was ever active, and ready for duty— brave as a lion, scorning danger. At Smyrna Camp Ground— or Culp's Farm, as it is called by some—he commanded the regiment, and won encomiums of praise for his skill and bravery. He built several bridges during the campaigns of the army, mention of which is made in the preceding pages.

Major Watson is no scholar, but a thoroughly practical man. He is rough and open-spoken, never mincing his words, but talks directly and plainly. He is nothing of a tactician, but an earnest, go-ahead fighter. If a duty was to be performed, no matter how dangerous, he sought to accomplish it. He was liked much by the soldiers, was always one with them, and put his own hand to any work with which he had to do. The boys of the old Third Brigade will never forget him.

MAJOR GEORGE W. PHILLIPS was born in the township of Adams, Berkshire County, Mass., on the 5th of November, 1821.

His ancestors are of English stock, and settled in Rhode Island. His grandfather was a soldier in the war of the Revolution. His parents removed to Illinois in 1841, when George was twenty years of age. He studied medicine with Dr. G. W. Richards, of St. Charles, Illinois, an able and accomplished physician and surgeon, and Professor of Theory and Practice in the Medical Department of the La Porte University, Indiana, at which institution Phillips graduated in the class of 1846-7.

He settled in practice in Wisconsin, but in 1850 went to California to seek a better field for a fortune. In 1854 he returned, and settled in Dixon, Illinois, where he has since resided. In 1859 he received the prize offered by the Illinois State Medical Society, for the best Essay, subject to be chosen by the writer. The Essay submitted was, "On the Effect of Climate on Tuberculous Disease."

Upon the organization of the SEVENTY-FIFTH ILLINOIS, he was commissioned surgeon, dating the 18th of September, 1862. At Perryville he was appointed Brigade Surgeon, which position he held until his resignation, for physical disability, on the 10th of May, 1863. Major-General Jeff. C. Davis indorsed upon his resignation papers a flattering testimonial to his worth as a medical officer. At Perryville and Stone River he was selected by the Medical Director to perform the operations in one of the field hospitals. When, in 1864, the call was made for One Hundred Day troops, he re-entered the service as Surgeon of the One Hundred and Fortieth Illinois. Arriving at Memphis, he was again appointed Brigade Surgeon, and was in the battle of Memphis on the 21st of August, 1864, when Forrest made his famous dash into that city. Here he lost a favorite horse, one which had accompanied him previously. His regiment was mustered out of service on the 29th of October, 1864, when he resumed his practice in Dixon.

Dr. Phillips is a very able physician, and a fine surgeon. He is a thoroughly conscientious man, and as an officer, did his duty faithfully and impartially. His skill saved many an arm and limb; and many a soldier holds him in grateful remembrance. Few surgeons acquired a more brilliant reputation for ability and faithfulness than he.

I can not but mention, in this connection, the services rendered by Dr. Abbott, of Dixon, Illinois, Surgeon of the Eightieth Illinois, who, during the summer of 1863—his own regiment having been captured in Streight's raid into Georgia—served as Surgeon of the SEVENTY-FIFTH ILLINOIS, working zealously and well. He, too, is distinguished for his surgical knowledge; and at Missionary Ridge performed some wonderful experiments. He is an ornament to the profession.

JOHN C. CORBUS, of Brooklyn, Lee County, came out as First Assistant Surgeon, appointed September 2d, 1862; resigned from ill health, June 19, 1863. While on duty at a hospital on the Stone River battle field, he was taken prisoner, but was released after a few days.

HENRY UTLEY, of Como, Whiteside County, came out with the regiment as Second Assistant Surgeon, appointed September 18, 1862. Immediately after the Perryville battle, he was put in charge of wounded who could not be removed from that vicinity, and was kept there until he resigned, December 10, 1862, for physical disability.

CHESSELDEN FISHER, of Freeport, Lee County, was Assistant Surgeon in the Seventy-fourth Illinois Volunteer Infantry; was appointed Surgeon of the SEVENTY-FIFTH, August 1, 1863. He resigned Nov. 22, 1864.

OCTAVE P. F. RAVENOT, a native of Paris, France, and a resident of Chicago, Cook County, was appointed First Assistant Sur-

geon, November 14, 1863, and promoted to Surgeon of the SEV-
ENTY-FIFTH ILLINOIS, in place of Chesselden Fisher, February
23, 1865. On the 25th of February, 1864, he was sent to look
after a soldier, who was wounded the previous day, and who was
necessarily left on the withdrawal of the troops from Buzzard's
Roost during the night of the 25th. On his return to camp near
Ringgold, he fell in with Wheeler's cavalry forces, by whom he
was taken prisoner, and was sent to different Southern prisons—
Dalton, Atlanta, Andersonville, Macon, Savannah, and Richmond, and returned to the regiment, September 13, 1864, at
Atlanta. Except the time passed in his captivity, he has been
with the regiment—close with it—in the different battles and
engagements.

WILLIAM F. CORBUS, of Brooklyn, Lee County, came out as Hospital Steward with the regiment, and was faithfully on duty
during the entire term of service, except a brief interval from
sickness, at Nashville, in 1864.

ORLANDO L. FRENCH was born on the 8th of June, 1829, in
Bridgewater, Vermont. He learned the cabinet maker's trade,
and worked at it for several years in the East. In 1851 he removed to Dixon, Illinois. He subsequently went to Minnesota,
but returned to Illinois in 1854. He enlisted as a private in the
SEVENTY-FIFTH ILLINOIS, and was appointed Quartermaster Sergeant. On the 3rd of May, 1863, he was commissioned Adjutant. He made a brave and efficient officer, and served with
credit in every battle fought by the regiment, save that of Perryville.

JOHN REMINGTON is a resident of Dixon, Illinois. He was commissioned regimental Quartermaster, and in the winter of 1862, or
spring of 1863, he was appointed Division Quartermaster, on the
Staff of Major-General Jeff. C. Davis, and afterwards was commissioned Captain and A. Q. M. In the spring of 1864, he was
commissioned Quartermaster of Volunteers, with the rank of
Lieutenant-Colonel. In January, 1865, he resigned and returned
to his home. He was an efficient officer, active and energetic,
and much of the time was entrusted with Government property
amounting to millions of dollars.

JAMES REED is also from Dixon, and enlisted as a private in
Company A. He was soon after detailed as Quartermaster's
clerk; and subsequent to Remington being commissioned as Captain, he was made regimental Quartermaster. He was a pru-

dent careful officer, closely attentive to his business, and continued in the position to the end.

EZEKIEL GILES is a shoe-maker, in Dixon, Illinois. He was originally a Lieutenant, but on the 20th of December, 1862, was promoted Captain, *vice* Watson, Major. He resigned on the 23rd of May, 1863.

WILLIAM PARKER is a printer by trade, and for many years has had charge of printing establishments. When enlisting Company A, he was connected with the Dixon "Republican and Telegraph." He was ever brave, and one of the free and easy officers of the regiment. He was an excellent soldier, companionable, and at all times ready for adventure.

FREDERICK O. HEADLEY is a shoe-maker by trade, and resided in Dixon, Illinois. He entered the service as Orderly Sergeant, but on the 20th of December, 1863, was promoted a Lieutenant. He was on detached duty for some time ; but mustered out with the regiment.

GEORGE W. PUTNAM is a farmer's son, and resides near Dixon. He enlisted as a Corporal in Company A, but finally reached the rank of Orderly Sergeant. He was a most faithful soldier, and I feel it proper, and but justice, to mention him in this connection. He well merited, although he never received, a commission. True and tried, firm in principle, and highly moral, he was a fit example for the imitation of those who, alas! became recreant to the principles of their manhood, and forgot them in the soldier.

CAPTAIN CHARLES R. RICHARDS was born in Lennox, Madison County, N. Y., on the 3rd day of April, 1824. When fifteen years of age, he moved to Ohio, where he lived eleven years, married, and was a mechanic by trade. He moved to Lyndon, Illinois, in the fall of 1850. Enlisted in Company B, SEVENTY-FIFTH ILLINOIS. He was a most worthy officer.

SECOND LIEUTENANT ELISHA BULL was born in Erie County, N. Y., in 1828. Lived at Lyndon, Illinois, when the SEVENTY-FIFTH was organized. Enlisted in 1861, in the Thirty-third Illinois. Was discharged as a musician of that regiment under orders of the War Department, mustering out regimental bands. Was at home but one week, when he re-enlisted in Company B, SEVENTY-FIFTH ILLINOIS. After the battle of Nashville, Tenn., he was detailed in command of brigade ambulance train. He was a faithful officer, and liked much by the men.

FIRST LIEUTENANT EARNEST ALTMAN, a German by birth, was a merchant in Morrison. He was afterwards promoted to Captain. He was wounded at Lancaster, Ky., Oct. 14, 1862, and resigned Feb. 1, 1863. This wound was the cause of his resignation. He was an upright man, and showed great heroism for the time he was in the service.

GEORGE W. SHAW was born in Rome, N. Y., on the 12th of December, 1835, and was by profession a civil engineer. Moved West in 1857, and settled in Prophetstown, Whiteside County, Illinois. Became a druggist, and afterwards County Surveyor, which position he still held when he went into the army. He was detached on the 17th of January, 1863, by order of Colonel P. Sidney Post, as Topographical Engineer. Upon the reorganization of the Corps, Oct. 10, 1863, he was returned to his company. He was detached a second time, Nov. 4th, 1863, as Topographical Engineer, by order of General William Grose. Remained in that position until Oct. 27, 1864. He was as brave as the bravest.

PRENTISS S. BANNISTER is the son of an honest, intelligent farmer, and was born in St. Lawrence County, N. Y. Moved West, and settled with his father's family at Union Grove, Whiteside County, Illinois. He was promoted from a Sergeant to a First Lieutenant, and was a fine officer.

The memoranda for the sketches of Captain Frank Bingham, and Lieutenant Henry Parrott, of Company C, are mislaid.
The former came out as a Sergeant, and won his promotion by faithful service. He was appointed to the position of Acting Assistant Adjutant-General on the Staff of General William Grose. Upon the muster-out of the regiment, he was relieved, and General Grose addressed him the following letter:

HEADQUARTERS THIRD BRIG., FIRST DIV., FOURTH A C., }
NEAR NASHVILLE, TENN., June 11, 1865. }

Special Orders, No. 48.

Captain Frank Bingham, Acting Assistant Adjutant-General of this Brigade, his term of service being about to expire, is hereby relieved.
It is proper to notice that for the Captain's long and efficient service in this capacity, he deserves well of his country. Brave, competent, and ever ready for duty—gallant comrade, good-bye.

WILLIAM GROSE,
Brigadier-General Vols., Comd'ng.

To
CAPT. FRANK BINGHAM, }
Seventy-fifth Illinois Vols. }

The latter was for some time a Sergeant, but was promoted Second Lieutenant on the 6th of May, 1863. During the Atlanta campaign, he had charge of the brigade ambulance train, and distinguished himself for his daring on the battle-field. At the time of the Nashville battle, he was aid-de-camp to General Grose, and was severely wounded. He retained this position until mustered out. He was fearless, even to recklessness, kind hearted, genial, and companionable; esteemed by all, and a great favorite with all his regiment.

A. McMoore was born in Cumberland County, Pa., in 1819, and was a house joiner by trade. He settled in Illinois in 1837. Enrolled for service July 28, 1862. His residence is Sterling, Illinois, and at the time of his enlistment he was a dry goods merchant. He was taken prisoner at Stone River, Dec. 31st, 1862, and enjoyed the hospitality of the military prison in Atlanta, and afterwards, that of Libby Prison, Richmond, where he remained until March 30th, 1863. He was exchanged May 17th, and rejoined the command June 8th, 1863. He was a good officer, but a strict disciplinarian; and near the end of the war was brevetted Major.

First Lieutenant Joseph E. Cobbey was born in 1824, in Miami County, Ohio. He did nothing to distinguish himself, and the record specifies that he resigned for the good of the service.

Edward H. Barber was born in 1827, in Vermont. He was engaged in farming when he entered the service. He was wounded at Perryville, and resigned in consequence. He was a true soldier.

Lieutenant F. A. Caughey, was born 1839, in Lancaster County, Pa., settled in Illinois in 1859, and was butchering when he entered the service. Was mustered, September 2d, as Sergeant, promoted successively to First Sergeant, Second Lieutenant, and First Lieutenant, and was for some time A. A. Q. M., Ordnance train, First Division, Fourth Corps.

Lieutenant Richard L. Mangum, born in Philadelphia, Pa., 1820, stone mason by trade. Mustered in Corporal, promoted to Sergeant, then to First Sergeant, and again to Second Lieutenant, May 22nd, 1863. Wounded June 4th, 1864, and resigned January 4th, 1865.

William S. Frost is a farmer of Lee County, Illinois, and by his experience in California, and elsewhere, was well calculated to deal with men. A wound at Perryville disabled him temporarily; and another, before Atlanta, becoming infected with gangrene, rendered him unfit for the field, and led to his honorable discharge on the 23rd of January, 1865. He was highly esteemed in the command for bravery and faithfulness in duty.

FRANKLIN H. EELS is a harness maker, in Sublette. His first encounter with the enemy cost him his life. A rebel bullet pierced his forehead, while bravely doing his duty at Perryville, having already shown strong characteristics for a good officer.

JAMES H. BLODGETT is a teacher, from Amboy, Illinois. He was temporarily disabled by a wound at Perryville, and was again wounded and taken prisoner at Stone River. Unable to procure leave of absence at times, and unwilling to leave the command at certain other times, favored in his own health and that of his family, he was never away from his company except by wounds and imprisonment. He had the honor of leading several skirmish charges on the enemy's lines, and was brilliantly successful. He looked after the interests of his men with care, and was an officer of high moral character. He rose from a Second Lieutenancy to a Captaincy.

JAMES HILL, Sergeant in Company E, is a shoemaker from Lee Centre. He was taken prisoner at Stone River. His imprisonment resulted in sickness, and he was discharged. Meanwhile, a commission was received for him at the regiment, as Second Lieutenant, but he never accepted it.

JAMES DEXTER entered the service as a Sergeant, and was successively promoted to a Second and First Lieutenancy. He is a well-to-do farmer in Sublette, and has a strongly marked character for earnestness, and was a most gallant and worthy officer. He received a wound at Perryville, which disabled him for months. For some months he was in command of the Pioneers. Truer soldier never marched to the field.

JAMES McCORD was born in Nawtawnards, in the County Down, Ireland, on the 28th of January, 1820. He came to this continent in 1842, and settled in Canada West. He moved to Wisconsin in 1845, and afterwards to Illinois. He is a carpenter and joiner by trade, and enlisted as a Sergeant of Company F, SEVENTY-FIFTH ILLINOIS. He was promoted to First Lieutenant, and finally to a Captaincy; and was in every battle and skirmish in which the regiment was engaged.

JAMES D. PLACE was born in Ackworth, N. H., on the 17th of August, 1830. He came to Illinois in 1853. He is a railroad engineer and enlisted as a Sergeant. On the 15th of August, 1863, he was commissioned a Second Lieutenant; but the company not being up to the maximum number of men required, he was never mustered. He was a good soldier, and missed no engagement save Nashville, and then he was sick in hospital.

CAPTAIN JOSEPH WILLIAMS was a grain merchant of Franklin Grove. He was taken sick soon after entering the service, and resigned in December, 1862.

FIRST LIEUTENANT DAVID SANFORD, afterwards promoted Captain, was a teacher in Carthage, Ogle County. Was taken sick from the exposures after the Stone River battle, and resigned in May, 1863.

SECOND LIEUTENANT ROBERT L. IRWIN received two wounds from buckshot, and one from a minie ball, at Perryville—the latter quite serious, and leading to his resignation in April, 1863. Previous to this he had been commissioned as First Lieutenant, but had not been mustered as such. After his return home, Dr. Brainard, of Chicago, took out part of the hip bone, and his situation, for two months, was very precarious. His health, after this, became firm again, and in the latter part of 1863, he engaged in recruiting for this regiment. In February, 1864, he reported for duty, with thirty-seven recruits, and soon after was commissioned Captain of Company G. At the battle of Nashville, Dec. 16, 1864, as the regiment charged the rebel rifle pits, he was struck down by a musket ball, but it proved a severe rather than a dangerous wound, and caused but a short absence from duty. The recruiting done by Captain Irwin was the only special effort to obtain recruits for this regiment. He was a most competent and worthy officer, beloved by all who knew him.

SERGEANT WILLIAM VANCE, promoted to First Sergeant, then to Second Lieutenant, and again to First Lieutenant, was in command of the Company most of the time from April, 1863, to the muster of Robert L. Irwin as Captain. He was sent to Chattanooga for additional transportation soon after the occupation of Atlanta, and performed the duty so much to the satisfaction of the Quartermaster's Department, that he was permanently detailed for duty with the trains on his return, and remained there ever after.

SAMUEL BENDER, successively private, Corporal, and Sergeant, was never absent from his command for a single night in the whole term of service.

JOHN L. NEWTON was born in Morgan County, Ohio. At twenty he came to Illinois. Enlisted as a Corporal in Company H, and was promoted, during the war, to a First Lieutenancy. He was some time in command of the Pioneer Company, and finally in charge of the Division Ordnance Train. He executed his duties promptly and well.

ROBERT HALL was a resident of Whiteside County, Illinois, and upon the outbreak of the war, enlisted as a private in the Twelfth Illinois, and at Fort Donelson was badly wounded, a ball entering the right shoulder and lodging just above the right lung. It frequently gave him trouble afterwards. He came out in Company I as a First Lieutenant, but upon the organization of the regiment, was commissioned Captain, Kilgore being pro-moted to Major.

His career is so thoroughly portrayed in this book, that it needs no comment here. And his glorious fall at Culp's Farm on that immortal day, the 4th of July, 1864, crowns him as a hero ever more.

He was tall and commanding in appearance, with features depicting nature's true nobleness. He was kind of heart, genial in manners, a friend to all who deserved well, and loved by all. He possessed no education, save that acquired by contact with the world; but in that was eminently sound and practical. He was as brave a soldier as ever drew a sword in our country's defence, and his whole soul was in our cause. His death was much lamented in the army, and at home. A monument worthy the patriotism of Whiteside County should be erected over his grave, and her citizens will prove recreant to the memory due an illustrious martyr in their cause, if they fail to do it.

Lee County forgets her dead, and the graves of the noble Levanway and Stevens, who fell in the forefront of battle at Shiloh, still lie unmarked by monumental slab or shaft, a burning stigma upon its citizens and his friends.

AMOS B. SEGUR was born at Rumford, Oxford Co., Maine, on the 5th of March, 1820. He is a painter by trade, and enlisted in Company I as Sergeant. On the 22d of March, 1863, he was commissioned Second Lieutenant, and upon the death of Captain Hale, he was promoted Captain. He is an unpretending man, fully up to his duties, and ever ready to perform them.

EZEKIEL I. KILGOUR was the third son of Colonel E. Kilgour, and was born in Cumberland County, Pennsylvania. Moved with his father to Whiteside County, Illinois, in 1836. He was a Republican in politics, in religion an Old School Presbyterian, and a farmer by occupation. He volunteered as a private in Company I, and assisted materially in raising and recruiting it. He was appointed Sergeant, and promoted to Second Lieutenant. Distinguished himself by heroic bravery at Perryville ; afterwards was taken sick, caused by exposure in the service, and died at Nashville, Tenn., on Christmas evening, A. D. 1862. His remains were taken to his home at Sterling, Illinois. He entered hopeful of seeing this war ended, and the Union restored'; but died ere the great iron wheel had performed a single revolution.

LEWIS E. CHUBBUCK was born August 2d, 1838, at Royalton, Niagara County, N.Y. He lived with his parents until seventeen years of age, and then engaged in teaching a district school. He continued to teach winters, and use the wages to attend school. At the age of twenty engaged as a clerk at Medina, N.Y., with a dry goods merchant. Not being suited with the business, he accepted the appointment to fill a vacancy as student at the State Normal School, at Albany, N.Y. Entered the Sub-Senior Class ; commenced teaching again in the fall of 1860, and the next spring went to Illinois. Was teaching at Erie when he enlisted as private in Captain W. M. Kilgour's company. Was at once detailed as clerk at Post Headquarters, and upon the organization of the SEVENTY-FIFTH ILLINOIS, was detailed as clerk at Regimental Headquarters. On August 20th, 1863, was appointed Sergeant-Major. On August 4th, 1864, received commission as First Lieutenant, Company I, and was immediately detailed as Acting-Adjutant. He was never absent from the command for a single day, unless sent on duty. He served in that position until November 20th, 1864. While Sergeant-Major he did the duty of Adjutant without help, during Sherman's campaign from Pine Mountain, June 11th, 1864, to Atlanta, July 25th, 1864. He was ever diligent and competent for any trust.

CAPTAIN D. M. ROBERTS was born in Luzerne County, Pennsylvania, and moved to Wyoming, Illinois. At the time of organizing Company K, he was a farmer and Justice of the Peace. He was wounded at Perryville through the hips, and disabled for further field duty. Returning, he was put on detached duty, which position he ever after held in various departments.

WILLIAM H. THOMPSON was born in Luzerne County, Pennsylvania. At the time of enlistment he lived in Viola. He was a farmer, and was wounded at Perryville. Returned to duty, and

15

finally died of consumption. The regiment lost in him a good man and soldier.

ISAAC L. HUNT was born in China, Wyoming County, N. Y. Moved west to Pawpaw, Illinois, in October, 1855. Was a farmer by occupation. He came out as Second Lieutenant, and was promoted to First Lieutenant. He was a fine officer, one of the best in the regiment, and was so considered by all. He did excellent service.

ORIGINAL ORGANIZATON

AND SUBSEQUENT CHANGES IN THE

FIELD, STAFF, AND NON-COMMISSIONED STAFF;

ALSO—COMPANY OFFICERS.

FIELD AND STAFF OFFICERS.

NAMES.	RANK.	DATE OF MUSTER.	REMARKS.
George Ryan	Colonel	Sep. 2, 1862.	Resgd. Dec. 20, 1862.
John E. Bennett	Lieut. Col	" "	Prom. Colonel, Feb. 1, 1863; Brev. Brig. Gen., April 5, 1865.
Wm. M. Kilgour	Major	" "	Prom. Lieut. Col., Feb. 3, 1863.
George W. Phillips	Surgeon	Sept. 18, "	Resgd. May 16, 1863.
John C. Corbus	Ass't Surg.	Sept. 2, "	" Jan. 19, 1863.
Henry Utley	Ass't Surg.	Sept. 18, "	" Dec. 10, 1862.
Jerome W. Hollenbeck.	Adjutant	Sept. 2, "	" Dec. 19, 1862.
John Remington	Reg. Qr. M'r.	" "	Prom. Capt. and A. Q. M., Nov. 24, 1863 ; Lt. Col. and Q. M., — 1864.
William H. Smith	Chaplain	Sept. 12, "	Resgd. March 5, 1864.
Chesselden Fisher	Surgeon	Aug. 1, 1863.	" Nov. 22, 1864.
Octave P. F. Ravenot.	Ass't Surg.	Nov. 14, "	Prom. Surgeon, Feb. 23, 1865.

NON-COMMISSIONED STAFF.

Silas D. Frost	Sergt. Major.	Sep. 2, 1862.	Prom. Captain, Aug. 19, 1863, in U. S., Col. Infantry.
Orlando L. French	Q. M. Sergt.	"	" Prom. Adjt., May 3, 1863.
Wm. Parkhurst	Com. Sergt.	"	" Discharged.
Wm. F. Corbus	Hos. Steward.	"	"
Hezekiah Stewart	Fife Major	"	"

COMPANY A.

James A. Watson	Captain	Sep. 2, 1862.	Prom. Maj., Dec. 20, 1862.
Ezekiel Giles	1st Lieut.	"	" Prom. Capt., Dec. 20, 1862 ; Resgd. May 23, '63.
William Parker	2d Lieut.	"	" Prom. 1st Lieut., Dec. 20, 1862 ; Prom. Capt., June 19, 1863.
Fredk. C. Headley	1st Sergt.	"	" Prom. 2d Lieut., Dec. 20, 1862 ; 1st Lieut., June 19, 1863.
Alfred K. Buckaloo	Sergeant	"	" Prom. 2d Lieut., June 19, 1863; died March 17, 1864.
Horace Judson	"	"	" Reduced, Oct. 26, 1862 ; cause, detailed as saddler.
Wm. J. Cogswell	"	"	" Dischd., March 8, 1863.
Joseph A. Hill	"	"	" Dischd. May 28, 1863.
John Williamson	Corporal	"	" Red. at his own request, Oct. 26, 1862.
Lewis H. Burkett	"	"	" Prom. to Sgt., May 28, 1863.
Edwin J. Jones	"	"	" Deserted Oct. 3, 1862.
Isaac E. Barr	"	"	" Reduced, detailed ; prom. to Sgt., Oct. 28, 1862.
George W. Putnam	"	"	" Prom. to 1st Sgt., June 19, 1863.
Ezra Cooper	"	"	" Prom. to Sgt., May 1, 1863 ; died Jan. 12, 1865.

.15

NAMES.	RANK.	DATE OF COMMISSION OR APPOINTMENT.	REMARKS.
David H. Wagner.....	Corporal	.... Sep. 2, 1862.	Prom. Sgt., May 1st, 1863.
Anthony Zimmer......	"	.... " "	Reduced at his own request, May 1, 1863.
Adoniram J. Collins...	"	.... May 1, 1863.	Prom. Sgt., June 19, 1863; commd. 2d Lt. Col. Regt., Dec. 31, 1863.
George J. Messer	"	.... " "	Prom. to Sergt., July 1st 1864.
Warren A. Howland ..	"	.... " "	Prom. Sgt., Jan. 15, 1865.
Fred. A. Clark..	"	.... " "	
John Williamson......	"	.... " "	Died in a Rebel Prison, Jan. 3, 1864.
John Beal, Jr.......	"	.... " "	
Charles Haupt........	"	....June 19, 1863.	
Isaac E. Barr	"	....July 1, 1864.	
Calvin DeFrain	"	.... " "	
William C. Moseley ...	"	.... " "	
Gideon Purbaugh.....	"	....Jan. 15, 1865.	
James Reed..........	Private.	....	Prom. 1st Lt. and R. Q. M., Aug. 15,1864.
Christopher Wheeler ..	"	....	" Asst. Surg., 8th Tenn. Cav., May 22, 1864.
Wm. Parkhust........	"	....	
Orlando L. French....	"	....	Prom. Q. M. Sergt., Sept. 2, 1862.

COMPANY B.

John Whallon	Captain	Sept. 2, 1862.	Resgd. Feb. 22, 1863.
Albert M. Gillett......	1st Leut....	" "	Resgd. Feb. 25, 1863.
James Bleau..........	2d 'Lieut....	" "	Killed Oct. 8, 1862.
Charles R. Richards...	1st Sergt.....	" "	Prom. 1st Lt., Apr. 29, 1863; to Capt., June 29, 1864.
Elisha Bull	Sergeant ..	" "	Prom. 2d. Lt., June 4, 1863.
James McDearmon....	"	" "	Dischd. Dec. 22, 1862.
Joseph E. Case	"	" "	Dischd. Jan. 28, 1863.
Chauncey B. Hubbart.	"	" "	Dischd. March 26, 1863.
Alonzo Caday	1st Corporal..	" "	Dischd. Jan. 17, 1863.
Wm. A. Slaymaker ...	"	" "	Dischd. Dec. 5, 1862.
Chas. A. Sperry......	"	" "	Prom. Sergt., July 1, 1864; Trans. to V. R. C., Feb., 13, 1865.
Samuel J. Starr......	"	" "	Trans. to Invalid Corps
Asaph C. Deming.....	"	" "	Died June 20, 1863.
George R. Adams	"	" "	Prom. to Sergt., July 1st, 1864.
Alonzo A. Higley	"	" "	Died Oct. 15, 1862.
Oscar K. Hubbard	"	" "	Killed Oct. 8, 1862.
Samuel H. Eye.......	Sergeant ..	May 1, 1863.	Prom. 1st Sergt., June 4, '63.
Milton D. Strunk	"	Jan. 1, 1864.	
Wallace W. Daniels...	"	......	Trans. to Engineer Corps, July 27, 1864.
David Hillyer	"	....Aug. 1, 1863.	
Martin Barkman......	Corporal	"	
Wallace W. Wilkins ..	"	....July 1, 1864.	
Levi Strunk	"	.... "	

COMPANY C.

John F. Bennett	Captain	Aug. 9, 1862.	Prom. Lieut. Col., Sept. 2, 1862.
Ernest Altman	1st Lieut.....	"	Prom. Capt., Sept. 2, 1862; resigned Feb. 1st, 1863.
George R. Shaw.......	2d Lieut.....	"	Prom. 1st., Lieut., Sept. 2, 1862; Capt. March 22, 1863.
Thomas G. Bryant	1st Sergt....	Aug. 15, 1862.	Prom. 2nd Lieut., Mch. 22, 1863; Died April 12, 1863.
Henry C. Ranatt......	Sergeant	"	Prom. 2d Lieut., May 6, 1863.
Edward Taudemp.....	"	"	Transf. to Invalid Corps, Aug. 1, 1863.
Irving W. Heathen....	"	"	Died Feb. 22, 1863.
Prentis J. Bannister...	"	"	Prom. 2d Lieut., Sept. 2, 1862; to 1st Lieut., March 22, 1863.
Samuel Roberts.......	Corporal	"	Prom. Sergt., Sept. 2, 1862; discharged April 11, 1863.
Stephen W. Smith	"	"	Appointed 1st Sergt., Aug., 1864.
Robert D. Talbot......	"	"	Appointed Sergt., May 5, 1863.
James L. Brackar.....	"	"	Appointed 1st Sergt., May 5, 1863; Sergeant Major, Aug: 4, 1864.
John Weldon	"	"	Appointed Sergt., Sept. 1, 1863.
Alfred Pollard........	"	"	Appointed Sergt., May 1, 1863.
William H. Judd	"	"	Transf. to Invalid Corps, Aug. 15, 1864.

NAMES.	RANK.	DATE OF COMMISSION OR APPOINTMENT.	REMARKS.
Albert H. Brace	Corporal	Aug. 15, 1862.	Dischd. April 20, 1864.
L. Edson Bacon.......	"	.... Sep. 2, 1862.	Transf. to 1st U. S. Engineers.
William M. Lane	"	.... Feb. 22, 1863.	Reduced at his own request. Nov.
Lyman D. Chase.......	Corporal	Mar. 11, 1863.	Killed at Smyrna camp ground. .
Oscar A. Seely..	"	.... Nov. 7, 1863.	Promoted Sergt., Aug. 4.
Burton F. Hosworth...	"	" "	
Charles Lehun	"	.... July 1, 1864.	
Vivaldo Talcott	"	.... Aug. 30, 1864.	
George W. Fairbanks..	"	" "	
Daniel W. Smith......	"	.... Dec. 16, 1864.	
James Leahy	"	" "	
George W. Fuller.....	"	.... Jan. 1, 1865.	
Samuel Snyder	"	" "	
Charles Redford	Private.....	......	Prom. Q. M. Sergeant, May 4, 1863.
S. D. Roberts....	"	....	Prom. Drum-Major, June 1, 1863.
J. M. De Groodt	"	....	Prom. Com. Sergeant, Nov. 1864.

COMPANY D.

A. McMoore..........	Captain	Sep. 2, 1862.	Resigned.
J. E. Cobbey	1st Lieut....	"	" Resigned.
E. H. Barber	2d Lieut....	"	" Resigned.
Abner Miller	1st Sergt.....	"	" Died Sept. 30, 1862.
F. A. Caughey........	Sergeant	"	" Promoted 2d Lieut., Jan. 2, 1863; 1st Lieut., April 17, 1863.
M. L. France.........	"	.... "	" Discharged.
J. M. Sterns.........	"	.... "	" Transf. to Invalid Corps, July 1, 1863.
E. S. Harris.........	"	.... "	" Prom., Dec. 15, 1862.
George Newton, Sen...	Corporal	"	" Prom., 1st Sergt, June 30, 1863; discharged April 4, 1865.
R. L. Mangan	"	.... "	" Prom. 1st Sgt., April 8, 1862; 2d Lieut., April 17, 1863; resgd. Jan. 4, 1865.
Benjamin Cohenour ...	"	.... "	" Prom. Sergt., June 29, 1863; reduced Aug. 27, 1863.
Henry McCartey......	"	.... "	"
Daniel Aument	"	.... "	" Discharged May 6, 1863.
Enoch Long	"	.... "	" Color guard at Perryville; discharged March 7, 1863.
J. A. Ballou...	"	.... "	" Reduced by Court Martial, Dec., 1863.
Daniel Ingerham......	"	.... "	" Discharged March 10, 1863.
William Emmett......	"	.... Oct. 1, 1862.	
Barney McGrady	"	.... Oct. 9, "	Discharged March 14, 1863.
John Stauffes	"	.... Nov. 22, "	Promoted 1st Sergt, April 4, 1865.
Joseph C. Journey	"	.... Jan., 1863.	
Seth W. Coats	"	.... Mar., "	Reduced by Court Martial, Feb., 1864.
John W. Sheaffer.....	"	.... April, "	Promoted Sergt., Aug. 27, 1863.
Hugh L. John.........	"	, ... "	" Discharged August 10, 1863.
E. H. Scott...........	"	.... "	" Promoted Sergt. June 1, 1863.
George Newton, Jr....	"	... Aug., "	Reduced Jan. 1, 1865.
C. R. Steadman......	"	.... Nov., "	Promoted Sergt., Jan. 1, 1866.
Ezra W. Arey	"	.... Mar., 1864.	Promoted Sergt., April 4th, 1865.
Leonard H. Richards..	"	.... "	"
Thomas Diller	"	.... Jan. 1, 1865.	
Richard Arey.........	"	.... Feb. 1, 1865.	
Patrick Daley	"	.... Apr. 4, 1865.	

COMPANY E.

William S. Frost	Captain	Sep. 2, 1862.	Disch. on acct. of wounds, Jan. 23, 1865.
Franklin H. Eels	1st Lieut....	"	" Killed Oct. 8, 1862.
James H. Blodgett	2d Lieut....	"	" Prom. 1st Lieut., Dec. 31, 1862; Capt., Jan. 31, 1865.
James H. Barker......	1st Sergt....	"	" Killed Oct. 8, 1862.
Henry Hill, Jr........	Sergeant	"	" Discharged March 7, 1863.
James Dexter........	"	.... "	" Prom. to 1st Lieut. Jan. 31, 1865.
Cyrus W. Sawyer.....	"	.... "	" Dischd. Dec. 11, '62.
Harlow F. Chadwick..	"	.... "	" Trans. to Ind. Corps, Sept. 1, 1863.
George W. Wheat	Corporal	"	" Missing since Oct. 8, '62.
Oliver A. Wood	"	.... "	" Dischd. Jan. 8, 1863.
Harrison Hale	"	.... "	" Prom. to Sergt. ; dischd. May 2, 1863.
Charles Stewart,......	"	.... "	" Dischd. May 5, 1863.

NAMES.	RANK.	DATE OF COMMISSION OR APPOINTMENT.	REMARKS.
Aquilla Christopher...	Corporal	.... Sept. 2, 1862.	Prom. to Sergt. Feb. 8, 1863; dischd. Feb. 14, 1865.
Wm. H. Sawyer........	"	.... "	" Dischd. May 5, 1863.
John Stiltz	"	.... "	"
John Snorer	"	.... "	" Deserted Feb. 23, 1863.
Geo. T. Fessenden	"	.... Dec. 16, 1862.	Prom. Sergt., July 1, 1863.
Sylvester S. Nash. ...	"	.... Dec. 6, 1862.	
Jonathan F. Colwell...	"	... "	" Died Apr. 7, 1863.
Isaac Yocum	"	.... Jan. 1,	" Prom. Sergt., Sept. 1, 1864.
George M. Houk	"	.... Jan. 1, 1863.	Prom. 1st Sergt., Feb. 17, 1865.
David D. Myers.......	"	.... July 1, 1864.	Prom. to Sergt., Feb. 15, 1865.
August Degner........	"	.... "	"
John Nass	"	.... "	"
Wm. P. Packard......	"	.... "	"
Myron J. Peterson	"	.... "	"
Norman Jewett	"	....April 1, 1865.	

COMPANY F.

Addison S. Vorrey	Captain	..... Sep. 2, 1862.	Died Aug. 13, 1854.
James Tourtillott	1st Lieut....	"	" Resigned Apr. 21, 1863.
Dennis Hannifin	2d Lieut....	"	" do Apr. 21, 1863.
Benj. J. Warren	1st Sergt....	"	"
James McCord........	Sergeant	"	" Prom. 1st. Lieut., Aug. 15, 1863; Capt. Apr. 1, 1865.
John Dolan..........	"	.... "	" Dischd. Mch. 5, '63.
Sheppard Reynolds....	"	.... "	" Dischd. Dec. 17, 1862.
James D. Place	"	.... "	" Commissioned 2d Lieut., Aug. 15, 1863.
William Armstrong ...	Corporal	"	" Dischd. Jan. 29, 1863.
Emanuel Van Osdell...	"	.... "	" Transfd. to U. S. Eng.Corps,July 27,'64.
Elisha T. Tourtillott ..	"	.... "	" Dischd. Aug. 3., 1863.
Charles R. Gregory ...	"	.... "	" Transfd. to Invalid Corps, Nov. 1, 1863.
George W. Niver	"	.... "	" Prom. Sergt., Aug. 22, 1863.
Edwin E. Faunce	"	.... "	" Prom. Sergt., Aug. 23, 1864.
D. B. Walker........	"	.... "	" Dischd. Jan. 12, 1863.
William Doran	"	.... "	" Deserted Oct. 19, 1862.
Hugh Carlile	"	.... Au. 14, 1863.	
John C. Harmon	"	.... "	"
George R. Loncks.....	"	.... "	" Prom. Sergt. Aug. 23, 1864.
Aaron O'Neil.........	"	.... Aug. 1, 1864.	
Earnest Warnick.... .	"	.... Sep. 1,	"

COMPANY G.

Joseph Williams	Captain	..... Sep. 2, 1862.	Resgd. Dec. 19, 1862.
David Sanford	1st Lieut....	"	" Prom. Capt. May 2, 1863; resgd. June 13, 1863.
Robert L. Irwin	2d Lieut.....	"	" Comd. 1st Lt. April 19, 1863; resgd. for disability, April 29, 1863.
Manly E. Brown	1st Sergt.....	"	" Killed at Perryville.
Charles Twomhley	Sergeant	"	" do do
Wm. Taylor..........	"	.... "	" Died Mch. 12, 1863.
Wm. Vance...........	"	.... "	" Prom. 1st Sergt., Apr., 1863; to 2d Lt., May 2, 1863; 1st Lt., Apr. 11, 1864.
Joseph Mumma.......	"	.... "	" Transf. to V. R. Corps, Jan. 1, 1865.
Cornellus Brinkerhoff..	Corporal	"	" do do Aug. 1, 1863.
George W. Hittle.....	"	.... "	" Died Nov. 12, 1862, of wound.
Joseph Winehranner ..	"	.... "	" Dischd. Mch. 16, 1863.
Jonathan Shrock......	"	.... "	" Prom. 1st Sergt., May 3, 1863; dischd. Apr. 6, 1863.
Walter Gilbert	"	.... "	" Died Mch. 19, 1863.
Caleb Forbes	"	.... "	" Killed at Perryville.
William Shults	"	.... "	" Dis. Dec. 12, 1862, left arm amputated.
James Dysart.........	"	.... "	" Dischd. Apr. 18, 1863; died soon after.
Daniel E. Spafford	Sergeant	Ap. 27, 1863.	Prom. to 1st Sergt., Apr. 6, 1864.
Brison Leonard	"	Nov. 1,	"
Robert L. Irwin.......	Captain	My. 20, 1864.	His re-enlistment was as a private.
Samuel Bender.	Corporal	Nov. 1, 1863.	Prom. to Sergt., July 1, 1864.
Geo. W. Carr	"	July 1, 1864.	
Addison A. Heckart...	"	.... "	"

COMPANY H.

NAMES.	RANK.	DATE OF COMMISSION OR APPOINTMENT.	REMARKS.
John G. Price.........	Captain.....	Sep. 2, 1862.	Resigned Feby. 8, 1863.
J. W. R. Stambaugh..	1st Lieut.....	" "	Pro. Capt. Feb. 9, 1863; trans. to Eng. Corps, Feh. 1, 1865.
Ahner R. Hurless.....	2d Lieut.....	" "	Resigned April 22, 1863.
Frank Bingham...	1st Sergt.....	" "	Prom. 1st Lieut., Mch. 22, 1863; Capt. Feh. 25, 1865.
Alfred Cantelo........	Sergeant	" "	Dischd. Feb. 25, 1863.
Seth Hawkins.........	"	" "	Dischd. April 20, 1863.
John Q. Strape........	"	" "	Died of wounds, Oct. 15, 1862.
Saml. Tracy,........	"	" "	Dischd. Aug. 5, 1863.
John L. Newton.......	Corporal	" "	Prom. 2d Lieut., May 16, 1863; 1st Lt., Mch 1, 1865.
Oliver Oshorn.........	"	" "	Prom. Sergt. Aug. 5, 1864.
Benj. F. Banning......	"	" "	Reduced Oct. 8, 1863.
Fred. Mitchel.	"	" "	Prom. Sergt. Aug. 29, 1863.
P. L. Wolfe...........	"	" "	Prom. 1st Sergt. Aug. 8, 1864.
Joseph Malden........	"	" "	Deserted, Oct. 8, 1862.
Joseph Boyer..........	"	" "	Transf. to Co. A, Sept. 25, 1862.
E. S. Webster........	"	" "	Dischd. Feb. 20, 1863.
John Yeager.........	1st Sergt....	May 16, 1863.	Died of wounds, Aug. 3, 1864.
Walter S. Angell......	Sergeant	Aug. 3, 1864.	
D. S. Angell..........	Corporal	Jan. 1, 1865.	
James Morehead......	"	" "	
Hezekiah Stewart......	Private......	......	Apptd. Fife Major, July 1, 1863.

COMPANY I.

Wm. M. Kilgour......	Captain.....	Au. 13, 1862.	Prom. Maj., Sept. 2, 1864.
Roht. Hale.......	Captain.....	Sep. 2, "	Killed at Ruff Station, Ga., July 4, 1864.
Joel A. Fife....	1st Lieut.... ...	" "	Trans. to V. R. Corps, Nov. 8, 1863.
Ezekiel J. Kilgour ...	2d Lieut.....	" "	Died, Dec. 26, 1862.
Amos B. Segur.......	1st Sergt....	" "	Prom. 2d Lt., Mch. 22, 1863; Capt. Aug. 6, 1864.
Saml. Orcult...	Sergeant ...	" "	Appointed 1st sergt., Mch. 22, 1863.
Augustus Johnson.....	"	" "	
James R. Montgomery.	"	" "	Killed Oct. 8, 1862.
Edson W. Lyman......	"	" "	Hon. Dischd., Mch. 9, 1863.
Martin L. Johnston....	Corporal	" "	Appointed Sergt., Mch. 1, 1863; killed July 22, 1864.
James H. Woodhurn..	"	" "	Sergt. Oct. 8, 1862.
James W. Gordon.....	"	" "	Reduced at his own request, Mch. 1, '64.
Levi Moates.........	"	" "	Appointed Sergt., May 1, 1863; reduced Mch. 1, 1864.
Charles L. Marcellus..	"	" "	Transf. to V. R., Corps, Sept. 10, 1864.
Alvey Henson........	"	" "	Dischd. Mch. 4, 1863.
Sylvester Chapman......	"	" "	Transferred to V. R. Corps.
Jacob Rhodehamel....	"	" "	Appointed Sergt., March 1, 1864; killed at Resaca, Ga., May 14, 1864.
Benjamin W. Doty....	"	Mar. 1, 1863.	Sergt. July 1, 1864.
Cornelius C. Gerhart..	"	Feb. 1, 1864.	
Edmund G. Lathrops ..	"	Mar. 1, "	Sergt. 22, 1864.
David R. Moulton....	"	" "	
John Freck......... .	"	July 1, "	
David Bryson., ...	"	July 22, "	
Daniel Schryver.......	"	Nov. 1, "	
Lewis E. Chulluck.....	Private......	....	App. Sergt. Major, Aug. 20, 1863; 1st Lieut., Aug. 4, 1864.

COMPANY K.

David M. Roberts. ...	Captain.....	Sep. 2, 1862.	
Wm. H. Thompson....	1st Lieut.....	" "	Died, Feh. 25, 1864.
Isaac L. Hunt........	2d Lieut.....	" "	Prom. 1st Lieut. July 1, 1864.
Frank Atherton.......	1st Sergt....	" "	Dischd. Nov. 18, 1862.
Berkley G. Barrett. a.	Sergeant	" "	Prom. 1st Sergt., Dec. 18, 1862.
John Ryan	"	" "	Reduced, cause long sickness.
Jonathan N. Hyde	"	" "	

NAMES.	RANK.	DATE OF COMMISSION OR APPOINTMENT.	REMARKS.
James C. Howlett.....	Sergeant	Sept. 2, 1862.	Reduced, cause absence.
Wm. Nettleton	Corporal	"	Prom. Sergt., Dec. 18, 1862.
John A. Hunt.........	"	"	Dischd. Feb., 18.
James H. Thompson...	"	"	"
Joshua C. Wills..	"	"	"
Walter V. Simons.....	"	"	Prom. Serg., Jan. 1, 1864.
Stephen A. Tarr.......	"	"	Dischd. Dec. 6, 1862.
Edward J. Rice.......	"	"	do do
John A. Shondy	"	"	Prom. Sergt. Jan. 1, 1864.
De Witt J. Abrams....	"	"	Prom. Sept. 1, 1864.
Wm. M. Atherton.....	"	"	Prom. Jan. 1, 1864.
John Dilts............	"	"	Prom. Jan. 1, 1864 ; reduced July 19,'64.
Orlando B. Jones	"	"	Prom. Jan. 1, 1864.
Merritt Nuller........	"	"	Prom. Dec. 18, 1864.
Eben Backus..........	"	"	Prom. Dec. 18, 1864 ; Dischd. Feb. 8 ; 1865.

REGISTER OF DEATHS.

COMPANY A.

Alfred K. Buckaloo, 2d Lieut., March 14, '64, chronic diarrhœa ; Ezra Cooper, Sergt., Jan. 12, '65, diarrhœa ; Privates—William Stackpole, Dec. 20, 62, died in Insane Asylum ; David Howard, Feb. 18, '63, chronic diarrhœa ; Stephen R. Welshons, Feb. 26, '63, typhoid fever ; Alexander Rosenbaum, May 23, '63, apoplexy while on picket ; Charles H. Mostetter, Nov. 18, '63, chronic diarrhœa ; John R. Richards, Dec. 17, '63, chronic diarrhœa ; William H. Stewart, Dec. 30, '63, chronic diarrhœa ; John A. Cookson, Jan. 29, '64, of wounds received June 16, '64 ; Geo. H. McIntire, June 28, '64, chronic diarrhœa ; John Williamson, Corporal, Jan. 3, '64, died in rebel prison ; Alexander Dorn, Private, Sep. 28, '64, died in rebel prison.

COMPANY B.

Killed in Action—Corporal Orson K. Hubbard, Oct. 8, '62 ; Privates—Seymour Baker, Oct. 8, '62; Benjamin Chamberlin, Oct. 8, 62; John Early, Oct. 8, '62; Oscar M. King, Oct. 8, '62; Robert Millier, Oct. 2, '62; Lyman P. Shaw, Oct. 2, '62; Luman Wilder, July 20, '64; 2d Lieut. James Blean, Oct. 8, '62.

Died of Wounds and Diseases — Corporals—Asa C. Deming, disease, June 20, '63; Alonzo A. Higley, wounds, Oct. 15, '62. Privates—Frank Abner, wounds, Nov. 7, '62; Silas C. Bessee, wounds, Nov. 7, 62; Levi Dummer, disease, Jan. 17, '63; Emory M. Deming, wounds, Jan. 7, '63; David B. Dumars, wounds, Sept. 2, 1864; Alonzo Gaylord, wounds, Oct. 14, '62; Marion A. Holden, disease, Feb. 3, '63; Pascal Hawley, disease, Aug. 20, '63; Henry Jones, disease, Dec. 19, '62; Wesley J. Pike, wounds, Oct. 15, '62; John Pringle, disease, Dec. 6, '62; Robert K. Thompson, wounds, Nov. 5, '62; Azariah Wick, wounds, Sep. 20, '64.

COMPANY C.

George W. Olivor, died of wounds, Nov. 7, '62; David P. Perry, rubeola, Jan. 2, '63; Warren Young, pneumonia, Jan. 26, '63; Irving W. Hanshaw, apoplexy, Feb. 27, '63; Robert Mathew, typhoid, April 11, '63; Lieutenant Thomas G. Bryant, congestion, April 12, '63; Michael Mack, diarrhœa, Sept. 16, '63; Wm. Tranger, Jr. (unknown), Dec. 28, '62; Wm. Tompkins, diarrhœa, Dec. 7, '64; Wheeler Pratt, diarrhœa, Dec. 27, '64.

COMPANY D.

1st Sergt. Abner Miller, disease, Oct. 1, '62; Eugene L. Bessie, typhoid, Nov. 8, '62; Harvey Brink, typhoid, Nov. 22, '62; Amos McCarty, typhoid, Jan. 2, '63; Wm. H. Tracy, typhoid, Jan. 11, '63; Theodore M. Aldridge, heart, Jan. 18, '63; Harvey Mahan, diarrhœa, Feb. 2, '63; Daniel H. Miller, diarrhœa, March 20, '63; John H. Hauver, diarrhœa, Nov. 18, '63; Jacob Coughenour, wounds, Dec. 22, '62; Azariah Wicks, wounds, Sept. 20, '64.

COMPANY E.

Privates—George Kramer, Dec. 25, '62, congestion of brain; John W. McLain, Jan. 23, '63, rubeola and erysipelas; Edward S. Smith, April 27, '63, not specified ; Joseph J. Hodges, Dec. 19, '62, typhoid fever; Corporal Jonathan F. Colwell, April 7, '63, consumption; Privates—Eugene A. Chadwick, Feb. 3, '63, not specified; Charles E. White, Aug. 16, '63, chronic diarrhœa; Charles McLain, March 18, '64, typhoid fever; Thaddeus A. Spafford, Oct. 14, '63, in rebel prison, unknown; Chauncey M. Sawyer, Feb. 6, '64, small pox.

COMPANY F.

Captain Addison S. Vorrey, erysipelas, Aug. 13, '64; Privates—Alonzo E. Allen, disease of the lungs, Dec., '62; James Campbell, inflammation of bowels, Feb. 9, '63; Geo. P. Nellis, bronchitis, Sept. 19, '64; John Kelly, scurvy and dropsy, Aug. 27, '64; Samuel Shore, congestion of lungs, Feb. 10, '63; John M. Spencer, pneumonia, April 17, '65.

COMPANY G.

Samuel Piper, Musician, Dec. 1, '62, Nashville, Tenn.; Privates—Wm. W. Clark, Feb. 16, '63, Nashville, Tenn., pneumonia; Redrick Taylor, Jan. 26, '63, bronchitis; Joseph Mersale, Feb. 28, '63, Murfreesboro, pneumonia; Sergeant William Taylor, March 12, '63, Murfreesboro, pneumonia; Private John Stevens, March 17, '63, Murfreesboro, pneumonia; Corporal Walter Gilbert, March 19, '63, Nashville, small pox; Privates—Alexander Long, April 15, '63, Murfreesboro, consumption; William Harvey, June 12, '63, Murfreesboro, brain fever; Irvin W. Thomas, Feb. 21, '64, Nashville, small pox; John Tobyne, Springfield, Ill., small pox; Wm. A. Andrews, Feb. 24, '64, Nashville, inflammation of lungs; Rush Smith, May 16, '64, Nashville, pneumonia; Paul G. Wetzel, July 29, '64, Vinings, Ga., flux; Alfred H. Yothers, Sept. 29, '64, Kingston, Ga., chronic diarrhœa; Reuben Rowley, Feb. 9, '65, Memphis, Tenn., small pox.

COMPANY H.

John O. Strate, wounds, Oct. 15, '62; Frank Ford, wounds, Oct. 30, '62; Mathew Maiden, Oct. 28, '62; James Arnold, disease, date unknown; James D. Cherry, wounds, date unknown; Milton C. Hicks, disease, Feb. 21, '63; Cyrus Walker, disease, Feb. 2, '63; David Seitz, disease, March 1, '63; Michael O. Kane, wounds, date unknown; Patrick Mailey, disease, Feb. 4, '63; James Mailey, disease, Aug. 10, '63; Elijah Douglas, disease, date unknown; John Yeager, wounds, Aug. 3, '64.

COMPANY I.

James R. Montgomery, Sergeant, Oct. 8, '62, killed in battle of Perryville, Ky.; Privates—Washington J. Williams, Francis E. Brown, John Brubaker, Oct. 8, '62, killed in battle of Perryville, Ky.; Franklin Marcellus, Oct. 15,

'62, died of wounds received in battle of Perryville, thigh amputated; Almon Baker and Charles W. Case, Nov. 12, '62, died of wounds received in battle of Perryville; James L. Canfield, Dec. 10, '62, disease; Paschal Hawley, Jan. 20, '63, measles; Alonzo P. Johnston, Jan. 26, '63, disease; John W. Wilson, Jan. 17, '63, disease; Samuel L. Martindale, Feb. 12, '63, John F. McClery, Feb. 20, '63, disease; Charles A. Webb, Feb. 5, '63, disease (small pox); William E. Stroud, April 17, '63, disease; Jacob Rhodehamel, Sergeant, May 14, '64, killed in action, battle of Resaca; Ephraim Welden, Private, June 2, '64, killed in action, Kenesaw Mt., gun shot; Martin L. Johnston, Sergeant, July 22, '64, killed on skirmish line by shell from our own battery; Privates—William Hampston, Sept. 2, '64, killed in action at battle of Lovejoy's Station, (shell); Gilbert W. Jennings, Dec. 16, '64, killed in action battle of Nashville (gun shot); Sylvester Chapman, Dec. 16, '64, killed in action battle of Nashville (shell); Ezekiel L Kilgour, 2d Lieut., Dec. 25, '62, died of disease (consumption); Robert Hale, Captain, July 4th, '64, killed in action at Culp's Farm, Ga., while on duty as brig. officer of the day ; John Early, Oct. 8, '62, killed at Perryville.

COMPANY K.

Wm. H. Thompson, 1st Lieut., consumption, Feb. 25, '64; Joseph Miller, wounds, Nov. 2, '62; Benjamin Kipp, heart disease, Dec. 17, '62; Wm. G. Dean, wounds, Nov. '62; Silas Pringle, wounds, Nov. '62; Jacob D. Fuller, disease, Nov., '62; Wm. D. Baisley, rubeola, Jan. 18, '63; Fletcher Bickery, typhoid, Aug. 18, '63; George Dormey, wounds, June 30, '64.

RECORD OF CASUALTIES

IN THE SEVERAL ENGAGEMENTS DURING THREE YEARS OF SERVICE.

Battle of Perryville, Ky., Oct. 8, 1862.

FIELD AND STAFF.

Wounded—Major William M. Kilgour.

COMPANY A.

Wounded—Privates Jos. B. Crawford and John R. Richards.

COMPANY B.

Killed—Lieut. James Blean; Corporal Orson K. Hubbard; Privates Seymour Baker, Benjamin Chamberlain, John Early, O. M. King, Robert Millier, L. P. Shaw. *Wounded*—Captain John Whallen ; Sergeants J. McDearman and J. E. Case ; Corporals Alonzo A. Higley, Frank Abner, W. A. Slaymaker, and G. R. Adams ; Privates Silas C. Bessee, A. Gaylord, W. J. Pike, R. K. Thompson, Benj. F. Bessee, David B. Dumars, David Houston, J. C. Mears, P. O'Hara, James Scott, Thomas McDonald, John Pendleton, Thomas Brown, John Bacon, Henry Ege, E. J. Garrison, and Henry Jones.

COMPANY C.

Killed—Privates Nathan Myers, William Grunderman, and George S. Millins. *Wounded*—Sergeant I. W. Hanshaw ; Privates Edward Cleveland, G. W. Oliver, A. A. Cass, S. C. Early, J. S. Gillett, Seymour Harrison, Henry Leonard, Thomas Mason, G. W. Oliver, H. P. Fistner, Peter Root, Miles F. Wooley.

COMPANY D.

Killed—Privates Henry Bowman and F. P. Meservey. *Wounded*—Lieut. E. H. Barber ; Sergeant M. L. France ; Corporal Enoch Long ; Privates J. Coughenour, R. Goshen, H. Kramer, I. Stater, Wm. Wiggins, and N. W. Darrow.

COMPANY E.

Killed—Lieut. F. H. Eels ; Sergeant J. L. Barker ; Privates J. Akin, Ole C. B——, A. M. Gage, E. McKune, J. Wolcott, S. J. Yeast. *Wounded*—Captain W. S. Frost ; Lieut. James H. Blodgett ; Sergeants James Dexter, C. W. Sawyer ; Corporals O. I. Wood, H. Hale, J. Snover ; Privates Wm. Hickland, G. H. Barker, E. Fisher, W. Hannon, S. Johnson, D. B. Long, P. K. Mittan, C. Maes, N. Montgomery, M. J. Peterson, and Francis Tracy.

COMPANY F.

Wounded—Sergeant S. Reynolds ; Corporals O. R. Gregory, D. B. Walker ; Privates J. B. Ayres, F. D. Brown, Dennis Finn, P. Honan, W. F. Loucks, Charles Lambert, and Samuel Stewart.

COMPANY G.

Killed—Sergeant M. E. Brown ; Corporal C. Forbes ; Privates Rathburn Bly, H. Frost, Tubal Keen, A. McNeal, A. Weaver, J. W. Warner, Marion Wade. *Wounded*—Lieut. Robert L. Irwin ; Sergeant C. Twombley ; Corporal George Hittle ; Privates Isaac Wisler, Eben Fish, O. Atwood, George Cable, Wm. Clark, C. Chromstar, J. Davis, P. Garrison, L. Hillery, A. A. Hechert, C. Powers, J. Sturdevant, I. Thomas, J. Taylor, A. N. Timothy, and Oswald Wetzel.

COMPANY II.

Killed—Privates M. Heizer, C. Hollicher, H. Sheridan, T. O. Taylor, D. B. Ustick, and George Williams. *Wounded*—Sergeant J. O. Strate ; Corporal E. Webster ; Privates F. Ford, M. Maiden, J. D. Cherry, J. Hauprich, J. Morehead, H. Pickle, D. Steele, P. Hoffman, A. Johnson, D. Bruce, Benjamin Corbin, R. Chappel, M. O. Kane, E. Landis, P. Mailey, and John Yeager.

COMPANY I.

Killed—Sergeant James R. Montgomery ; Privates W. F. Williams, F. E. Brown, J. Brubaker, John Early. *Wounded*—

Sergeant E. W. Lyman ; Privates F. Marcellus, A. Baker, Chas. W. Case, A. McKenzie, C. W. Freeman, E. D. Welden, J. Crane, and S. L. Martindale.

COMPANY K.

Killed—Privates Z. Atherton and Geo. Brittain. *Wounded*—Captain D. M. Roberts ; Lieut. W. H. Thompson ; Sergeants F. Atherton, J. N. Hyde ; Corporals J. C. Wills, S. A. Farr, J. A. Shoudy, E. J. Rice ; Privates J. L. Baisley, G. Beemer, W. A. Conant, W. H. Christie, F. M. Case, W. Y. Dean, F. Dormoy, George Dormoy, C. H. Golding, E. E. Hallenbeck, George Hallenbeck, N. Halleck, H. Henrie, J. Miller, T. Spencer, Joseph Miller, H. Merwin, J. N. Steen, S. Pringle, B. F. Radley, C. Sutton, and Franklin Harkins.

In a slight skirmish near Lancaster, Ky., October 14, 1862, Captain E. A. Altman, of Company C, was severely wounded—the only one in the regiment.

Battle of Stone River, from Dec. 26th, 1862, to Jan. 6th, 1863.

COMPANY A.

Wounded—Private A. J. Collins.

COMPANY B.

Wounded—Sergeant C. B. Hubbard.

COMPANY C.

Killed—Private Washington L. Woods. *Wounded*—Privates H. M. Bunn, and G. W. Fuller.

COMPANY D.

Wounded—Private Aurand Aurans.

COMPANY E.

Wounded—Lieutenant James H. Blodgett.

COMPANY F.

Wounded—Corporal E. T. Tourtillott ; Private Samuel Shore.

COMPANY G.

Wounded—Privates John Kizer, E. J. Larry.

COMPANY H.

Wounded—Private James Morehead.

COMPANY I.

Wounded—Captain Robert Hale ; Privates O. Orcutt, J. Collins, W. Hampton, and August Quade.

Company K, none.

During this battle, 21 officers and men were captured. During the campaign of Chickamauga the Seventy-fifth Illinois lost, in prisoners, 8 men.

Reconnoissance before Dalton, February 22d to 28th, 1864.

FIELD AND STAFF.

Wounded—Major James A. Watson.

COMPANY A.

Wounded—Privates T. S. Caffrey, and Nicholas Mossholder.

COMPANY C.

Wounded—Privates O. A. Seely, and Daniel W. Smith.

COMPANY H.

Wounded—Sergeant M. F. Wolf.

COMPANY K.

Wounded—Corporal James H. Thompson.

Battles around Resaca, Ga., May 9th to 16th, 1864.

COMPANY A.

Wounded—Private Thomas Wood.

COMPANY I.

Wounded—Private Norman Brooks.

COMPANY K.

Wounded—Corporal O. B. Jones; Private J. Turk.

Battles around Cassville and Dallas, May 19th to 27th, 1864.

COMPANY D.

Wounded—Private Elisha Drew.

COMPANY E.

Wounded—Sergeant A. S. Christopher.

Battles around Dallas, June 1st to 5th, 1864.

COMPANY F.

Killed—Private Owen Doudel.

COMPANY G.

Wounded—Private George Fill.

COMPANY I.

Wounded—Private L. E. Matthews.

Pine Mountain, June 13th to 18th, 1864.

COMPANY A.

Wounded—Private J. N. Cookson.

COMPANY K.

Wounded—Privates Fred. Dormoy, and A. E. Fuller.

Battles around Kenesaw Mountain, June 19th to July 1st, 1864.

COMPANY A.

Wounded—Sergeant Lewis H. Burkitt; Corporal W. A. Howland; Privates J. B. Crawford, A. Zimmer, Calvin DeFrain, and J. L. Backus.

COMPANY B.

Wounded—Private John Pendleton.

COMPANY D.

Wounded—Lieutenant R. L. Mangum.

COMPANY F.

Wounded—Private John Kelley.

COMPANY G.

Wounded—Private Charles C. Bowers.

COMPANY H.

Killed—Privates D. L. Pierce, and Joseph Hauprich. *Wounded*—Sergeant. John Yeager; Privates Charles Fox, and Jacob Funt.

COMPANY I.

Wounded—Private Justis M. Reynolds.

COMPANY K.

Wounded—Private George Dormoy.

Battle of Culp's Farm, Rough Station, or Smyrna Camp Ground, July 3rd and 4th, 1864.

COMPANY C.

Killed—Corporal Lyman D. Chase.

COMPANY F.

Wounded—Privates Aaron O'Neal, Daniel Burns, and Joseph Carr.

COMPANY H.

Wounded—Private Dennis Fletcher.

COMPANY I.

Killed—Captain Robert Hale. *Wounded*—Private Charles W. Freeman.

COMPANY K.

Wounded—Sergeant J. N. Hyde ; Corporal G. W. Newton ; Privates A. Wick and Silas Richardson.

Chawahoochie Heights, July 9, 1864.

COMPANY G.

Wounded—Private Charles S. Brunson.

Peach Tree Creek, July 19th to 22d, 1864.

COMPANY I.

Wounded—Private Richard Trye.

COMPANY K.

Wounded—Private Marcus S. Plant.

Before Atlanta, from July 23d to August 28th, 1864.

COMPANY B.

Wounded—Private Jacob Howe, Aug. 15.

COMPANY E.

Wounded—Captain Wm. S. Frost, July 23 ; Private Fred. Schleicht, Aug. 15.

COMPANY F.

Wounded—Corporal Hugh Carlile, Aug. 22.

COMPANY G.

Wounded—Private Charles C. Bowers, Aug. 19.

COMPANY H.

Wounded—Private Stephen Thompson, Aug. 12.

COMPANY K.

Wounded—Private Ira M. Baker, July 23.

Lovejoy's Station, September 2d, 1864.

COMPANY A.

Wounded—Privates Joseph Gruver, and Gideon Purbaugh.

COMPANY C.

Wounded—Private William P. Squires.

COMPANY E.

Wounded—Lieut. James H. Blodgett; Corporal David D. Myers.

COMPANY F.

Killed—Private John Murphy.

COMPANY G.

Wounded—Sergeant A. J. Timothy.

COMPANY K.

Killed—Private Francis Mills. *Wounded*—Privates John E. Ayler, Henry Pott, and Charles Hewitt.

———

Columbia, Tenn., November 25, 1864.

Wounded—Corporal W. P. Packard.

———

Nashville, Tenn., December 15 and 16, 1864.

COMPANY C.

Wounded—Lieut. Henry Parrott; Privates Byron Willilon, and H. E. Talcott.

COMPANY F.

Wounded—Private Thomas Haley.

COMPANY G.

Wounded—Lieut. Robert L. Irwin ; Private Frank Whalen.

———————————————

REGISTER OF DESERTERS.

———

Company A—Corpl. Edwin J. Jones, Oct. 3rd, 1862; Joseph Cromwell, Oct. 3rd, 1862; Willis Fredenburg, Oct. 3rd, 1862; Proctor D. Oaks, Oct. 3rd, 1862.

Company B—Daniel S. Baker, Nov., 1862; Levi J. Clark, Oct. 4th, 1862; Daniel Houston, Oct., 1862; Gaylord M. Jennings, June, 1863.

Company C—Albert Barber, Aug. 20th, 1862 ; Wm. Barber,

Aug. 20th, 1862; Leonard Pratt, Oct. 27th, 1862; Joseph W. Bump, Jan. 1st, 1863.

Company D—Dunlant Murry, Oct. 6th, 1862; James H. Stewart, October 6th, 1862; Benjamin Coughenour, May, 1863.

Company E—Corpl. John Snover, Feb. 23rd, 1863; Wm. Beaton, Dixon, Ill., Sept. 26th, 1862; Alexander Long, in the field, Nov. 30th, 1862; Elias Fisher, Louisville, Ky., Dec. 23rd, 1862; John Grunert, enlisted in 17th Illinois Cavalry while exchanged prisoner from Perryville; Dennis Carrol, Stone River, Dec. 30th, 1862.

Company F—Corpl. Wm. Doran, Oct. 19th, 1862; James O'Garr, Sept. 27th, 1862; Edwin Crimmins, Sept. 27th, 1862; Wm. H. Stewart, Oct. 19th, 1862; James H. Stewart, Oct. 19th, 1862; Cornelius McFadden, Oct. 19th, 1862; Patrick Holland, Dec. 10th, 1862; Benj. F. Cammon, Jan. 8th, 1863; Phillip McCormick, Feb. 10th, 1864.

Company G—Daniel E. Sheaslain, in the field, Dec. 10th, 1862; Eugene Sullivan, in the field, Dec. 10th, 1862; Morgan Williams, in the field, Dec. 10th, 1862; John Berneter, Oct., 1861, from Louisville, Ky., paroled prisoner; Peter Sower, Oct. 27th, 1864, from hospital, Jeffersonville, Ind.

Company H—Jacob D. Echelberger, Oct. 5th, 1862; Newton Brown, Oct. 4th, 1862; Joseph Maiden, Oct. 8th, 1862; David A. McBride, Jan. 20th, 1863; George H. Benham, Jan. 15th, 1863; Simon Reynear, Sept. 1st, 1863; Augustus O. Clark, April 30th, 1864.

Company I—August Quade, June 1st, 1863.

Company K—J. Poindexter, Sept., 1862; Frank Harkins, Feb. 22d, 1863; James Hall, Oct. 26th, 1862; Menzo Coffin, Dec. 4th, 1862.

A TABULAR HISTORY OF THE ORGANIZATION AND

DURING ITS PERIOD OF SERVICE IN

	No. Date of Muster.	No. since Commissioned.	No. Received by Transfer.	TOTAL GAIN.	No. Killed.	No. Died of Wounds.	No. Died of Disease.	No. Transferred.	No. Resigned.	No. Discharged.	No. Dismissed.	TOTAL LOSSES.	Strength at date of Muster-out.
						OFFICERS.							
Field and Staff......	8	4	...	12	...	...	...	...	1	5	...	6	6
Non-com'd Staff....	...	...	...	...	...	...	...	...	...	...	...	...	...
Company A	3	2	...	5	...	...	1	1	1	...	...	3	2
" B........	3	2	...	5	1	...	...	...	2	...	...	3	2
" C........	3	3	...	6	...	...	1	1	1	...	...	3	3
" D........	3	2	...	5	...	...	...	...	2	1	...	3	2
" E........	3	2	...	5	1	...	...	...	...	2	...	3	2
" F........	3	2	...	5	...	...	1	...	2	...	...	3	2
" G........	3	2	...	5	...	...	...	...	3	...	...	3	2
" H........	3	2	...	5	...	...	...	1·	2	...	...	3	2
" I........	3	2	...	5	1	...	1	1	...	...	...	3	2
" K........	3	...	...	3	...	...	1	...	...	...	...	1	2
TOTAL,..........	38	23	..	61	3	...	5	5	18	3	...	34	27

This Tabular Statement is verified by

CHANGES IN THE SEVENTY-FIFTH ILLINOIS VOLS.,

THE ARMY OF THE UNITED STATES.

				ENLISTED MEN.									
No. Date of Muster.	No. Recruits.	No. Received by Transfer.	TOTAL GAIN.	No. Killed.	No. Died of Wounds.	No. Died of Disease.	No. Discharged.	No. Transferred.	No. Commissioned.	No. Dropped as Missing.	No. Deserters.	TOTAL LOSSES.	Strength at date of Muster-out.
4	....	6	10	....	....	....	....	2	2	....	....	4	6
89	3	....	92	....	1	11	18	10	4	....	5	49	43
80	2	....	82	8	8	5	16	16	2	....	4	59	23
98	20	....	118	4	2	8	26	41	3	....	4	88	30
91	9	....	100	2	2	10	32	12	2	....	3	63	37
87	13	....	100	7	3	10	21	20	2	1	6	70	30
61	4	....	65	2	1	6	16	6	2	....	8	40	25
87	32	...	119	14	3	14	18	42	2	....	5	98	21
85	....	....	85	8	6	7	17	16	2	....	7	63	22
88	7	6	101	12	1	11	28	17	1	....	1	71	30
84	12	....	96	4	4	4	24	18	....	....	4	58	38
854	102	12	968	61	31	86	216	200	22	1	47	663	305

Regimental and Company Records.

ERRATA.

On Page 44, line 19, in place of "right," say "left."

On Page 68, line 19. After the name, "Geo. G. Messer," add, "and Privates Joseph Watson and John Catnaugh."

On Page 72, line first, "Gibbons" should be "Gibson's."

On Page 117, line 17. After the name, "George G. Messer," add, "and Corporal W. A. Howland;" and in place of "a most trusty soldier," read "trusty soldiers."

Page 139, 2d line. "One company" should read "one wing," as one-half of the regiment was engaged in the movement.

Page 163, line 12. For "Johnson," read "Johnston."

The name of Colonel Kilgour is misspelled "Kilgore," throughout the book.

Page 207. The copy of the Farewell Address given me contains only the names of three staff officers. The original one was signed by all. I regret I do not remember the names of the Act. Asst. Quartermaster, Asst. Com: Subsistence, and the Junior Act. Aid-de-Camp.

Page 91, line 10. I am informed that Lieutenant Colonel Kilgour was in command the entire time of the march to Chattanooga. Colonel Post's report states that Colonel Bennett assumed command at this time. Probably it is incorrect.

www.ingramcontent.com/pod-product-compliance
Lightning Source LLC
Chambersburg PA
CBHW020117030726
47498CB00006B/2142